The Resurrection of Lady Ramsleigh

The Lost Lords
Book Four

Chasity Bowlin

Copyright © 2018 by Chasity Bowlin
Print Edition

Published by Dragonblade Publishing, an imprint of Kathryn Le Veque Novels, Inc

All rights reserved. No part of this book may be used or reproduced in any manner whatsoever without written permission, except in the case of brief quotations embodied in critical articles or reviews.

Books from Dragonblade Publishing

Dangerous Lords Series by Maggi Andersen
The Baron's Betrothal
The Viscount's Widowed Lady

Also from Maggi Andersen
The Marquess Meets His Match

Knights of Honor Series by Alexa Aston
Word of Honor
Marked by Honor
Code of Honor
Journey to Honor
Heart of Honor
Bold in Honor
Love and Honor
Gift of Honor

Legends of Love Series by Avril Borthiry
The Wishing Well
Isolated Hearts
Sentinel

The Lost Lords Series by Chasity Bowlin
The Lost Lord of Castle Black
The Vanishing of Lord Vale
The Missing Marquess of Althorn
The Resurrection of Lady Ramsleigh

By Elizabeth Ellen Carter
Captive of the Corsairs, *Heart of the Corsairs Series*
Revenge of the Corsairs, *Heart of the Corsairs Series*
Shadow of the Corsairs, *Heart of the Corsairs Series*
Dark Heart

Knight Everlasting Series by Cassidy Cayman
Endearing
Enchanted
Evermore

Midnight Meetings Series by Gina Conkle
Meet a Rogue at Midnight, book 4

Second Chance Series by Jessica Jefferson
Second Chance Marquess

Imperial Season Series by Mary Lancaster
Vienna Waltz
Vienna Woods
Vienna Dawn

Blackhaven Brides Series by Mary Lancaster
The Wicked Baron
The Wicked Lady
The Wicked Rebel
The Wicked Husband
The Wicked Marquis
The Wicked Governess
The Wicked Spy

Highland Loves Series by Melissa Limoges
My Reckless Love
My Steadfast Love

Clash of the Tartans Series by Anna Markland
Kilty Secrets
Kilted at the Altar
Kilty Pleasures

Queen of Thieves Series by Andy Peloquin
Child of the Night Guild
Thief of the Night Guild
Queen of the Night Guild

Dark Gardens Series by Meara Platt
Garden of Shadows
Garden of Light
Garden of Dragons
Garden of Destiny

Rulers of the Sky Series by Paula Quinn
Scorched
Ember
White Hot

Highlands Forever Series by Violetta Rand
Unbreakable
Undeniable

Viking's Fury Series by Violetta Rand
Love's Fury
Desire's Fury
Passion's Fury

Also from Violetta Rand
Viking Hearts

The Sons of Scotland Series by Victoria Vane
Virtue
Valor

Dry Bayou Brides Series by Lynn Winchester
The Shepherd's Daughter
The Seamstress
The Widow

Table of Contents

Chapter One 1
Chapter Two 9
Chapter Three 16
Chapter Four 24
Chapter Five 32
Chapter Six 44
Chapter Seven 60
Chapter Eight 75
Chapter Nine 84
Chapter Ten 98
Chapter Eleven 105
Chapter Twelve 113
Chapter Thirteen 123
Chapter Fourteen 131
Chapter Fifteen 136
Chapter Sixteen 148
Chapter Seventeen 157
Chapter Eighteen 165
Chapter Nineteen 173
Chapter Twenty 185
Epilogue 202
About the Author 207

A shipwreck near Castle Black sees Dr. Nicholas Warner risking his life to save a woman from the churning sea. As he pulls her to the safety of the shore, the villagers are stunned by her presence. She is no stranger to them. They identify her as Viola Grantham, Lady Ramsleigh, wife of the recently deceased Lord Percival Ramsleigh... a woman who supposedly died nearly two years earlier. The mystery and scandal surrounding her only draws him in further, adding fuel to the fire of the immediate connection he feels to her.

Viola, thanks to her cold, unfeeling father, her abusive husband and his profligate nephew, has no trust for men and very little use for them. But there is something about Dr. Warner that she cannot so easily dismiss. Drawn to him seemingly against her will and better judgement, she confides in him about the son she bore in secret, the heir to her late husband and that she had only returned to secure his future and his place in society.

As they spend more time together, their feelings for one another deepen. But their happiness and growing affection for one another are threatened by Viola's past. The late Lord Ramsleigh's nephew, Randall, will not willingly give up the title, even if his aunt has returned from the dead and is presenting a child as the true heir to the title. In fact, there is nothing he will not do and no depths to which he will not sink, to ensure that never happens. He means to hold on to the title and the prestige that accompanies it by any means necessary... even if it means doing far more than just pretending that she is dead.

Will Viola be able to let go of the pain from her past and embrace the love of a truly good man? And even if she can, will Randall's plots and schemes cost her far more than just her chance at happiness?

Chapter One

THE INTERIOR OF the cottage was clean and neat, everything tidy and in its place. That had far more to do with the village woman who cleaned for him than with any proclivities toward tidiness himself. It wasn't that he was slovenly really, but a shirt or waistcoat tossed over the back of the chair and a news sheet spread across the table was hardly the end of the world. Still, it was nice to come home to a pot of stew simmering on the hearth and a bed that had been freshly made, even if it was unlikely he could make it to that bed in his current exhausted state.

Nicholas Warner settled deeper into the wing chair that faced the fireplace and rested his stockinged feet on the small, tufted ottoman that had magically appeared in his abode. It seemed that every day some new item of crockery, furniture or, heaven help him, a barnyard animal, manifested there. It was the way of being a country doctor. People rarely paid with actual coin but instead paid with the things he might have bought for himself had they done so. Of course, there was one particularly foul-tempered goat that he'd not have purchased for love or money. That beast had been deposited on his doorstep out of nothing more than spite. He wound up spending coin he didn't have himself to pay for one of the neighboring farmer's children to care for those animals.

It was almost as an afterthought that he retrieved the letter from the pocket of his discarded coat. It had been delivered to him earlier in the day but he had not yet had time to look at it. The seal on the back, pressed into ominously dark red wax, was ornate, heavy and painfully familiar.

Breaking the wax, he scanned the contents.

Doctor Nicholas Warner,

It is with my deepest regret that I must inform you of the death of our father, Edward Garrett, Lord Ambrose. The late Lord Ambrose suffered from a malady likely attributed to the many years of excess which he enjoyed.

Syphilis. Pox. A diseased liver likely from drinking so heavily for decades. Whatever it was, Nicholas tried to conjure some emotional response that was appropriate to hearing that his father had died, but he failed miserably. He hardly knew the man after all. Lord Ambrose had paid for his education and had purchased his commission in the Royal Navy, but all of that had been accomplished without the two of them ever occupying the same room together. The man had been nothing to him but a generous stranger. Rather than focus on that disturbing and shockingly morose thought, Nicholas returned his attention to the letter.

Despite his haphazard parenting, our late father has bequeathed a generous settlement to you in his last will and testament. When it is convenient for you to do so, please come to London. You will be welcome at the family's townhome, though family may be a slight exaggeration as I alone remain to carry on the family name. Again, as one orphan to another, I bid you welcome.

Sincerely,
Your heretofore unknown brother,
Cornelius Garrett, Lord Ambrose

Nicholas read the missive again. It was the only time in the entirety of his life that any member of his father's family had reached out to him. He didn't know his mother's family. Whatever actress, dancer, demirep or unfortunate housemaid had given birth to him, he'd been deposited with a family on one of Lord Ambrose's estates and then, when old enough, plucked from that home and put into a school.

There had been no interaction, no indication that anyone with whom he shared a blood connection would ever seek him out. Any childhood fantasies or foolish wishes to the contrary, he'd come to accept that he was merely an obligation to be discharged. But he supposed he should have some gratitude for that. He had the means to support himself and was viewed as a gentleman by most, when many of his ilk had been forgotten entirely, left to their own devices and whatever fate a cruel world held in store for them.

The note, while somewhat brief and abrupt, had been strangely welcoming nonetheless. But he was undecided on whether or not he should go. It seemed that establishing connections with them this late in his life might be nothing more than opening wounds unnecessarily. He had survived quite well for his thirty odd years without any interaction with them. It was an avenue fraught with potentially negative consequences. Regardless, he was too tired to decide.

Perhaps it was the heat of the fire, or the comfort of his favorite chair after a long day of tending to sick children and then a difficult birth, but he dozed there. His eyes drifted shut. He sank deeper into the chair and dreamed of a dark-haired woman. Her face was hidden. He saw nothing of her but the cascade of her dark hair and the lush curves of her body as he trailed behind her. In spite of the lack of contact between them, the dream was still intensely carnal. His ephemeral light o' love wore nothing but a diaphanous gown that draped elegantly over her figure and served more to highlight than to conceal the exaggerated curve of her hips, the narrow indentation of her waist, the heart-shaped bottom that stirred his blood and roused his body.

In his dream, she paused and waited, letting him draw close enough to see the fine, silken texture of the dark waves that cascaded over her shoulders and the velvety texture of her skin. As he reached for her, his hand brushing the satiny skin of her shoulder, a sharp tapping sound jolted him from the pleasantness of his dream. Sitting bolt upright in his chair, Nicholas shook his head and tried to make sense of where he was and what he'd heard. It was rare that he slept deeply enough to dream. Even more rare that a dream was so tantalizingly real to him. Still trying to ground himself to the here and now, and to identify the source of noise that awakened him, Nicholas tried to focus his sleep-fogged mind. Before he could do either, the door burst open to reveal none other than Graham, Lord Blakemore himself.

"You're needed," he snapped.

"Lady Agatha or Lady Beatrice?" he asked, instantly awake and alert, the dream forgotten in the face of a potential crisis. He referred respectively to Graham's mother who had overcome a long illness as well as an addiction to laudanum and Graham's new bride who was expecting their first child. Both women were his patients. But he had also come to view both of them as friends if not family.

"Neither. It's a shipwreck on the rocks below… I doubt there will be any survivors. You'll be more a pair of strong hands than a doctor on this occasion," Graham answered. The grimness of his expression told the truth of the situation far more than his sparse words.

Nicholas was already dragging his boots on. Shipwrecks were bad enough. But in the bitter cold of an early spring on the North Sea, the likelihood of survival was even slimmer. He didn't bother to don his coat as he'd only have to remove it once he arrived at the shore. They'd all be wading out into the waters to retrieve the bodies of those lost to the capricious whims of nature. Fewer layers to trap the damp cold against their skin and less weight while trudging through the water would be to their benefit.

Outside the small cottage, Graham was already mounting his own horse with another one waiting beside him for Nicholas.

"Do we know the kind of ship? Smugglers?" Nicholas asked as he hoisted himself onto the back of the borrowed mount. The man had uncanny foresight as it would have taken much longer if he'd been forced to saddle his own.

"If they are, they're not local. But I don't think so. There was nothing furtive about their movements," Graham answered. "I saw them earlier in the day heading south, flags and sails flying high, bright in the sun. The storm came up quickly and blew them back here."

Nicholas didn't ask how he knew it was the same ship. There were few enough that passed within viewing distance of their little spit of a coastline to imagine it could be anything else. He also didn't speak because he needed all his wits about him to navigate the steep path down to the beach. He might have trusted the horse more if he'd been born to the saddle. But like Lord Blakemore, he'd spent more time aboard ships than on horseback. He was an adequate horseman, but lacked the love for it many Englishmen possessed.

Sweat had beaded on his skin, despite the cold, by the time they reached the rocky beach. It could only be laid partially at the door of exertion. There was a strange rush of energy that came with facing such situations and it brought a visceral response—heart racing, sweating, muscles tensed and ready. It was a terrible thing to feel such excitement in the face of tragedy. But while it might have marked him heartless to some, it was that which allowed him to be good at his chosen profession. He'd learned to appreciate it during his days in the navy and later serving on less than respectable ships in the Caribbean as they prepped for battle or harsh weather. This was no different.

Villagers had already arrived, many of them fishermen in their small boats. It wasn't simply to help those poor souls that might be suffering or have already perished. Shipwrecks were an opportunity for riches and rewards that rarely came to those folks. Mercenary it might have been, but he didn't lay blame. In the course of his work, he'd seen the poverty of their homes. If they could scavenge something to use or sell, in his mind, they were welcome to it.

An older man was dipping torches into a barrel of oil and setting them alight, giving one to each man in queue. When he saw Nicholas, he waved the others aside and extended a torch in his direction. "They've found a few survivors, Dr. Warner. They're down the beach a ways though. Most of the poor souls will be needin' an undertaker more than a physician!"

Nicholas said nothing, simply accepted the torch and headed off in the direction indicated. Many of those that survived the wreck were quickly succumbing to the cold or to injuries sustained as the ship broke apart beneath them. On the beach, chaos reigned supreme. Survivors and casualties alike were pulled from the water and laid out upon the sand. He worked through the night, ignoring the cold, ignoring the ache in his bones and the pounding in his head as he helped those he could and closed the unseeing eyes of those for whom he was too late. In many ways, he had transcended the limits of his own body, no longer feeling the exhaustion or the cold. His focus was such that he could ignore his own discomfort in those moments.

Others had ceased looking for survivors at all and were simply bent on scavenging what could be saved from the debris of the ship and its doomed cargo. As dawn broke, a skirmish erupted between two men over a small cask of brandy. As they struggled, grappling with one another for possession of the item, they tripped, collapsing onto the broken body of one of those unfortunate souls whose life had been claimed by the rushing waters of the sea.

Furious, Nicholas rose. "You worthless, grasping bastards! Fighting over a cask of second rate brandy atop the corpses of the men who died trying to bring it to shore! Have you no shame?"

"This ain't no second rate brandy!" one of the men protested, still grumbling and attempting to elbow his competition in the ribs to wrest control of the contraband.

Nicholas was no longer paying attention to them. His eyes had been drawn to something beyond the beach, bouncing in the rough waves. A flash of red and then it was gone. He strained to see it again as the tide ebbed and flowed. Another wave crested and there it was again. A woman in a red gown. "Get a rope," he growled.

"It ain't worth hanging us over!" the other man said in defiance.

"Look out there, you fool! Do you not see her?" Nicholas demanded.

Dutifully, if the two miscreants could ever be described as such, they stared at the crashing waves for a second until the flash of red appeared again. "Likely just a bolt of cloth, Doctor. Ain't no use in drowning yerself, too!"

"Get a rope for me to tie about my waist while I make my way to her," he barked. "Even if it's too late to save her, I'll not leave her out there to be preyed upon by the fish."

"Aye, Doctor," the first man said. "You can have the brandy, you old sot," he added to his companion and headed off in search of rope.

The other man eyed the cask with delight. "It's a fine brother I have, Doctor. A fine one! Every time I have a sip of me brandy, I'll be drinking to him for giving up his claim to it!"

Nicholas was still shaking his head when the drunkard's brother returned with a length of rope. "It ain't long enough. We'll need men to make up the distance... I'd ask me brother, but he'll likely not put down his barrel of brandy."

"He will, or he'll die for it," Nicholas said with conviction even as he hastily tied the heavy rope about his waist, looping it in a way that it was unlikely to come loose even in the rough waves. When that was done, he removed his boots and waded into the water. The cold of it took his breath and made his muscles cramp. Forcing himself to relax, to ease into the water and not fight the sensations, he slowly made his way past the breaking waves to the figure that bobbed just out of reach.

Every wave rocked him back, the force of the water lifting him off his feet. Still, he pressed on. The nearer he got, the more certain he was that it was not simply a bolt of cloth. He could see the dark fall of her hair and the pale oval of her face. Blue with either death or cold, he had no notion of whether he was rescuing a woman or retrieving a body. He only knew that he was determined to get to her, to bring her back to shore and do what needed to be done, regardless of her state.

He was chest deep in the water, frigid and hurting from it, when at last he could lay hands on the lid of the crate she floated upon. She was still and unmoving, her lovely face almost certainly a death mask. With one hand hauling her makeshift raft, he struggled to swim back to the beach. Had it not been for the men gathered there towing the line tied about his waist, he would likely have drowned with her.

It seemed to take ages. Each inch gained was a hard fought and won battle. Slowly, the beach seemed to be growing nearer, the distance shrinking until, at last, his feet touched in the shallower waters. But it was no less treacherous there. The waves knocked into him forcefully and he struggled to hold himself upright, to keep a firm grasp on the woman he'd retrieved from the sea.

By the time he reached the sand, he was gasping for breath, every muscle taut and nearly to a snapping point from the bitter cold. As he laid there, sand crusting his skin and soaked clothing, he noted how unnaturally quiet the men around him had become. Not a word was spoken on that stretch of beach. Each and every one of them had gathered around those broken boards and the woman who rested upon them, staring down at her not just with sadness at her passing but with what he instantly perceived to be recognition.

"Do you know her then?" he asked the man who'd held so fiercely to his brandy.

"Aye, Doctor. She's a dead woman."

"I understand that... but do you know her name?" Nicholas asked, wanting alternately to laugh and strangle the sot.

It was his brother who answered the question then, turning back to Nicholas with wide eyes and a pale face as if he'd seen a ghost. "What he means, Doctor, is that this woman has been dead for nigh on two years. Lady Ramsleigh, she be... and there's a marker in the boneyard for her in the Ramsleigh plot in the churchyard. I know, cause it were I that dug the grave and set the stone!"

Just then, the dead woman opened her mouth and gasped for air. The gathered men scattered like crows, almost as if the dead had truly risen.

Chapter Two

VIOLA GRANTHAM, LADY Ramsleigh, had thought death both imminent and inevitable as she floated on those broken boards in a rough sea. She'd slipped into the blackness of unconsciousness assuming it was a precursor to the eternal damnation that surely awaited her on the other side.

She no longer felt the cold, nor any of the pain that she ought to have after being tossed about the failing ship like a child's toy. Opening her eyes, she expected to be staring into the harsh light of dawn. But there was a man there, visible only in silhouette, as he blocked out the light.

"Are you injured?" he asked.

Perhaps she hadn't defeated death, after all. "Am I dead?" Her throat ached, parched and dry from the appalling amount of seawater she'd swallowed. It burned horribly to speak.

"No, but if we do not get you warm, you soon will be," he answered. "Before I move you, I need to be certain that you are not so gravely injured it would be more dangerous to do so. With your permission, Madame, I will perform a brief examination."

"Are you a physician, then?" she asked. Her brain was still muddled as she tried to differentiate the strange dreamlike state she'd been in from what was apparently her current reality.

"Yes," he replied. "I am."

To avoid the pain of speaking again, she nodded. It was a terrible mistake. She had thought herself too numb from the cold to feel pain. But as she moved her head, pain exploded in it. So much so that she cried out. Immediately, his hands were there, moving over her scalp through the wet and tangled mass of her hair to the large bump that had formed near the base of her skull.

"Can you recall if you were struck with something?"

"A particularly rough wave threw me from the bunk. I landed against the opposite wall," she said softly. Having stilled, the pain had subsided to some degree.

"I suspect that you have concussed your brain... but I also suspect that your spine may be bruised. As you have been able to move your limbs, I do not think it more severe than that. Only painful," he answered. "To make this as pain free as possible, I am going to use a piece of board and some strips of cloth to immobilize your head and neck before we take you up the path to the cliffs."

She still had not seen his face. His voice was kind and reassuring, his touch oddly gentle and far different from any of the men of her previous acquaintance. It was only when another man stepped closer, stepped fully behind him and blocked out more of the light still, that his shadowed face became clear to her. Handsome. Far too handsome for her peace of mind. Definitely too handsome to be trusted. But what choice did she have? "Do what you must," she said quickly, before she changed her mind and begged them to just let her die in the cold, wet sand.

He issued instructions like a general, barking orders to those around him like a man used to being obeyed. The man who'd been behind him moved to do his bidding and once more his beautiful face was hidden, blocked out by the light surrounding him. But she knew now what was hidden and because of that, any sense of trust was gone. When the other man moved behind her cradling her head in large rough hands and she was turned to her side by another, she felt them place the board behind her. They turned her onto her back once more and other boards were placed beside her head. Then a piece of cloth was used to tie her to the very bit of wreckage she'd floated on. Panic hit her then, panic at being tied down, at being immobile, at being once more in her life at the mercy of a man she did not know.

"It's only temporary," he offered soothingly, in the same gentle tones he'd used before, as if he understood her panic. "If we don't immobilize your neck and head before moving you, it could make the current damage worse if not permanent. As soon as we can safely do so, I will cut the bindings free."

Forcing herself to breathe, to ignore her instinct to struggle, Viola squeezed her eyes closed and pictured in her mind the only thing that had ever brought her peace. She thought of her son and steeled herself to do whatever was necessary for his sake. That was why she'd returned at all, to ensure his future.

When they lifted the broken crate, the pain was excruciating. Darkness crept in once more, closing out the light and sucking her back into the abyss of it. She didn't fight it. It was preferable to suffering the agony while conscious.

"She's dead, isn't she?"

Nicholas glanced over at his brandy cask-carting companion. He held the cask like a woman cradling an infant as they walked behind the small cart that was being led up the steep path to the cliffs above and the respite that would be provided for her at Castle Black. Given her identity, it was the most appropriate place to take a woman of her station. "No, she is not dead. She's unconscious, likely from the pain. Head and neck wounds are particularly agonizing."

"Oh, I know that, Doctor. I've knocked my noggin a time or two!" the man agreed, chortling heartily.

"Was there brandy involved?" Nicholas asked.

The man had the decency to at least appear sheepish. "There might have been some," he admitted ruefully. "Why do you reckon she's come back? And why do you reckon old Lord Ramsleigh told everyone she'd died?"

"Those are questions for her and for Lord Ramsleigh," he answered, keeping his gaze on his patient. Even in her unconscious state, he could see her grimace with pain as they hit ruts in the path or had to make one of the steep turns. In spite of her pallor and her obvious pain, she was likely the most beautiful woman he'd ever seen. When she'd opened her eyes and looked up at him on the beach, he'd been struck by the color of her eyes. A deep, pure violet, it was unlike anything he'd ever seen. Completely entranced by them, he'd been as much at risk of drowning in them as the sea he'd rescued her from.

"Can't ask a dead man," the brandy cradler cackled.

"Really dead or dead like she was?" Nicholas asked.

"No, he's really dead. Some six months back... just before Lord Blakemore returned. Lots of folks in these parts seem to be turning up resurrected. Odd, that."

"Odd, indeed," Nicholas agreed. A beautiful and presumed dead woman returns after a near fatal accident to take up her rightful place as the widow of a titled landowner. It was like something from one of those dreadful gothic novels Beatrice had taken to reading.

Why had she left to begin with? What other secrets was she hiding? What had been Lord Ramsleigh's motives for telling the world she had preceded him in death when that was clearly not the case? A dozen questions about her flitted through his mind and not a one of them had to deal with her present condition. For once in his life, he'd encountered a person who intrigued him more than their various medical conditions did. She was a mystery and one that he looked forward to solving. Glancing at her once more as the cart turned, he caught sight of her in profile. Every feature was perfection from her the perfect proportions of her forehead and the lightly arched dark brows to the tilt of her small upturned nose and the jut of a chin that warned him she would be a challenging woman. If he were honest, he could admit that his curiosity was sparked as much by the mass of black hair and a pair of fine violet eyes as the story of her resurrection.

They reached the top of the cliffs and she was transferred from the rickety handcart that had been carried by several men to a horse drawn wagon. Nicholas climbed up beside her. He looked askance at the brandy cask that was placed down beside him with a heavy thump.

It appeared he'd earned a follower.

"What in the world are you doing?" Nicholas demanded, eyeing the man with aggrieved horror.

"I'm helping, ain't I? Worked for old Lord Ramsleigh, I did. If'n anyone has questions 'bout who she is, I'd be the one to answer 'em, wouldn't I?"

Realizing that the man, in fact, had a point and that he could not continue to simply refer to him by his drink of choice, Nicholas asked, "And what is your name?"

"William Wells, sir," he said, and doffed his cap to offer a clumsy bow. "At your service, Dr. Warner."

Nicholas sighed. He had no doubt that the man would cling to his side as stubbornly as he clung to his cask of brandy. While he might have useful information, Nicholas had little doubt that the man was doing nothing more than assuring he had the most up to date gossip about the resurrection of Lady Ramsleigh. He'd be paid for it in free drinks at the local tavern, no doubt.

They made the remainder of the journey in silence. Upon arriving at Castle Black, the doors were flung open and a bevy of servants rushed out to assist. Most of them defined assistance as gawking at the unconscious woman. Clearly, word of her return had reached the house long before her battered body had.

"Has a room been prepared for her?"

"Yes, Doctor," the butler intoned as he looked disapprovingly at the unconscious woman. "But it would likely be best if she were not to remain at Castle Black overlong. She is a scandalous woman, after all… abandoning her husband! I cannot imagine what would be said of Lord and Lady Blakemore for entertaining such a woman here."

"Scandalous or not, she'll stay here until she's well enough to go elsewhere. And no one shall speak of her scandalous past, her husband or anything related to his erroneous report of her death. Is that clear?"

The edict came from the open doorway of the castle where Beatrice stood. She'd taken to her role as lady of the manor with aplomb. The butler, chastened, inclined his head and apologized, "Forgive me, my lady, if I have overstepped."

"There is no if. That was decidedly overstepping. But you are forgiven, and you will ensure that while she is here as our guest and under Dr. Warner's care, that she is not importuned in any way or harassed about whatever her past may hold. We are none of us without sin or blame," Lady Beatrice said sternly.

The butler, thoroughly scolded and slightly embarrassed, signaled two strapping footmen to come and carry the woman inside. As they passed her, Beatrice looked down at the patient and frowned. "It really is her," she said to Nicholas. "I thought it was exaggeration or perhaps simply mistaken identity, but it is Viola Grantham!"

"You know her then?" Nicholas was more than a little surprised. The events that had surrounded Graham's disappearance at sea and the nearly two decades before his return had kept the occupants of Castle Black terribly isolated.

"Ramsgate Hall is five miles inland from her... I would take long walks and Viola would ride frequently. Our paths crossed on occasion. And while I never called there and she never called here, we had a friendly acquaintance if you will. I was very disturbed when her husband reported her death. I feared that he was very unkind to her."

"You mean he abused her," Nicholas surmised. "It is not uncommon."

"Yes," Beatrice answered evenly. "Quite so. If she did abandon him and run away to heaven knows where, I certainly would not blame her a bit for it."

His mystery woman was growing more complex with every passing minute. "And Ramsleigh is dead now, and she's returned to claim the estate?"

"It might be very difficult for her to do so. Lord Ramsleigh's nephew, Randall Grantham, has taken up the title and the estate. He'd be unlikely to hand the land or the house over to his uncle's resurrected widow! Unless of course there is a child. But she's been gone nigh on two years and if she kept her child from his father—of course, that could be why she left when she did. Perhaps she was attempting to protect more than just herself?" she mused.

"I need to attend her. If she succumbs to the cold or the head injury I fear she has, we will never know," he replied gravely. "You should rest. You look pale."

"That is because I must cast up my accounts every day until at least tea time," she answered sharply.

"Drink ginger tea," he replied with a wave of his hand as he stepped into the cavernous great hall of Castle Black.

Chapter Three

It was late afternoon when Viola awoke, or so she supposed based upon the amount of sunlight that filtered in through the window. It was a rather grand room though entirely unfamiliar to her. The pale blue walls and matching bed clothes were lovely, if somewhat weathered by age. Still, it was far finer than anything she had enjoyed in the last two years. Her sojourn to her mother's family in Aberdeen had not been without its costs. They were poor working people, farmers, and she'd worked the land beside them. It had been a small price to pay for her own freedom and for the safety of her son.

Recalling the excruciating pain she'd experienced on the beach, she moved her head slightly, testing her body's response. It produced only mild discomfort, so she turned it a bit further. Immediately she stopped, but it had nothing to do with pain. A man slept in the chair beside the bed, his handsome face and windswept, dark hair easily recognizable from those fractured memories of her rescue. His feet, stripped of their boots, were propped on the edge of the bed as he dozed near her.

Searching her mind, though it only made her head ache to do so, she recalled that he had said he was a physician. He was certainly unlike any physician of her acquaintance. Most of those she'd encountered had been old, with paunches, a propensity for too much port and looked down their noses at her as they told her she was too clumsy if her husband had bothered to lie about the origin of her bruises. It was worse when he hadn't lied and one of the worthless bastards, Dr. Shepherd amongst them, had told her to stop provoking him. For that, she'd have had to stop breathing entirely as her very existence had seemed to provoke his unreasonable anger and vicious temper. There had been times when she'd wondered if perhaps he wasn't simply mad. But men of wealth and power did not find themselves in Bedlam, only their unfortunate wives did.

As if he'd sensed her inspection of him, the young doctor opened his eyes.

Their gazes locked, each one studying the other, taking their measure. His eyes were impossibly warm, so warm that just being under his gaze seemed to eradicate what she'd thought would be a permanent chill in her bones. But there was a danger in that, too, she knew. No man, no matter how handsome or kindly they appeared, was to be trusted entirely. And as the charged nature of their locked stares began to seep in, it was she who broke contact first. Looking away hurriedly as a guilty flush spread over her cheeks, she wondered at her own boldness far more than she wondered at his.

"I see you've come around. I rather feared you wouldn't... already being a dead woman and all." His voice was tinged with sardonic amusement, but like his gaze, it was warm and rich. It seeped into her and further kindled the fire that was building inside her. He was a dangerous man.

Frowning as much at his words as to hide her own reaction to him, Viola said sharply, "You speak in an unaccountably strange manner for a physician. Clearly, I am not dead. Or if I am, the afterlife is certainly not at all what I anticipated."

His lips quirked slightly in an amused smirk, as he replied, "You are Lady Ramsleigh, are you not? Wife of the recently deceased Percival never-to-be-called-Percy Grantham, Lord Ramsleigh?"

Her frown deepened. "Yes, Lord Ramsleigh was my husband. When word reached me in Scotland that he had passed, I returned. It seems you knew my husband well," Viola surmised from his words.

"We had not met. But upon your return, I have been regaled with many stories of him... most of them very unflattering. It appears he spent most of his time in London and very little of it here, even when he should have been rusticating in the country during his period of mourning... for you. But then, I think his time in London was likely welcomed by you. Eagerly anticipated even as it spared you his less than tender mercies."

Viola did not shake her head with the confusion that plagued her at his words. She was not foolish enough to make that mistake again. "I may have been the one struck about the head, Doctor, but it is you, I fear, who has become insensible! What is this infernal talk of my death?"

He blinked at her. "You really have no idea? You honestly have no notion that after you abandoned your husband—and likely for good cause—he told the entire community that you had perished! There's a casket holding heaven knows what and a gravestone, Madame, that bears your epitaph. It appears you succumbed to a fever, far too young and beautiful for this ugly world. It's quite moving."

It should not have surprised her. Not in the least. Percival had always been about saving face above all, at least for himself. He might have abandoned her happily. But because it had been she who had done the leaving, an elaborate fabrication had been woven to prevent others from knowing that he had been abandoned by his battered wife. She had known that her return would pose difficulties, but certainly not to that degree. His lies would complicate matters dreadfully, without a doubt.

"You'll forgive me, Doctor, for asking so boldly, but now that we've established how I supposedly died, perhaps you could enlighten me as to the nature of my late husband's death?"

He shrugged. "I cannot offer any certainty on that score. He preferred the archaic ministrations of Dr. Shepherd... leeches and bloodletting. Though I don't suppose I can protest too much as I did quite a bit of bloodletting today myself."

She frowned again, once more heartily confused by his words. "I don't understand."

He rose and moved to the side of the bed, sitting down beside her. It was instinctive, almost an involuntary reaction, for Viola to shrink back from him. His eyes darkened, filled with a kind of rage that terrified her. Yet, when he spoke, his voice was gentle, soothing her the way one would soothe a child. "I have no intent to harm you, Lady Ramsleigh. I need to check the wound on your scalp. There was quite a bit of blood trapped beneath the skin. The pressure from that was what was causing your pain. I made a small incision to drain away the blood and, hopefully, relieve the monstrous headache that resulted."

Viola could feel her face flush with the acute heat of embarrassment. He must think her a complete imbecile or, even worse, a timid mouse of a woman who skittered and cowed. In spite of everything, that was not who she was. It was certainly not who she intended to be going forward. "Certainly, Doctor. You may proceed."

"Allow me to help you sit up," he offered, extending his arm.

Reluctantly, Viola accepted it. It was strange to be so near a man again, stranger still that it was not a man that she found utterly revolting. Or even slightly revolting. If she were honest, not revolting at all. Even dazed with pain and near frozen from the cold, she'd looked at him and felt that spark of interest, of her own traitorous body responding to him. Now, feeling marginally improved and no longer fearing an impending death, that spark had given birth a blaze. Averting her gaze, she kept it locked resolutely on the carpet beyond the edge of the bed while he tended her wound.

NICHOLAS KEPT HIS temper in check, but only just. She'd shied from him like a dog kicked once too often. If Ramsleigh weren't already dead, he'd have been meeting the bastard with pistols at dawn. Brushing aside the still tangled and matted mass of her dark hair, he examined the rather nasty abrasion to the back of her head. The swelling had gone down greatly, so that was a relief. Moving on, he examined the small incision where he'd drained much of the blood that had pooled at the base of her skull. There was no fresh blood, and very little had seeped onto the bandage after it had been applied. The cold seawater that had all but frozen her stiff had likely helped on that score. It was hell on the body but excellent for wounds.

The borrowed nightrail she wore slipped from her shoulder just a bit, revealing a bevy of bruises. She had endured a great deal, not simply from the shipwreck and being tossed about on the open sea, but from her previous life with the late Lord Ramsleigh it seemed. He was reminded of a woman he'd cared for in Jamaica. Broken arms, dislocated shoulders, a broken nose, repeated falls and tumbles and clumsiness that could all be laid directly at the heavy fists of her brute of a husband. Of course, the similarities ended in their suffering. While that woman had been meek and downtrodden, offering no resistance, Lady Ramsleigh appeared to be cut from a very different cloth.

"Tell me, Lady Ramsleigh, did no one offer assistance to you when you were at the less than tender mercies of your late husband?" he queried. It was not a question he expected her to answer, but it was one he still felt compelled to ask.

"There was no one to help, Doctor. We did not entertain. While Percival was in London, I remained at Ramsgate Hall under the ever watchful eye of his most trusted servants. I was never permitted to call on any of the local gentry or the respectable ladies nearby. Most people assumed I was standoffish, aloof, or thought myself above such provincial entertainments and company. Very few realized that I would have done anything to have a single person to confide in during that time."

That she had not tried to hide her past or pawn him off with some painful excuses was something of a surprise. She offered the information brazenly, almost challengingly. "I see. And I take it that when your injuries were severe enough, you were treated by Dr. Shepherd?"

"I was. If one can call it treatment," she answered breezily.

"I detest that man," Nicholas said under his breath. "I've never encountered anyone who less deserved to call himself a physician. In my experience, he has done far more harm than good to every single patient that we have shared."

The conversation was more to keep her calm, to ease the tension between them and to put her at ease in his presence. It was quite obvious to him that she trusted few people and with very good reason. He wanted her to be at ease with him, to feel safe and secure in his presence. He also acknowledged that it had very little to do with his role as her physician and much more to do with the hollow feeling that settled in his stomach whenever she met his gaze. Battered, bruised, with wild hair and a haunted look about her, she should not have stirred his lust, yet she did. She also stirred a surprising tenderness inside him that was far more concerning.

"Out of curiosity, Doctor, how long have I been dead?" She'd couched the question in an idle tone, but it was apparent that she was concerned. And he had an inkling why.

"I imagine that your unfortunate demise occurred not long after you departed... likely before your child was even born."

She gasped softly. "How did you know?"

"I am a doctor, Madame. I examined you completely to treat and bandage all of your numerous, if somewhat trivial wounds. I am familiar enough with the effects of child bearing on a woman's body. How old is the child now?"

She was silent for a moment, so silent that he thought she might not answer at all. He sat back, moving toward the end of the bed so that he was looking at her face, meeting her dark gaze directly. It was less for his benefit than hers. He intended to let her take his measure and decide whether or not to confide in him. It was his most fervent hope that she would and he could not quite fathom why. Whether she chose to treat him as a confidante or not had no bearing on her well-being from a medical standpoint. And yet he felt compelled to earn her trust, to offer her the kind of comfort it was clear no one else had. He was not foolish enough to think he was being entirely altruistic. She was a shockingly beautiful woman and an enchanting mystery. Curiosity had been his downfall on more than one previous occasion.

"He has only just passed his first birthday," she answered. "And despite what others may suggest, he is a Grantham, though I have often regretted that for his sake."

"And why is that?" he asked with a frown, wondering at such an odd statement.

"I fear that whatever madness and rage drove my husband, whatever demons within him made him so violent and unpredictable, might be a disorder of the blood... something that would be passed from father to son. Are you familiar with such illnesses?" she asked.

And that was the reason for her willing confession, because he, as a physician, might offer her a peace of mind that she had been unable to attain independently. "I have seen such things... but I have also seen men and women who did not have a violent parent become quite violent themselves, and vice versa. I think it is determined by character more than blood and so long as you raise him to be brave and kind, I doubt his father's tendencies will ever present."

She let out a deep sigh, so full of relief, almost as if the weight of the world had suddenly been lifted from her slender shoulders. "I am occupying too much of your time, Doctor. Surely there were other patients who will require your assistance after an accident such as this one. There was a woman... I did not know her well. We met in Aberdeen. She wished to reach London and I needed an escort for the sake of propriety. I agreed to bring her as far as Yorkshire and put her on the stage to London. Do you know if she survived?"

"There were very few survivors and you were the only female rescued or recovered. I fear your companion was lost to the sea," he admitted regretfully.

She nodded. "When I am well enough, I shall go to the church and say prayers for her. Perhaps I can prevail upon the vicar to have a small monument placed for her in the churchyard... for all of the victims."

"I believe that is a fine idea, and I daresay he would be hard pressed to find any reason to refuse." Given that he'd likely been party to burying an empty box in what was to have been her grave, Nicholas thought, it might behoove the man to be moved by her request. Rather than say something out of turn or create more distress for her, he excused himself. "You were not the most gravely injured of the survivors, but you bore more ill effects from the cold sea than did the others. However, now that you are awake and sensible, I will go look in on them. I shall return after dinner to look in on you."

"That isn't necessary," she said. "I'm quite sore, but I imagine that I will recover well enough without further assistance. Thank you for your consideration, Doctor, but further services will not be needed."

Nicholas smiled. "That's good to hear. But it was not in the capacity of physician that I meant to visit again, Lady Ramsleigh."

"And in what capacity could it be, Doctor?" she asked skeptically.

That of a man who wanted her, even when he knew he shouldn't. But that was not something she was ready to hear, and he had not determined yet if acting on that desire would be wise for either of them. So he answered, "In the capacity of a friend, Lady Ramsleigh... it seems quite apparent to me that you may be in need of a few of those."

He walked out then, leaving her gaping after him as he made his way downstairs to ply the servants for any gossip he might find useful about Lady Ramsleigh and her liar of a late husband.

Chapter Four

THE SERVANTS OF Ramsgate Hall moved through the house like shadows. Eyes downcast, shoulders hunched forward, each moved as if expecting a blow to land upon their head at any moment. It was true enough. Lord Ramsleigh, both the former and the current, had heavy hands and vile tempers. Unlike his predecessor, the current Lord Ramsleigh wasn't a slave to his anger. His blows landed with fury and glee alike.

The rumors had already reached the house. They had likely reached Lord Ramsleigh before the unconscious form of Lady Ramsleigh had even reached Castle Black. He'd been in a rage since then, ranting and throwing things as he screamed about her conniving to steal what was his.

"I'll not give that worthless quim a single sovereign!"

The shout echoed down the corridors, followed by the soft spoken reply of his solicitor. "My lord, even if she is actually Lady Ramsleigh, the house is yours. Ramsgate Hall is entailed!"

"And the money, Weston? To whom does it belong?" Ramsleigh hissed, throwing an empty brandy snifter against the tiles of the hearth. It shattered, but offered no peace to the raving lord.

The solicitor swallowed nervously. "The marriage contracts were very generous to Lady Ramsleigh. And while very little of the funds that were transferred upon their marriage to your uncle will remain with the estate, there are options—"

A vase, likely a reproduction of a priceless artifact that had been sold off by previous generations, was tossed against the opposite wall to shatter. Shards of pottery flew in all directions. "I want her gone."

"My lord," the solicitor began again, brushing bits of porcelain from his coat, "If she is Lady Ramsleigh, then she abandoned your uncle... therefore, she violated the marriage contracts herself."

"And he faked her death to save face! The scandal will ruin us if you pursue this through legal channels," Randall snapped. "Everything would be frozen while we're tied up in the courts and I'd be living like a pauper! I will not have it, Weston. I will not. I shall find my own way of dealing with my resurrected aunt!"

The solicitor appeared stricken. "My lord, I must encourage you to proceed cautiously and not to allow your temper to get the better of you."

"My temper will not get the better of me, sir. I know precisely what must happen, and you will stay well out of it... or my aunt will not be the only casualty," he warned. "Is that perfectly clear?"

The solicitor nodded, his eyes glazed with fear. It was not the first time he'd witnessed the lengths to which Lords Ramsleigh would go to get their own way. He knew better than to cross anyone of that line. "Yes, my lord. Certainly. I will do whatever is required to assist you."

"Silence is the only assistance I require. Be gone from me, Weston. I cannot abide the sight of your quivering cowardice!"

After the solicitor had left, Randall moved back to the desk and plopped down into his chair. He propped his booted feet on the desk and tapped his finger against his chin as he considered. To get her where he wanted her, he'd have to get her ensconced at Ramsgate Hall. Given their past relationship and the unfortunate confession he'd made, it was unlikely for her to accept an invitation. Yet, she'd returned for a reason. What was it? What had brought the bitch back into his life now?

"I'll bury more than an empty box this time. The bitch will suffer... slowly and agonizingly, if need be, until she tells me the reasons for her return," he said softly. Decision made, he whistled a tune under his breath as he rang the bell pull.

One of the maids entered. She had that soft, blousy look about her, like she was sneaking cakes from the kitchen when cook wasn't looking. He didn't much care for that in a woman, but she'd do for the moment.

"Did you need something, my lord?" she asked softly, keeping her head down and her gaze locked firmly on the floor.

Randall walked toward her. Reaching out with one hand, he trailed it over her arm, up to the soft skin of her neck. "Oh, I need something... and you'll do nicely."

She let out a soft sob of fear and it sent a thrill through him like nothing else ever would. But her sobs weren't as sweet to his ears as Viola's shrieks had been, or the way she'd fought like a wildcat beneath him. This one would be meek and submissive. She'd sob with pain and fear, but she wouldn't fight the way Viola had. He'd kill his aunt, but he might indulge in her charms again first.

GRAHAM, LORD BLAKEMORE, entered Ramsgate Hall and frowned. While Castle Black was hardly a model of luxury given its ancient origins, he'd seen enough fine homes to recognize things were very wrong at Ramsgate. The servants were all remarkably timid, and yet the housekeeping was hardly up to par. Dust and cobwebs were present in abundance. Luxurious at one time, there were missing paintings and rugs, their shadowy silhouettes still visible. He had to wonder whether those absences were from Lady Ramsleigh's late husband or his successor.

"Is Lord Ramsleigh in?"

The butler looked, if such a thing were possible in the typically stoic servants, panic stricken. "He is not to be disturbed, Lord Blakemore. If you wish to leave a card—"

"Not to be disturbed means he is here," Graham insisted. "This isn't simply a social call. It's vital that I speak with him. I have news of his aunt, Lady Ramsleigh."

The butler's gaze shuttered immediately. "Lady Ramsleigh has passed away, my lord. Almost two years past."

Lies. The man knew she was alive. As Graham took his measure again, he realized that the servant had likely known all along, even when they were burying what was hopefully just an empty box in the churchyard. "Lady Ramsleigh has just been rescued from a ship that has run aground in the cove, sir. I assure you she lives and is recovering from her injuries at Castle Black as we speak. While Lord Ramsleigh may not wish to be disturbed, I've no doubt such news is just cause to do so."

"That is impossible," the butler insisted. But as he did, his gaze shifted to the left, toward a closed door that was likely the library.

"She was properly identified by Lady Blakemore, my wife—unless you wish to challenge her honesty," Graham said tersely. "If that is the case, my good man, we have more to disagree about than whether or not Lord Ramsleigh ought to be interrupted."

It was panic that had the butler backpedaling then. "No, my lord. I would certainly never dream of offering such insult to your wife or to the house of Blakemore. It was not my intent at all!"

"Step aside," Graham said. "I will see Lord Ramsleigh today and I will do so with or without your permission."

Reluctantly, the butler retreated, stepping back and shaking his head to the brawny footman who'd stepped forward to bar Graham's way. The footman immediately slunk back as well. Graham made for the door that had commanded the butler's attention earlier. With only a brief knock, he opened it and let himself in. The first sight to greet him was a weeping girl in a torn dress. A housemaid from the look of her, it wasn't difficult to ascertain what he had interrupted. Nor was it difficult to determine that she had been a less than willing participant. Her lip was bloodied and he could see the bloom of a large handprint on her cheek.

"Step outside, girl, and wait for me there. Or better still, collect your things and meet me at the front door. You'll not have to stay here," Graham offered.

The girl began weeping anew, but it was with obvious relief. She nodded affirmatively and ran from the library, her sobs echoing after her.

"Who the devil are you?" the dissolute man behind the desk demanded, even as he reached for a bottle.

"I am Lord Blakemore... come to inform you of the miraculous resurrection of your aunt, Viola Grantham, Lady Ramsleigh. But I daresay you and your household were well aware that she was not dead."

Lord Ramsleigh sneered. "It ain't her. Even if it is, she'll never be able to prove it... my uncle kept her well isolated here. Not a single person of quality would be able to vouch for her identity and the cooperation of villagers and servants can be bought easily enough."

The rage bubbling inside him was teetering on the brink of disaster. "Including those you've raped?" Graham demanded, unable and unwilling to keep the censure out of his voice.

"I'll do what I want with my bloody servants, now won't I? She'd have gotten a coin or two for her troubles," Ramsleigh said, his tone insolent and smug as he poured a healthy amount of liquor into a waiting glass. "All women are whores, Blakemore. Some just discover it sooner than others. I bet your own wife spreads her thighs much more willingly after you've tossed her a bauble or two, doesn't she?"

Graham didn't attack because he knew without question that it was precisely what Ramsleigh wished for him to do. "Speak of my wife again and I'll cut your tongue out and force you to eat it. I came here as a courtesy to inform you that she had returned. Given that this house and your company are not fit for a lady, she will remain as a guest at Castle Black and our solicitor will be in touch."

Stepping out into the hall once more, the door closed just as the glass shattered against it. The maid was there, her things tied up in a simple bundle. It was obviously all she possessed. But the girl had washed her face and stood with her spine straight, clearly eager to be away from the wretched pile that was Ramsgate Hall and its debauched master.

NICHOLAS HAD RETURNED only briefly to his own cottage on the estate, long enough to bathe and dress in clean clothes. An invitation to dine at the castle with the Blakemore family had been extended. Exhaustion weighed on him but so did temptation. He wanted to see her again, to take the measure once more of that wary look in her eye.

Viola, Lady Ramsleigh, was an enigma to him. By turns fragile and fierce; hauntingly beautiful and also, he sensed, impossibly damaged but far from broken. He found her compelling. It was easy enough to admit that there was little in his life to challenge him. His work with Lord Blakemore, to help him regain his memories, was progressing at a steady pace. Other than the usual fevers and accidents that plagued any small farming or seaside town, there was little to challenge him. There were eligible women in the village, to be sure, many who were far more appropriate to his station than a wealthy and scandalous widow would be. But he was not looking for marriage or for love. Entangling himself with an innocent young miss who would likely expect both of those things held no appeal to him.

And so, with only a few hours of sleep in the span of nearly three days, he found himself once more entering the great hall of Castle Black. The drawing room was lively with conversation and he turned in that direction. Lady Agatha was there, along with Lady Beatrice and Christopher, Graham's younger half-brother. The once sullen boy had managed to turn himself around and become at least moderately pleasant company. The wicked influences of his past were no more.

"Good evening, Lady Agatha, Lady Beatrice, Christopher. I take it Lord Blakemore has not come down yet?" he asked.

"More like he hasn't returned," Christopher answered. Both Agatha and Beatrice looked worried as the young man continued, "He made for Ramsgate Hall earlier today to inform the new Lord Ramsleigh that he's about to become the almost Lord Ramsleigh. Though, I suspect he'll buck at that given that the heir to the title is only an infant and not even in this country at the moment."

He likely would at that, Nicholas thought. And if he was anything at all like his late uncle, it could go very poorly for his patient. "I see. And is Lady Ramsleigh well?"

"Well enough," Beatrice answered. "I looked in on her just a bit ago and she was resting. She did not eat very much, claiming that her appetite was put off by nerves. Though she hardly seems the nervous sort, now does she?"

Nervous, no? The woman had a spine that might well have been forged in iron. But that didn't mean she was without fear. Nicholas would have excused himself to check on her but the doors opened once more and Graham stepped inside. His stormy countenance revealed all that was necessary about the nature of his meeting with the lady's relatives.

"Oh dear," Lady Agatha said. "I recognize that look. He is in high dudgeon! What on earth has that despicable man done?"

"You know Lord Ramsleigh?" Nicholas asked.

She nodded sagely. "I knew all of them, of course. They are local gentry and, at one time, we were friendly. But over the years, we stopped associating with them as their reputation and finances disintegrated. There was hope when the late Lord Ramsleigh married the girl that he would improve, but alas he did not. As to the new Lord Ramsleigh, Randall is his given name, he is not at all the thing. If his uncle was a bad apple, then he is an entire bushel of them."

Nicholas tucked that information away and turned back to Graham just as he saw a maid being ushered up the stairs. "You're abducting servants now?"

Graham tensed. "We'll speak of it privately. Beatrice, Mother, if you'd go into dinner, Nicholas and I will join you shortly."

The ladies left the room, Beatrice with a warning glance. "No dueling," she muttered as she left. Her tone was soft, but there was little doubt that it was an order that would be enforced.

"You didn't challenge him to a duel," Nicholas said. "Please tell me you did not challenge the bastard to a duel!"

"I did not, though he likely tried to goad me into it," Graham stated. Quickly, he filled in the gaps, revealing the interrupted attack on the maid and Ramsleigh's words. "He's denying her, of course, and the entire household is denying that they have any knowledge of Lady Ramsleigh's death being a fraud perpetrated by her husband. But it's lies. All of it. Whether they were complicit or simply cowed, I cannot say."

"Is the maid injured?" Nicholas asked cautiously.

"I do not believe he succeeded in carrying out his intentions for the girl." Graham's answer was just as discreetly worded. "Though, I daresay she may require some minor treatment for bruising and she has a cut on her lip where he struck her. It was my intent that she should stay on here as a maid to Lady Ramsleigh. The girl is acquainted with her from before."

"Which will further her claims should her nephew-in-law attempt to deny her place here," Nicholas surmised. "You are a cagey one, Lord Blakemore."

"We did serve on the same pirate ship, Warner," he reminded the good doctor. "You might not have come aboard willingly, but you stayed of your own volition."

Nicholas shrugged. It was true enough and there was little point in denying the accusation. He'd longed for adventure and that brief stint had provided it. "I'll check on the maid and then look in on Lady Ramsleigh. You needn't hold dinner for me. I'll have a tray in the kitchens after I'm done."

"Given that we are all but turning Castle Black into a hospital, you should stay here… I can send one of the servants to fetch your things."

Nicholas waved him off as he headed toward the stairs. "I'll go myself tomorrow and get what I need, but I will stay here for the interim. If for no other reason than your cook's lemon tart." And the mysterious, dark-haired woman who now rested above stairs—both haunting and haunted, she intrigued him more than anything or anyone else had in a very long time, if ever.

Chapter Five

VIOLA WAS RESTING, if one could call tossing and turning in bed such. It wasn't the fault of the bed at all. It was quite comfortable, in fact. It was her own wayward thoughts that led to her discomfort. The handsome doctor should not have been so much on her mind. He was a distraction she did not need given the very rough path that lay before her. Percival's decision to have her declared dead, or at the very least to have her "buried" to save face was a complication she had not anticipated. Precisely how did one return from the dead in the eyes of English law?

A soft knock on the door startled her out of her reverie. She called out for the visitor to enter. Her assumption that it would be one of the Ladies Blakemore could not have been more wrong. A young woman dressed very simply in a drab gown entered with her head cast down.

"Forgive the intrusion, my lady, I only wanted to let you know that I've come from Ramsgate Hall to attend you here."

Recognition dawned. "Margaret?"

"Maggie, my lady. Margaret is my name, but most have never called me that since it was my mother's name as well."

"How did you come to be here, Maggie?" Viola asked curiously as she sat up in bed. Immediately, she hissed with pain as her head throbbed and her bruised ribs protested.

The maid shot forward and tucked a pillow behind her quickly. "Forgive me, m'lady. I should not have come and startled you so."

"It was my own fault. I know well enough the catalogue of my injuries," Viola answered. And with the girl standing so close to her, she could just as easily make a catalogue of hers. "Is that Randall's handiwork?"

The girl blushed and nodded. "Yes, my lady. But he didn't—that is to say, Lord Blakemore arrived and offered me the position to come here and assist you at a very opportune time."

So he was caught in the act. "Is this the first time you've suffered his attentions, Maggie?"

"Yes, ma'am. I'm not the sort he likes really... not pretty enough or worldly like some of the girls are. Most times he ignored me like I wasn't even there. I was just unlucky today."

Because of her. Randall had been angry at her return and had looked for the nearest victim to inflict his rage upon. "I'm so terribly sorry."

Maggie looked up then, understanding in her gaze. "We've all got things to be sorry for, I suppose. I worked in that house for four years... long before you supposedly died. And I reckon I understand good as anyone else there why it was you left the way you did."

The burn of humiliation, the way it churned in her gut, was not a new sensation to her. It was one she had become agonizingly familiar with over the last few years. But with his handprint bruised on the girl's cheek and her lower lip split and swollen, it was easy enough to see that she did. "Yes, Maggie, I imagine that you do."

The girl nodded and stepped back. "Is there anything I can do for you right now, my lady?"

Another knock at the door prevented her from answering. She hadn't even called out to bid the person enter when the door opened and the doctor stepped inside. He had bathed and was freshly shaven, his dark hair combed back from his high brow and his eyes glittered not with vitality but with the slight madness of exhaustion. From the hollows beneath his eyes, it was clear that he'd had no rest or, at the very least, little enough of it.

"Ah, I see both of my patients have gathered to make my work easier then," he said congenially. His tone was mild, diffident and clearly intended to set the young maid at ease.

"My maid is injured and requires your assistance, Doctor. My injuries have already been treated," she reminded him.

"Treated, yes… monitored, no. They require frequent checks to ensure that infection is not setting in and that they are not worse than my first examination led me to believe. But I will tend to your maid first as it appears her wounds are a bit more acute," he said, again keeping his tone mild. He offered the maid a dazzling smile that was sure to set any young girl's heart racing no matter what she might have been through. "Ran into a bit of a bully, did you?"

"No, sir. Well, yes, sir. I don't know, sir," the maid stammered, clearly dazzled by his handsomeness. Finally with a sigh, she said, "I don't know what I should say to that."

"You don't need to say anything," the doctor said. "Come sit over here and let me take a look at your lip."

The maid crossed the room to the chair at the dressing table that he'd indicated, looking nervously back at Viola. Whether she thought she would be scolded for sitting in the presence of her betters or whether she was uncertain of Dr. Warner, Viola could not be sure. Whatever the reason, the maid's uncertainty faded quickly in the face his charm.

Dr. Warner made a few noncommittal sounds. "It's not done up too badly. How are your teeth? Nothing feels loose?" he asked.

"No, sir. He didn't hit me so hard, really. It was his ring what caught my lip."

"Of course, it was," he said, and there was a coldness in his tone that indicated he'd encountered such a thing before. "Likely a very large one, with a rather pointy setting by design. I've seen the like before."

From her vantage point, Viola watched him as he tended to the young woman. His touch was gentle, perfunctory and whenever he was within sight of his patient, his expression was even and mild. But when the girl had been seen to, a salve applied to the cut to ease the stinging and swelling, and she'd gone, his expression darkened to one of complete fury. "I ought to kill the bastard and be done with it."

"You cannot," she said, not even remotely offended at his language or tone. "While he is a bastard by deed, he is not one by birth. If you touch him, it will be you who hangs for it. He's a titled gentleman even if he can lay no claim to gentlemanly behavior."

"Do not be the voice of reason now, if you please," he implored. "Let me indulge my righteous anger for a few moments while I envision beating him to a pulp."

She chuckled in spite of herself and then winced at the sharp pain in her ribs. "Please do not make me laugh. And you may envision beating him all you wish, so long as you do not actually do so. I'd prefer not to see you go to the Fleet or the gallows."

He crossed the room to her bedside. "Tilt your head, if you please, Lady Ramsleigh. I need to check the incision here."

She did as he asked, once again marveling at how remarkably gentle his touch was. Never in her life had she encountered any man capable of such a tender touch. But as her knowledge of men was limited, it was no great wonder. "I'm certain it's fine, Doctor. But I would have your word about Randall. He is not an honorable man and I strongly suspect that you are. He would not fight fairly."

He smirked slightly. "You are making a number of assumptions about my character, Lady Ramsleigh. It might surprise you to know that I spent a great deal of my time in Jamaica in the company of pirates. Lord Ramsleigh might have a more difficult time than you imagine. You might also be vastly overestimating the degree of honor which I possess."

That was something of a surprise to say the least. Raising one eyebrow, she said, "Pirates?"

"Things are very different in the islands, my lady," he answered vaguely. "The swelling has gone done further. You should be able to get out of bed tomorrow but I wouldn't attempt to navigate the stairs just yet. They are dark and uneven in a house this old. Treacherous even under the best of circumstances."

"I will keep that in mind, Doctor," she answered. "But at some point, I must leave these rooms. I will have to return to Ramsgate Hall."

His expression hardened immediately. "No. That cannot and will not happen."

She'd been ordered about by men for so many years that, having experienced freedom in her current life, she took a great deal of umbrage to it. "Why on earth not? I'd like to point out that while you may be my physician, you are hardly my master, sir!"

"I lay no claim to the title of master. And while I may not count myself a gentleman, I do pride myself on behaving as one to ladies. Your nephew is thoroughly debauched and without conscience, Madame. If you need further reminders of that fact you have but to look at your maid!"

"I returned here, facing the prospect of social ruin, to claim to my son's birthright and my own fortune! I will not be put off!" It was more than social ruin. If the truth ever came out, that kind of scandal would haunt her and her child for the remainder of their days. To keep it from coming out, to keep Randall from bandying those painful rumors and half-truths to the world for his own end, she'd need to confront him and remind him of what it would cost him, as well. She could not do that from a borrowed bedchamber.

He opened his mouth to protest but stopped abruptly as there was a knock at the door. With a resigned sigh and a glower in her direction, he strode toward the door to greet whoever else had arrived.

Sitting up in bed, wearing a borrowed nightrail and wrapper, she was ill-prepared to have both Lord and Lady Blakemore enter the chamber.

Lord Blakemore didn't smile but there was humor in his gaze. "As your conversation could be heard in the dining room, we assumed you must have wanted us to be party to it."

Lady Blakemore shushed him. "He's being facetious, Lady Ramsleigh. We had decided to join you anyway as Lady Agatha was overtired and sought her chamber. Christopher, my brother-in-law, decided to go out with friends for the evening. We thought it best to join you here... and only in the corridor could we hear the obvious disagreement between you and Dr. Warner. Whatever could be the source of such friction?"

"I was insisting to Dr. Warner, Lady Blakemore, that I cannot remain at Castle Black indefinitely. My reasons for returning home remain, regardless of the somewhat altered nature of my return. Given my late husband's fabrications, I do not have the luxury of remaining here and avoiding my relatives, regardless of how unpleasant they may be," Viola explained.

All the easy affability he'd displayed at his entrance vanished as Lord Blakemore said, "You will not return to that house, Madame. If you must speak with your nephew-in-law, when you are recovered enough, I will accompany you there. Then after the fact, I will return you here to the safety of our home. It is not fit for the habitation of ladies and he is not fit for the company of the human race."

"My lord, I thank you for your concern, but Lord Ramsleigh—"

"Was on the verge of forcing himself upon a chambermaid while the remainder of his servants stood about in the hall, unwilling or unable to help her. Who would help you?" Lord Blakemore demanded. "I have already sent for my solicitor. He will be able to advise you on whatever must be done from a legal standpoint that you may regain control of whatever your inheritance or portion from your late husband's estate was to be."

"It is not so simple as that, my lord… I came here to make preparations for my son to take up his rightful place as the Ramsleigh heir. His nurse is to sail with him from Aberdeen at a later date when the weather is more certain," she said. "While a journey by water would be quicker and certainly less confining for a child so young, I fear that I may not be able to wait so long. I may need to send for them sooner."

She watched as Lord Blakemore's face darkened even further. His answer was blood chilling. "Then rest assured, Madame, the safest place for you is here with us. Were he to discover that you pose a threat not only to his fortune but his title, neither you nor your child would be safe from him. As to fetching your child and his nurse, we have several carriages and it would be no great difficulty at all to send for them."

It was Lady Blakemore who spoke then. "My dear, Lady Ramsleigh, a man who would force himself upon an unwilling woman is, at his heart, a self-serving creature. His wants and needs supersede even the most basic principal of not violating the body of another. Someone far wiser than I wish to admit once asked me if a man is capable of rape, why would he not be capable of murder? Then as now, I cannot formulate an appropriate response to that. Not wanting something to be true does not make it false."

"It could take months," she protested. "I could not be a burden to you for so long!"

"What burden?" Lady Blakemore said breezily. "I will soon be confined to the castle as I am warned that Blakemore babies tend to be impossibly large. What better time to have another woman present, specifically one who is not my mother-in-law and has gone through the experience of childbirth herself? I will likely pester you with so many questions you will wish me to the devil."

Left with little choice and with her own uncertainty of her ability to ensure her safety and the safety of her child in Randall's presence, Viola nodded her agreement. "I thank you for your hospitality and your assistance. You have all been too kind and generous to me by far."

Lord Blakemore took a seat before the fire and Lady Blakemore the one opposite him as servants entered carrying platters of food. The impromptu table was laid and another chair produced from somewhere for Dr. Warner. Viola remained in her bed, buried under the covers and picking at the tray of her dinner while the trio conversed easily. They made every effort to include her and she responded to their conversation as her parents had trained her to do. Her replies were witty, her conversation sparkling, but her mind was elsewhere. Was she putting Tristan in danger by bringing him to England? Would it even be possible to claim the title for him unless he was present?

NICHOLAS WAS AWARE of her preoccupation. That she was reconsidering her course of action spoke to her wisdom, though he suspected she might term it cowardice. For his part, he saw no valor in recklessly endangering her life, even if it was for her son. The boy would likely be far more grateful to have a mother than a title.

As dinner ended, Lord and Lady Blakemore said their goodnights and he was once more alone with her. It was highly improper, even in their rustic setting. But the inhabitants of Castle Black had grown used to their isolation in the years that Graham was missing. In turn, they were insulated from the judgement and censure found in society. To that end, he could sit in her chamber, unchaperoned. She was a widow, after all, and he was her physician. Given her current condition, it would hardly be viewed as a romantic assignation by anyone. And yet, sitting there alone with her, the fire flickering behind him, he recognized that it was very so much for him, whether she was in agreement or not.

"You've made a wise choice," he said. "Ramsleigh is dangerous. More so than you imagined… and if he views you as a threat, it will only get worse."

"I cannot remain here indefinitely," she stated, though the concern was voiced without her previous urgency. "The solicitors will get things in order and once Randall removes himself from Ramsgate Hall, I will take up residence there with Tristan. They will sail in April… it's only over a month away, but should be much safer."

"It should be. But that will not calm your nerves on the score until he is safely here with you, no doubt."

Her rueful smile was answer enough. "I miss him dreadfully. I won't regale you with stories of his accomplishments or gross exaggerations of what a smart, wonderful, well-behaved and thoroughly heaven-sent child he is."

"Is he all of those things?"

Viola's smile deepened. "Yes, along with being willful, a bit spoiled, and an avid pursuer of every speck of dirt he can manage to locate and place upon his person."

Nicholas laughed at that. "Not so different from grown men at all then, is he?"

"I suppose not. It will be difficult for him... the scandal of having a mother like me and a father like Ramsleigh. That's all bad enough without the farce of my fraudulent death! If Id' known—there's little use in recriminations, I fear."

Leaning forward in his chair, resting his elbows on his knees with his hands clasped loosely in front of him, Nicholas said, "You did not make your decision lightly. I daresay that, for you, leaving your husband was a prospect weighed, measured, and repeated again and again."

She didn't acknowledge that assessment, but grew very quiet. After a long and rather pregnant pause, she admitted softly, "My decision to leave Ramsleigh was more for my son's safety than my own. The Grantham men have violent tempers. I'd suffered a miscarriage once already as a result of it. When I discovered I was with child—well, I made the only decision that I could in order to protect myself and my son. I fled to my mother's people in Scotland, an aunt and uncle who were too poor to be of consequence to her or my father."

"And your parents were aware of this?" he asked.

She nodded. "They have not spoken to me since I left him, except to send me one letter urging me to return to my husband and not bring scandal to our family."

Nicholas frowned. Were they aware of her suffering? As if she'd read his mind, she continued, "They suggested that I would not have been beaten had I been a better and more obedient wife. My father even went so far as to say that Ramsleigh was within his rights and that it was his moral duty as my husband to discipline me... discipline. It's laughable now but, at the time, it nearly broke my heart."

Had her entire family actually forsaken her? Had her life been so filled with people who were clearly unworthy? "They know you live and said nothing when Ramsleigh buried whatever it was in a coffin under your name?"

She nodded. "Yes. They must have, I suppose. I've little doubt that it was my father's suggestion. Better to have a dead daughter than an errant one."

Nicholas rose and crossed to the window. Drawing back the curtains, he peered out into the darkness. Beyond the cliffs, he could make out the glint of moonlight on the white-capped sea. "Has no one in your life ever fought for you? Defended you?"

She smiled. "My maid... who is now Tristan's nurse. She remained behind with him in Aberdeen to see to his care. My mother's relatives whom I stayed with are quite aged. They never had children of their own and I like to think that my presence there, and Tristan's, brought some joy into their lives. They are poor people. Simple farmers and I helped them where I could. I sold enough of my jewels to ease their burden somewhat. They have been kind to me. I am not without allies, but those I possess lack the power and social cache that would have been necessary to stand up to my husband and now to my nephew-in-law."

"That is no longer true. Lady Blakemore recognized you immediately. She will vouch for your identity, as will the maid who came here from Ramsgate. No doubt, if pressed, your parents would have to. And I daresay, when it comes to his grandson inheriting the title and Ramsgate Hall, your father may become slightly more supportive of your cause."

Her expression shifted, her lips turning downward in sour bitterness. "I don't care if he does. In truth, if I never speak to either of my parents again, I'll be content. To my father, I was never anything but chattel to be bartered. But he'd made that clear even from my earliest memories of him."

"And your mother?" he pressed. "Have you no desire to reconcile with her?"

It was a subtle alteration, a tightening of the muscles of her face and a tension that settled over her features. He'd found the tender point, the one part of her past that hurt the most. It had been inadvertent, but it was true nonetheless.

"It is my mother's unwavering devotion and obedience to my father, even in the face of seeing me battered and bruised, that I find unforgivable. Knowing the love I have for my own son, it makes her behavior even more unconscionable. I am better off without her in my life. And I will not willfully expose my son to such weakness of character."

Her quiet resolve was admirable. Her rigidity on the matter was a testament to just how deeply that betrayal had scarred her. Having no real recollection of his own mother, and having had a father who could not have cared less for his by-blows, so long as they stayed well out of the public eye, he understood the loneliness of being without a family. "I'm sorry they hurt you... and disappointed you. But this is hardly a conversation conducive to your recovery and I have allowed my own curiosity about your past to interfere with my actions as your physician. You should rest, Lady Ramsleigh, and think of these distressing things no more tonight."

She cocked her eyebrow. "You are not the least bit scandalized by me, are you? That I ran off, left my husband, gave birth to a son that most will call a bastard, and have now returned for the most mercenary of reasons—to claim the money that should be mine at my husband's demise? None of that puts you off, does it? Yet, talk of my family and the utter lack of sentiment for them, you find distasteful."

He sighed in answer, lifted his gaze upward in a thoughtful manner as he formulated a reply. When at last he spoke, his words were not the condemnation she had anticipated. "Not distasteful... but distressing. It bothers me more than I care to admit that you endured such abuse at the hands of your husband and that those who should have cared for you the most did not dare to intervene on your behalf. It infuriates me, actually. And discussing it further will benefit neither of us. As to your leaving him and returning after his death—that was simply pragmatism at work and is an admirable quality."

"And my son... the one whose parentage will always be suspect?" She threw the challenging question at him almost as if lobbing a volley of munitions. He had little doubt that she was making every reasonable attempt to create obstacles between them, to disperse the strange sensation of intimacy that existed between them and had almost from the outset. *Because she was too drawn to him for her own peace of mind, or because she wished to ease his feelings without bruising his ego?* Nicholas wasn't sure which he preferred to believe.

Nonetheless, he did smile then. "I'd hardly be the one to cast stones whether he is or is not. As a bastard myself, I have a good deal of empathy on the matter. Goodnight, Lady Ramsleigh."

Chapter Six

ON THE THIRD day after a ship, unknown to him, had run aground on the Yorkshire coast, The Right Honorable Sir James Daventry was enjoying his evening brandy when a knock interrupted his contemplation of his most recent mistress. The woman was becoming entirely too clingy by far and it was requiring increasingly expensive gifts to mollify her. Those two things combined were reason enough to rid himself of her altogether. But she was remarkably lovely and skilled. Her company was tolerable so long as she wasn't in one of her moods. She didn't put on airs of being a greatly intelligent woman, nor did she try to speak to him of things women had no business indulging in. Business, politics and religion were not areas where the feminine brain could easily grasp even the most basic tenants, to his mind.

Unlike his wife and his errant daughter, he thought. At least his wife—dried up, brittle and so far past her prime he could hardly recall a time when she'd even been pretty much less desirable—had learned her place and no longer dared to question him. Viola had never learned hers. From the very moment of her birth, the girl had been a trial to him. All he'd wanted was a son to carry on his name, but his wife had failed to produce one and the physician had declared her infertile afterward, not that he'd any interest in bedding her again. So he'd been saddled with a useless daughter whom he would have to dower and parade through society.

It had been a stroke of luck when Percival Grantham had caught sight of the girl and sought him out for a match. Some men might have questioned a man of Percival's age seeking a match with a girl who was barely out of the schoolroom. For Daventry, it had been nothing short of a godsend. He could avoid the expense of launching Viola into society by marrying her off when she was too young to know any better.

But, of course, it had not worked out quite that way. She'd shed pitiful tears aplenty, begging him not to sell her off to a man thrice her age. He'd ignored them and even urged Ramsleigh to take a firm hand with her, not that the man had required much urging in that regards. Of course, he'd failed to tame her just as Daventry himself had. If the sudden appearance of the newly-minted Lord Ramsleigh was any indication, that had not changed.

"What do you want, Randall?" he asked. He refused to address the man by title. He wouldn't acknowledge the disparity in their station since he certainly didn't view the younger man as his equal, much less his better.

"Your bitch of a daughter has inconveniently resurrected herself," Randall replied, stalking the length of the room and back, over and over again. He was far too agitated and aggressive for the action to be termed pacing. "What are you going to do about it?"

"Not a thing," Daventry answered, his tone flippant. Viola was no longer his problem. He and Randall's uncle had hatched their plan to declare her dead, to split the inheritance left to her by her maternal grandfather and no one was to be the wiser. But he'd had an inkling then that Viola might return at some point, and so he had been careful to craft his role as a grieving father in such a way that no one could ever doubt him. The simple truth was, he'd spent the entirety of Viola's life ignoring her presence. It hadn't altered his life much at all to have to pretend she had shuffled off the mortal coil. Other than the damned inconvenience of their mourning period and how much it had limited his social opportunities, it had truthfully changed nothing at all. "I did not attend her funeral or see her body. It's joyous news to me that she survived her abusive husband by whatever means necessary and now that he is gone, has returned to the bosom of her family."

Randall stopped his stalking and crossed the expanse of the room. When he was standing just on the other side of the desk, he placed his clenched fists atop it and leaned in, "You're in this, too, Daventry. You cannot pretend otherwise, at least not with me. You and my uncle devised this scheme together and then split what was to have been her inheritance. If need be, I'll expose your involvement and then your pristine reputation will be ruined just as mine is!"

James laughed in incredulity. He would not be threatened by the likes of Randall Grantham. Titled or not, the entire family was beneath him in dignity. "As if you'd be believed! You're a dissolute rake, a wastrel and ne'er-do-well. The entirety of the ton knows you for what you are, Randall. That's why they've shut their doors to you."

Ramsleigh smiled coldly, his eyes gleaming with vengeful delight. "Their drawing rooms may be closed to me, Daventry, but I am still a member of their clubs. I still attend the same hells and brothels as the most esteemed men of our society do. And there are any number of ladies who would refuse me entrance to their parlors but invite me into their boudoirs. And let us not forget to mention how grateful they are for the services I provide there! You think yourself safe from rumor and innuendo? You are not above it, sir, and you'd do well to remember that."

James felt the faintest flicker of apprehension. It was true enough that despite his drinking and whoring, Randall was still a handsome enough and occasionally charming enough man to turn a lady's head. If he did manage to utter those damning whispers into the right ears, it could have devastating consequences. His sole purpose in convincing the elder Ramsleigh to go ahead with the deception surrounding Viola's rumored demise was to maintain their current status. The return on his latest investments had not been what he had anticipated and, as such, their financial survival had been dependent upon gaining access to the money left to his missing daughter. Ramsleigh had been in the same boat himself, though it hadn't been poor investments that had caused his financial woes. Drinking, gaming and whoring had brought about the other man's ruin. It wasn't the first time.

If Viola had truly returned and those funds would have to be produced, he would be unable to do so. "What is it that you require for your silence then?" James demanded.

"Only that you come to Yorkshire and persuade your daughter to take herself back to Scotland and rusticate there before something unfortunate were to happen to her. If she doesn't, that box in the churchyard will contain more than rocks," Ramsleigh warned.

"Kill her then," James snapped. "The world already believes her dead. It's a much more expedient solution!" In fact, so long as he didn't have to dirty his own hands, it was the best option for everyone involved.

Randall eyes him coldly. "She's safely ensconced at Castle Black under the care of the newly-returned Lord Blakemore and his new wife. Suffice it to say, my first encounter with Lord Blakemore did not go well. I will not be welcomed there to sway Viola to our way of thinking."

"You threatened him? You are a blasted, hotheaded fool!" Daventry reached for the bottle of brandy on his desk and poured a healthy amount into his glass. Before he could lift the glass to his lips, Randall wrested it from his hands and drained it entirely.

When he was done, Randall wiped his mouth. "No doubt if anything were to happen to her, they would not take kindly to it. There are ways to end her, ways that will have no verifiable connection to either of us. But it's risky and will result in scandal neither of us can afford. Our best bet is to send her packing, and that duty falls to you. As for the threat of putting someone in that grave that bears her name, I meant you, Daventry. If you attempt to burn me on this, I will see you dead."

"Get out," James uttered. "I'll see to her. And you, you wretched beggar, will never darken my door again."

"Just so she goes, Daventry... I don't much care how you do it or what you say to her to make it happen. I'm not giving up all that I've gained here."

On that point, they were in agreement. The generous settlement that had been left to Viola by her grandfather had been claimed upon her death and divided equally between himself and Viola's late husband. His financial woes had not been quite so desperate as Ramsleigh's, but he would feel the loss of it. Of course, it had always been about more than just the money. It had been the height of insults for it to have been tied up in such a way that it would be forever beyond his reach unless Viola's husband was generous or unless Viola, as a widow, decided to share the largesse of her grandfather with her own family.

Ramsleigh, with two mysteriously dead wives already and no heirs, hadn't been chosen at random. James had seen the greed in him. While on a purely objective level, he'd understood that his daughter was beautiful and would appeal to men, he hadn't understood just how much until Ramsleigh approached him. The man's desperate need to possess the girl had worked to James' favor and they'd agreed then to share Viola's inheritance once she reached the age of twenty-five and the funds would be distributed. But then she'd left, fleeing Ramsleigh's heavy hands. Faking her death and getting the funds released to her husband had been the only way. For a moment, Daventry considering killing Randall outright. Only the threat of scandal and the possibility of consequences should he fail stayed his hand. It was not worth the risk to himself and all that he had built.

"I'll talk to her," Daventry agreed.

"You do that. Because if I have to invoke my plans to get rid of her, it will not be a merciful death," Ramsleigh warned, before turning on his heel and leaving as quickly as he'd entered.

Daventry watched the other man go. He really didn't care one way or another if or how Viola died. All he cared about it was appearance. If it came to light that Viola had lived, that she had fled her husband, abandoned him and run off to heaven knew where, it could reflect poorly upon him. Ultimately, that was what he needed to focus on.

How he despised Randall, just as he'd despised his predecessor. They were weak men, controlled by their base urges and their tempers. It was regrettable that he'd ever felt the need to involve himself with them. But shedding himself of his daughter and finding a husband for her who would be willing to give him a portion of her inheritance had been vital at the time. Frustrated and in a foul temper himself, Daventry picked up the glass Randall had taken from him earlier and clutched it in his hand. The urge to throw it and watch it smash into slivers was overwhelming.

After a charged moment where he considered giving in to a vulgar display of temper, Daventry placed the glass once more on his desk and exited his study. He strode out into the corridor, still drafty from Ramsleigh's exit. His wife was standing on the stairs, her face pale and wan, one hand clutching the banister. It would be easy enough to send her tumbling down them, to see her broken like a doll on the floor. For just a moment, he willed it to happen, but she proved to be steadier on her feet than he wished and the laudanum she was dosed with daily should have allowed. He'd need to have a word with the kitchen staff about that.

"Who was here? I heard shouting," she uttered in the same, soft, sing-song voice that he'd come to despise. Never mind that it was the laudanum he'd been slipping into her food for years to keep her quiet and compliant that made her such a puppet. It still grated on his nerves.

"It is none of your concern. Go back to your room," he commanded.

"I heard them mention Viola..." she protested, though her voice trailed off and she looked away, clearly distracted.

"It was the new Lord Ramsleigh expressing his belated condolences on her death," he lied.

"But why would he go to the trouble now? It's been two years!" A confused frown marred her face as she tried to puzzle it out for herself.

It was dangerous to let her think. Just because he'd dulled her wits with the drug didn't mean she lacked them entirely. "You're overwrought and need to drink your evening tonic lest you have another spell," he snapped and waved to a footman to escort her back to her chambers. To the butler, he added, "See to it that she gets an extra dose of her special medication tonight, Fenton."

"Certainly, sir," the butler replied.

There was no judgement, no censure. The man simply accepted his duty and performed it. James smiled tightly. If his wife had been able to do that, he wouldn't have had to resort to drugging her. And he would have had a son instead of the useless whore of a daughter who continued to plague him. "And fetch my coat. I'm going out for the evening." He had a mistress to get rid of.

VIOLA WAS SEATED in the drawing room. It was her first day out of her chamber and in company. She found Christopher, Lord Blakemore's younger brother, to be charming if somewhat jaded for one so young. Lady Beatrice and Lady Agatha, as they'd insisted on being called to avoid confusion, were both delightful. Lord Blakemore was an enigma, however. He was rougher mannered and coarser in his appearance than a titled gentleman typically was. Of course, she knew the rumors about his disappearance from before her own escape—that he'd been lost at sea, presumed dead by most, and now, it appeared, had miraculously returned.

He stood on the far side of the room, drinking brandy and conversing softly with Dr. Warner. The good and much too handsome doctor was another enigma, and one that had occupied far too many of her thoughts already.

To herself, she could recognize it for what it was. Attraction. It was not a state she had anticipated finding herself in—to be drawn so to a man. Certainly not after her marriage and the atrocities she'd suffered nearer the end of it. But even then, she'd understood that not all men were like Percival, or Randall, or even her father. She'd seen men who were kind and attentive to their wives and children. She'd known that to be truth not because of the actions of those men, but because she'd seen their wives lean into their touch, their children rush to greet them. All without fear or hesitation. Certainly most of them had been farmers or those working on her husband's lands. But if such kindness and genuine caring for one another could be had in such low and often arduous circumstances, it only stood to reason it could exist elsewhere as well.

She was seeing that borne out before her eyes in the interactions of Lord Blakemore and Lady Beatrice. They were so obviously, painfully in love with one another that it almost hurt to look at them. Not even in the early stages of her courtship with Percival had she thought herself in love with him. It had been, from the outset, more about making an advantageous match than having a happy and loving marriage. But he'd revealed his true colors on their wedding night and on far too many of the nights that had followed. Any visions she might have entertained of love, of passion, or even of something as simple as contentment had vanished in the face of his cruelty.

Jealousy. Envy. It was an ugly thing to feel for those who had been so kind to her, but feel it she did. She envied their ease with one another, their obvious affection, and when they thought no one else was looking, the passion that burned so clearly in their eyes for one another. What would it be like to feel such things for a man and to have those feelings returned?

"You are awfully deep in thought, my dear."

The observation came from Lady Agatha. Lady Beatrice had risen and crossed the room to stand next to her husband and Dr. Warner, so impossibly handsome in his dark evening clothes and with his black hair brushed away from his face. "I was just thinking how rare it is and how wonderful for them that they are so much in love."

"It is," Lady Agatha agreed. "They both deserve happiness. Graham suffered so much when he was taken from us so young... and Beatrice has always been like a daughter to me. Of course, there are those who take exception to her lack of fortune, who feel that Graham should have married better."

"And do you think he should have?" Viola asked. It was an impertinent question, one that she should not have asked. But luckily, Lady Agatha did not take offense.

The older woman smiled. "My dear, I believe that there is no better reason to marry than for love... and to those who would think otherwise, I hold them in no contempt. Only pity."

"I've been impertinent in asking... but I feel no inclination to stop just yet. Did you marry for love, Lady Agatha?" Viola asked. Her own marriage had been the furthest thing from it. She'd pleaded with her father not to force her into marrying Lord Ramsleigh, but all of her pleas had fallen on deaf ears. A man thrice her age whose first wife had died from a fall while riding alone with him and whose second wife had tumbled down the stairs in the dead of night with no witnesses. It hadn't taken very long in her marriage to realize that it had likely been Lord Ramsleigh's temper that had ended her predecessor's lives and not their own clumsiness.

"I did not. I married because he was wealthy, charming, handsome and all those things that a young and foolish girl can so easily become infatuated with," she admitted ruefully. "But I was lucky. My Nicholas was a kind man, with a loving and forgiving nature. I did not love him when I wed him, but I haven't the words to tell you how much I loved him when I finally had to say goodbye to him."

Viola turned to look back at the couple. They were standing impossibly close to one another. There was nothing inappropriate in their behavior or vulgar, yet the intimacy between them was a palpable thing. Envy filled her, but not jealousy. She did not begrudge them their happiness and she certainly had no designs on Lord Blakemore, but there was something in the way that they were so obviously connected to one another that sparked longing inside her. What would it feel like to be so close to another person? Other than her son, she had no notion of what it felt like to show simple affection for another human being.

Glancing away, she noted that Dr. Warner had vacated his post to Lord Blakemore's right and was approaching her. Her stomach fluttered nervously in response.

When he reached them, he bowed to Lady Agatha and then to her. "If you'd like, Lady Ramsleigh, I thought I'd offer to take you for a stroll in the gardens before dinner."

"That would be lovely. You should join him, my dear," Lady Agatha encouraged. "Beatrice has taken over the gardens and done some truly marvelous things there."

"It would hardly be proper," she protested, "to walk alone with a gentleman and no chaperone." Because she was too drawn to him for her own peace of mind, because she could not trust herself not to spill more of her secrets and to further build on the strange intimacy that already existed between them.

"Nonsense!" Lady Agatha waved her hand dismissively. "You are a widow, my girl… the rules are very different for you now than when you were a young debutante! And he is your physician after all. What could be the harm?"

What, indeed? Left with no recourse and very little room to wriggle out of it, Viola smiled. "Of course. I'd be happy to join you."

"Or at least willing," he chided softly.

She didn't respond to that goading tone, but offered a baleful stare as she took his proffered arm. As they neared the French doors that led out onto the terrace and the garden beyond, she stated firmly, "I dislike being maneuvered, Dr. Warner."

"I only issued an invitation," he replied evenly. "The maneuvering was entirely the enterprise of Lady Agatha. Perhaps your grievance should be directed to her."

"As I am here on her charity, that would hardly be appropriate, would it?"

"Then it is duly noted. Now, may we not enjoy the mild weather and what promises to be a lovely sunset?" The question was posed with a not insignificant amount of amusement.

"You are laughing at me."

"A bit," he agreed. "I understand your reticence but, I assure you, I have no designs on your virtue."

"I am a widow as Lady Agatha pointed out. My virtue, as it were, is no longer a concern."

He looked at her then, all traces of amusement gone from him and a dark, almost predatory expression in its place. "I had intended," he said, "To simply go for a walk with you... I won't deny my attraction, nor will I deny that I mean to act upon it, but I had not thought to do so tonight. However, pointing out that your apparent lack of virtue is not an obstacle does not help the cause."

"That isn't what I meant at all," she protested.

"So it isn't. I have complete control of my actions, Lady Ramsleigh, and you are entirely safe with me. My actions will be all that are proper and gentlemanly, even if my thoughts are another matter entirely."

It was a dangerous game to play with him, and yet she found herself far more curious and far more titillated than was good for either of them. "And what, precisely, are those thoughts, Doctor?"

"Nicholas," he corrected. "My name is Nicholas. And when we are alone, there is no reason that you should call me anything else. My thoughts, Madame, are too carnal even for the jaded ears of a widow."

"Are you trying to seduce me, Nicholas?" she asked, her tone direct and revealing none of the trembling excitement or paralyzing fear she felt at the thought. After the hellish torment she'd suffered at Percival's hands, it was a strange sensation to actually desire a man's company, much less his touch. But she could admit to herself, even without knowing yet whether or not she would act upon it, that she did desire his touch and so much more.

"That would depend upon your willingness to be seduced... Viola."

Viola drew in a deep, shuddering breath and then admitted something to him that was dangerous for them both. "I have not yet decided."

He smiled. "Then, no. I am not trying to seduce you... yet. When you do decide, kindly pass along the information and I'll adjust my intentions accordingly."

With that phrase hanging between them—half-promise and half-threat—they strolled through the garden in a not quite comfortable silence and admired Lady Beatrice's handiwork.

WILLIAM WELLS WAS in his element—the tavern. Seated at one of the tables near the fire, drinking ale he hadn't had to pay for, he was well into his cups. He was also retelling, and embellishing, the story of the good doctor's dashing rescue of a woman who ought to have been a corpse. So long as there was a fresh pair of ears to hear it and a hefty purse to pay for his ale, he'd tell it until he ran out of air.

"Get a rope, he says!" William snapped loudly. "How he saw her, bobbing in that dark water, I'll never know. Eyes like a hawk the man has! Stripped off his boots, tied that length of rope about his waist and waded up to his chest in water so cold I don't even know how he survived it. Some thought he'd gone mad… didn't believe there was a woman out there a'tall. But I knew it. I could see it in his eyes. That wasn't madness. It were courage unlike anything I'd ever witnessed. Not even in battle!"

Two aged women, traveling together to take the waters at Matlock in Derbyshire, were positively enraptured by the tale. They were leaning forward, their eyes as wide as saucers, their hands clenched so tight on the chair arms that the seams of their gloves were straining with it.

William paused, cleared his throat, coughed a bit, then smacked his lips as if he were as parched as a desert. "I don't think I can go on, ladies. My throat's plum dried out on me, it is!"

"Nonsense!" the elder of the two cried out. "Innkeeper, refill this man's tankard immediately!"

Tarley, the innkeeper, nodded his head. If William had ordered the drink himself, his response would have been entirely different. As the ale was going on the tab of those that could pay, Tarley was a bit more amenable to it.

When the tankard was placed before him by the sweet-faced serving girl, William smiled, but he only had eyes for the drink before him. Taking a healthy swallow of the brew, he let out a heartfelt sigh. "My thanks to you, ma'am. Your generosity has done this old soldier a world of good!"

"Yes, yes! Of course. Now tell us about the doctor... is he a handsome man?"

The question had been posed by the younger of the two, though not by more than a decade. Still, it appeared she had a heart for romance, that one.

William grinned. "Oh, now, I wouldn't be calling another man handsome would I? But you can ask Dora there... Dora, is the doctor a handsome man?"

The serving girl smiled that dreamy smile that always seemed to accompany mentions of the doctor to any of the womenfolk in town. "He's the most handsome man I ever seen," she said, her voice coming out like a soft, winsome sigh. "Hair as black as night, cutting a fine, tall figure of a man, he does. And gentle... oh, ladies. I watched him care for my little brother when he fell out of a tree and broke his arm. Never seen a man so tender and careful with a child in my life."

"There you have it, ladies," William said, unwilling to share the spotlight for too long. "Now, where was I?"

"He was wading out into the waves to go and rescue her!"

"Yes, yes," William agreed. "I held the rope tight, not wanting to let the good doctor be washed away as he fought Poseidon himself to save her! None of us could even see the woman, just a dark shape in the water. But that sure he was that she was out there!" Knowing that the ladies had a penchant for the romantic, William embellished more than a little. "It was like he could feel her, I think... knew her presence, he did. Like it was some sort of mystical connection!"

"Soulmates," the woman whispered, wide eyed and wondrous. "Oh, heavens. Please tell me he saved her. After all that and for her to die in his arms, I couldn't bear it!"

"He reached her and just in time. The waves were picking up, you see. The tide was coming in and in that cove, with them rocks, it's a dangerous place to be. But he got to her, and he hauled that piece of wreckage with her splayed on it all the way back to the beach... with us, my brother and me, tugging on that rope to keep it tight and true.

And that, ladies, is when the story became even more interesting..." William raised his tankard, drinking heavily until he could tip it up and let the last drops fall from it onto his lips.

"Innkeeper," the older woman shouted again, "keep the ale coming for this poor gentleman. Why, I cannot imagine how anyone could utter such a tale of dashing bravery and not be thoroughly parched from it!"

William grinned, tipped his dirty hat in thanks and continued on. All the while, another man sat in the darkest corner, taking in the tale for all it was worth. He had no use for stories, but information was another matter entirely. And if Lady Ramsleigh had returned, then likely the new Lord Ramsleigh would want something done about it. Timothy Cobb had never wanted to work hard, but he didn't mind working dirty when it was called for.

Smiling to himself, he listened to William's vivid tale, carving out the bits and pieces of truth from the wildly embellished whole. When it was done, he tossed a coin on the table and rose, heading out into the darkness. Ramsgate Hall wasn't far and the moon was high and bright in the sky to light his way.

The short walk cleared his head, lifting the fog of the numerous tankards of ale he'd indulged in. Reaching the house, he didn't knock at the front. While he might have resented knocking at the servant's entrance, his greed surpassed his pride in sin. It was the housekeeper that answered, her gray hair tucked up in a cap and a heavy, wool wrapper shrouded tightly about her. As if anyone would want the wrinkled goods it concealed, he thought with a bitter laugh.

"It's late to be calling," she scolded.

"I have some information for his lordship that will not wait. He'll not be happy to hear it on the lips of every gossipmonger in this town on the morrow, now will he?" he replied.

"You can wait for him in the study, then," she said. "I'll send a footman to fetch him!"

Too dangerous to send a maid, he thought. Lord Ramsleigh did love to pluck the most reluctant fruit. Cobb tipped his hat to the housekeeper and walked past her into the darkened hall of the mausoleum that was Ramsgate. He'd never liked the place. It pressed in on a person, heavy and dark, like the grave it was for so many. Old Lord Ramsleigh had gone through three wives in that darkened tomb. Well, two at any rate, he corrected with a chuckle.

It was a long wait, long enough for him to have seated himself comfortably and nearly dozed off in one of the wing chairs that flanked the desk. The flick of a blade at this throat woke him quickly enough. Bringing his hand up, he touched the shallow cut there, his own blood coating his fingertips.

"That wasn't called for, now was it?" he asked calmly.

Ramsleigh stood before him, cleaning the blade with his handkerchief. Dressed only in breeches and an open shirt, the man looked more pirate than nobleman. "That depends entirely upon your reasons for disturbing me at such an hour. They'd better be good, Cobb, or you'll get more than a shaving nick."

"William Wells won't shut his gob," Cobb said. "He's telling tales to every traveler what passes through the inn and can buy him a pint. If you want to keep the return of your aunt quiet, you'll need to shut him up quick."

"And I assume you'll want the job? And to be well compensated for it?" Ramsleigh queried.

"I might. And any other jobs what might come my way from it… a man's got to eat, after all," Cobb replied.

"Then you'll shut Wells up, by any means necessary… and you'll be borrowing his methods. I can't kill her," Ramsleigh said. "Not outright. It's too suspicious. But this is a small village, poor and angry for it. They are rife with superstition and that anger and those backward beliefs are the tools we will use to end her miserable life."

"I'm all ears, your lordship," Cobb said.

"One simple word is all that will be required to turn the lot of them against her," Ramsleigh said. "Witch."

Cobb shook his head. "They won't try anyone for witchcraft, my lord. It's no longer a crime!"

"It wasn't a trial I was after, Cobb, but a mob. Stir them up. Rile them to the point of action and then unleash them upon her!"

"The lot of them would hang for it in the end," Cobb said.

"Do you honestly care?" Ramsleigh shot back.

Cobb shook his head. "Not a bit, your lordship. Just need to be certain all the cards is on the table, is all."

"So long as they are effective in eliminating the threat of Viola Grantham, I've no qualms about sending half the inhabitants of this village to hell. See to it, Cobb. But eliminate Wells first. Perhaps, his unfortunate demise will be attributed to the very darkness that my aunt has brought back to Blackfield with her."

"In other words, don't shoot him. Make it look like the devil did it."

Ramsleigh laughed. "My dear, Mr. Cobb, the devil did do it... we are simply his agents."

Chapter Seven

SEATED IN THE morning room, working to repair a piece of embroidery that Lady Beatrice had mangled beyond imagining, Viola was still wracked with indecision. Her wounds had largely healed. Even the lingering headaches had vanished. The only thing preventing her from acting upon her desire to pursue the handsome doctor was her own indecisive nature.

It had been two days since their pre-dinner stroll in the garden, two days since he'd told her of his desire for her and his lack of intent to seduce her—or at the very least, his postponement of any intent to seduce her. He'd made it quite obvious that in order for any sort of seduction to begin, she would have to offer an express desire to be seduced by him. It wasn't that she was uncertain of her desire. But she found the idea of having to profess such a thing to anyone had left her somewhat befuddled. What precisely did one say in such a situation?

"You appear to be quite deep in thought, my dear!"

The observation had come from Lady Agatha, whom Viola was quickly realizing missed little. Whatever ill health the lady might have suffered in the past appeared to have little to no impact on her current mental acuity. "I am very sorry, Lady Agatha. I fear my conversation has been very lacking this morning."

"Nonsense, my dear! It is not your duty as a guest to entertain me... but as your hostess, it is my duty to see to your comfort. And it does appear to me that you are troubled. If I may be so bold, I might hazard a guess that it is our dear Dr. Warner who so occupies your mind."

Viola could feel the blush stealing over her cheeks. "I don't know what you mean," she denied quickly and unconvincingly.

Lady Agatha laughed softly. "My dear child, and I say this with complete affection, you are a terrible liar."

Viola dropped the embroidery onto her lap. "He is a very handsome man. And more charming than he ought to be."

"And you are more charmed than you think you ought to be," Lady Agatha observed sagely.

Viola could feel the blush heating her cheeks as she nodded her agreement. "You must think me terribly wicked!"

"I think you delightful, my girl, but terribly unhappy. As for any wickedness, you are a widow, my dear. That affords you a great deal of freedom. So long as you are discreet, there is no reason that you should not live your life precisely as you please," Lady Agatha said. "I understand that my advice might be somewhat shocking, but I—well, I knew enough about your husband to imagine that the marriage was not a happy one. As such, it would not surprise me if you did not wish to marry again. That does not mean you should be devoid of companionship forever."

Deciding to be as candid as Lady Agatha had been, Viola replied, "I confess to having had those same thoughts myself, my lady, but I am entirely ignorant of how one undertakes such a thing! I am quite uncertain how to proceed."

"I daresay if you provide the appropriate cues, he will be more than content to take the lead on the matter."

Viola smiled. "This is a most irregular conversation."

"This is a most irregular household, my dear," Lady Agatha answered evenly. "We are too far removed from society here to care what its dictates are. Instead, I choose to care only for the happiness of this house's inhabitants."

There was much more to it than that, Viola realized. There was a sadness about Lady Agatha, a worldliness as well. She was a woman with a past, too. Emboldened by that realization, Viola confided, "My husband was... he was not a kind man. If he possessed a shred of gentleness in his soul, I certainly never bore witness to it. I admit to having an attraction to the doctor, Lady Agatha, but I'm enjoying being attracted to him far more than I imagine I will enjoy being his lover.'

Lady Agatha put down her embroidery, placing it in her lap with care. She was quiet for a long moment, obviously considering her answer with great care. "It is unfortunate that young women are so sheltered that they have no notion what to expect before marriage. I understand that knowledge leads to temptation and temptation to ruin... but someone should have spoken with you frankly beforehand. If he was rough with you, or even cruel, that is a product of his own twisted desires and has nothing to do with what would typically take place between willing and, I daresay, eager participants. What you experienced at the brutish hands of your husband will have little or no similarity to what could take place between you and Dr. Warner."

"Nicholas—" Viola stopped herself abruptly. It was terribly inappropriate to refer to him so familiarly. Even with the conversation they were having, it seemed to her a terrible faux pas. "Dr. Warner appears to be a very kind man. I do not think he is at all similar to my late husband either in temperament or behavior... but I am also not the hopeful girl I was before I married Percival. I am very much afraid, Lady Agatha, that the issue is not Dr. Warner at all. It's simply me and all the doubts and fears I cannot allay."

Lady Agatha reached over and placed her hand over Viola's. "Nicholas was my husband's name. Did I tell you that?" At a shake of Viola's head, she continued. "I was, in my youth, a terrible wife—and an unfaithful one. The very inappropriate man to whom I gave my affections could well have ruined us all and possibly sent us to the gallows. I was wicked and yet my husband forgave me. He loved me, even when I had failed him so terribly. I say this to you now, Viola, to tell you that there is great deal in your Nicholas that reminds me of my own. He is not kind because he expects things in return, or because he thinks it will sway you to what he desires. He is kind because it is who he is. He will be patient with you, because that, too, is who he is. Do not let fear keep you from love, my dear, even if it is a fleeting sort of love."

"He doesn't love me and I don't know if I can let myself love him."

Lady Agatha laughed. "My dear, you say that as if you have a choice! We do not choose to love. Love chooses us!"

Viola was allowing that knowledge to sink in, basking in the reassurance and the hope that had been offered, when the butler entered. "There is a visitor, my lady," he said, "For Lady Ramsleigh."

"Who is it?" Lady Agatha asked.

"He will not give his name, my lady. But insists on speaking with Lady Ramsleigh immediately," the butler replied, clearly offended by the presence of such a rude individual.

"It could only be one of two people," Viola reasoned. She was rather proud of how calm and serene her voice sounded, at least to her own ears. Especially since she was quaking with fear inside. "It will be my nephew-by-marriage, the new Lord Ramsleigh, or it will be my father, here it his behest."

"Show him in," Lady Agatha commanded. When the butler was gone, she said, "If it is your father, I will leave you. If it is Lord Ramsleigh, I will not. Also, I will ring for extra footmen to be present lest he shares similar violent tendencies to his uncle."

"Lady Agatha, his violent tendencies surpass his uncle's," Viola answered honestly. "If my husband was a brute, then his nephew is nothing short of a monster."

A moment later, an older and distinguished-looking gentleman stepped into the room. His disapproving frown and cold gaze settled on Viola instantly. "I see it is true," he said.

"Hello, Father. And yes, it is true. I am very much alive... though I strongly suspect you were well aware of that," she answered. He had written her in Aberdeen, after all, informing her that she would never again be welcome in his home and that he and her mother had disowned her entirely. He'd spoken at length of the shame she'd brought to him, of disobedience and willfulness, selfishness, and a complete lack of care for the dishonor of her family. Meanwhile, he'd sold her to a man thrice her age who had already buried two wives under mysterious circumstances.

"You should not have returned," he snapped. "It would have been better for all concerned had you simply stayed dead!"

"Well, I did not... nor do I have any intention of returning to Scotland and rusticating on a farm. I am the widow of Lord Ramsleigh. As such, I am entitled to the inheritance my grandfather left me... or whatever remains after my husband squandered so much of it."

"You abandoned him! You broke the marriage contract. I daresay the current Lord Ramsleigh could take this to the courts and have every single sovereign awarded to him!"

"I did not abandon my husband... I fled his abuse in order to protect my unborn child," she answered just as forcefully. "Randall is only Lord Ramsleigh for as long as Tristan is not here to claim the title. When he arrives, Randall will find himself deposed and I will take over the running of Ramsgate Hall and all of the Ramsleigh holdings until such time as my son is able to see to them for himself."

If she'd wanted to shock him, she'd certainly succeeded. His face paled considerably and his breathing took on a ragged quality. She thought he might very well be having apoplexy. Even worse, she had to admit that a part of her wanted him to. She had never loved her father, but she hadn't hated him. Not until the truth of his involvement in the false declaration of death had been confirmed.

"Yes... I have a son. He is but a year old and was conceived before I left for Scotland—before you and my husband declared to the world that I had died so that he could save face and you could get a portion of the money my grandfather had left in trust for me," she continued. It was purely conjecture on her part, but his motive was entirely confirmed as his gaze narrowed and his lips pulled back in an expression that could only be described as feral. "Did you think I was too stupid to understand your motives? That I wouldn't be able to see your greed at work in all of this? Percival was all bluster and temper. He'd have searched to the ends of the earth if for no other reason than to drag me back and punish me for what I had done. It was you who convinced him to do otherwise by appealing to his greed!"

"You will not speak to me that way!" he shouted in response, his face purpling with rage.

"I had not thought to speak to you at all," Viola answered evenly. "Your only contact with me following my leaving Ramsgate Hall was to state emphatically that I was dead to you. I find it best for all around if we leave matters in just that way. Good day, Father."

"I'll do whatever is necessary to see that you and your bastard child get not a penny! Do you understand me?"

Viola smiled, but it was a cold expression, mirroring one that she'd seen on his face for most of her life. "Far better than I'd like to. Please do not make me ask the servants to throw you out... I'd prefer it, as would Lady Agatha, no doubt, if you'd leave of your own accord."

"I will leave. I will be paying a visit to Lord Ramsleigh and informing of your intent to pawn off some bastard as the rightful heir. This will not stand, Viola. It will not!" He turned on his heel and stormed out as quickly as he'd entered.

Lady Agatha exhaled sharply. "What an unpleasant man! I'm so terribly sorry, my dear, that you have had nothing but the worst of men in your life. It's little wonder you are hesitant about Dr. Warner! Rest assured, he is cut from a much different cloth."

"On that we are in agreement... but if my father and Randall intend to bring Tristan's paternity into question, embarking on a torrid affair with anyone is hardly the way to secure my son's future." Even now, her late husband and his worthless relatives—and her own— were controlling every aspect of her life.

"It isn't as if you're taking out in advertisement in the *Times*! You are both under one very respectable roof and may do as you please."

It was a tempting suggestion, but Viola understood far better than Lady Agatha just how ruthless both her father and Randall could be. "I will consider it," she stated simply.

DAVENTRY HAD BROUGHT two letters with him, well prepared in advance. One was to inform Randall that he had succeeded in gaining Viola's cooperation. The second was to inform him that Viola was once more proving difficult and he should proceed with his own enterprises. Carefully worded, neither of those missives could be perceived in any way to pertain to criminal activity. Weighing them in his hands, they felt completely identical in heft and size. Yet with one of them, he would be signing his own progeny's death warrant.

For a moment, he allowed that thought to resonate within him. In the end, like so many other things in life, it failed to spark any true sentiment. His pause had been more to measure his own actions and decide what would ultimately be the best course for him. There had been no thought about morality or sinfulness, or even any tender feelings he should have had for the young girl he'd watched grow into womanhood. At one point in time, she'd been an asset. Now she was an obstacle. As with all obstacles, she would be removed.

"Driver, return me to the inn. I will sup there while you see this letter delivered to Ramsgate Hall. When your task is done, fetch me and we will be rid of this wretched place."

"Yes, sir," the driver acquiesced.

Daventry settled back against the well-padded squab seats of his barouche. Viola had sealed her own fate, he reflected.

THE ONLY INN that the small village of Blackfield-on-Went was somewhat below his normal standards. As Cornelius wiped the bread crumbs and spattered ale from the table with his handkerchief, he realized what a gross understatement of the facts that was. He'd arrived later than anticipated. The small cottage he'd been directed to that was supposed to house his half-brother, Blackfield's only physician, had proven to be empty.

To the serving girl, he said, "Pardon me, but where might I find Dr. Nicholas Warner?"

The girl stepped back immediately, a look of panic on her face. "Are you ill, sir?"

Cornelius didn't utter the long suffering sigh that her response begged for. Instead, he smiled politely. "Not at all. He is a relative of mine and I have arrived in town unexpectedly. I thought to visit him while I am here."

"Oh!" the girl said, in obvious relief. "Mr. Tarleton doesn't like to have sick folks at the inn, sir. He insists it's very bad for business. We had a gentlemen casting up his accounts in here a month back and I've never had to clean so much in my life!"

Given that it was unlikely the place had been cleaned since, Cornelius nodded. "I'm certain it was terrible. About Dr. Warner..."

"He's likely up at Castle Black, sir. He and Lord Blakemore are quite thick with one another!"

That was helpful information, at least. Hoping that Castle Black was more hospitable than its name implied, Cornelius dropped several coins on the table and rose. "Bring a pot of tea and whatever food is about that is least likely to induce illness."

The girl either didn't understand that he was speaking in jest or was too intimidated by either him or Mr. Tarleton to laugh. Instead, she scurried away to do his bidding as quickly as possible. Alone again, Cornelius sat back and gave his surroundings deeper study. The inn was old. The wood furnishings were worn and scratched from use, and the cleanliness was less than pristine to be sure. But the building showed signs of recent repair and was in passably good upkeep.

The patrons were an odd assortment of locals and travelers, as the stage and another carriage had arrived there at the same time he had. In one corner, a group of local men were deep in conversation, casting furtive glances about the room. Smugglers, he thought, but if they were, they were doing poorly at it. Each one was dressed in clothing little better than rags and while they might work on the water, from the looks of them, they'd never much been in it.

"I'm telling you, it ain't natural!" the swarthiest amongst them said forcefully. His voice had risen just enough that even Mr. Tarleton, the innkeeper, looked up and leveled a warning stare at him.

"You can give me the evil eye all you like, Tarley," the man continued. "But you was saying the same thing last night over a pint before William Wells started in on his epic tale! She were dead! We all knew it. Watched them cart her out in that box and put her right in the ground, we did!"

"Saw them cart out a box," Tarleton replied. "That's all. I never seen what was in it and neither did you, Timothy Cobb! You'll not be stirring up trouble in my establishment with your superstitions and nonsense! Get on with you now!"

The man, Timothy Cobb, rose to his feet, swayed slightly and then lifted his hand in the tradition of all great orators as he began to pontificate. "There's been evil at that house for decades... alls I'm suggesting is that maybe it weren't the old lord who was the root of it! Or maybe he corrupted her! All I know is the dead ain't supposed to come back and if'n they do, it means nothing but trouble for the living!"

"And what do you suggest we do about it?" one of the men asked. He was clearly leery of getting into trouble, but also easily swayed by the opinions of his friend and apparent leader.

"What we always did with witches and those that were in league with the devil," Cobb said. "We drive her out of town!"

"And if she won't go?"

"Then she burns for it!" Cobb emphasized the violence of his belief by banging heartily on the rafters, sending showers of dust down onto the tabletops.

Several of the travelers, a few women among them, gasped in alarm. Tarleton, realizing that the would-be zealot in their midst was potentially costing him business, bristled. "That's enough out of you. Drink down that last pint and be gone with you... and not another word about witches and the devil! The only devil in here is you, Timothy Cobb! Disturbing my customers and making these fine folks think we're a bunch of backwards fools!"

Cobb gripped his tankard, drained a goodly portion of the ale and let the rest run in disgusting rivulets from the corners of his mouth down onto his dirt-encrusted shirt. Finally, with a loud and rather pungent belch, he wiped the back of his hand across his mouth and staggered toward the door.

Curious, Cornelius checked his watch. It was only three in the afternoon. For a man to be that drunk that early, he had to have started at first light or possibly continued from the previous night. Either way, Timothy Cobb was trouble to be sure.

The serving girl returned carrying a tray with bread, some rather suspect cheese and pot of tea. "Tell me, girl, who was he speaking of?"

She shook her head. "I don't want to utter the name lest he's right, sir. If she is in league with the devil and I speak of her... it might bring ruin to my whole family!"

Cornelius considered pressing the issue, but it was only to appease his own curiosity and not because he had any need or desire to involve himself. He glanced down at the unappealing fare placed before him and made a split-second decision. He would seek his half-brother at Castle Black.

"How do I reach Castle Black from here?"

"You'll need a horse. It's too far to walk! Follow the main road out of town toward the coast. It's the big house on the hill above the sea. It's nearly impossible to miss!"

"Excellent... my carriage is being repaired, hence my unexpected stop here in Blackfield. The wheelwright is to call here when it is ready. You will send word to me at Castle Black if I have not yet returned. There will be additional coin for you, if you do."

The girl nodded in vigorous agreement. "Aye, sir. I'll see it's done!"

Cornelius moved toward the door just as it blew open, landing against the other wall with a heavy thud. The man who entered was known to him, though they were not friends. It was impossible for anyone to be truly friendly with Daventry. The man was a colder fish than any pulled from the Atlantic.

He eyed Cornelius with disdain. "Lord Ambrose," Daventry

acknowledged.

"Daventry. What brings you to Blackfield?" There had been some scandal about the man's daughter being wed to Ramsleigh he recalled. What a nightmare that was!

"Family affairs... nothing to concern yourself with," the other man replied dismissively. "And you? You are quite far afield from London."

"A broken carriage wheel while returning to London, in fact," Cornelius answered. "And I have distant relatives in the area. I'm off to Castle Black to inquire with them now."

The man's face darkened, his thunderous expression turning even darker at the mention of Castle Black. "I am not surprised that a member of your family would have truck with the liars and thieves that inhabit the place. I bid you good day, Lord Ambrose!"

Not only dismissed but insulted by a gentleman he outranked, Cornelius found himself bemused rather than affronted. It was becoming a common occurrence as all of his father's sins were coming home to roost. He had little doubt that the cut direct would be something he would quickly become accustomed to.

At the stable, he procured a horse, if one could call the sway-backed nag such a thing, and headed in the direction of the castle as he'd been directed. What should have taken no more than half an hour took nearly two. Not only was the horse he'd been given sway-backed, it was stubborn, disobedient, never met a blade of grass or weed it did not feel inclined to ingest. If he hadn't known better, he'd have thought that the stable master disliked him. As he'd spoken a grand total of ten words to the man, he wasn't entirely certain how he'd managed to give offense, but clearly he had.

During his longer than necessary ride, he was still thinking of Daventry and whatever he might be doing in Blackfield. To the best of his recollections, the man's daughter had died some time ago, and Ramsleigh as well. Surely, there would be no reason for him to have dealings with the newly-named Lord Ramsleigh. Randall was the worst kind of blackguard—not the thing at all.

As he neared the castle, Cornelius saw two gentlemen, both dark-haired and the appropriate age to be his half-brother. But it was the gentleman to the left who drew his attention. There was a portrait of his father as a younger man, before his dissipated life had taken its heavy toll on him, and that gentleman could have posed for it.

"Dr. Nicholas Warner, I presume?" Cornelius said as he drew his mount up near theirs.

"I am Dr. Warner," the gentleman replied. "How may I be of service?"

"You can help me put this animal out of its misery... I've seen worthier horseflesh on donkeys," Cornelius replied. "But alas, I should introduce myself. I am Cornelius Garrett, Lord Ambrose—your half-brother."

NICHOLAS' EXPRESSION REMAINED inscrutable, more from years of practice than from effort on his part. He had not expected that his newfound family connections would come seeking him out. Recalling the letter and the mention of a settlement, it began to make more sense.

"I'll sign whatever documents are required to disavow the inheritance. I've no desire to have anything more from the man who sired me than what has already been given—the ability to support myself," Nicholas replied.

Lord Ambrose was silent for a moment, as if taking his measure. When the man spoke again, his tone was mild, almost apologetic. "You misunderstand, Dr. Warner... my being here is more of a coincidence than anything to do with our father's last will and testament. Though, I daresay, you should learn the particulars of the settlement before refusing it so vehemently. I was traveling to London from our great aunt's estate near Edinburgh when my carriage became disabled. I had thought this an opportunity to become acquainted with one another... assuming you are amenable to that."

Nicholas surveyed the gentleman dispassionately. There was a slight similarity in their appearance, though his own coloring was much darker. To his mind, that only made matters worse. He'd have been far happier if there had been no family resemblance at all. He resented it, he realized—resented sharing anything with the family for whom he'd been nothing but a dirty secret. "I can hardly refuse, can I?"

"I don't see why not," Lord Ambrose mused. "Given the scandals that have boiled over, one right after another, following father's demise, most people have… I can't think of a single house in all of London where I'm truly welcome these days, including my own. So, yes, Doctor, you may certainly refuse. And given our father's treatment of you, you would be well within your rights to do so. I would only beg your consider one thing, sir."

"And what is that?" Nicholas demanded.

"That I am, thankfully, not our father."

Nicholas didn't know quite what to make of the stranger before him claiming such kinship. The man was well dressed, gave every appearance of being a gentleman, and yet he had none of the haughtiness that was so typical of those of a higher class. He seemed, in fact, to be amused by all of it, rank and scandal alike. "It is not my house to welcome you to," Nicholas responded vaguely, alleviating himself of the responsibility in that situation.

"By all means," Graham interjected, "Join us, please. My mother will be delighted to have someone else to fuss over and no doubt Lady Ramsleigh will be relieved as well that mother will have someone else to fuss over. She can be a bit overwhelming."

"Lady Ramsleigh?" Lord Ambrose queried. "I understood that she had passed some time ago."

"It is my understanding," Nicholas answered sharply, "that she fled an abusive husband and he put about rumors of her death, going so far as to fake her burial in order to save face at having been abandoned for his cruelty."

Lord Ambrose held up a staying hand. "I meant no disrespect to the lady, Doctor. But that news does answer two questions that I have stumbled upon today. The first is why on earth, Mr. Daventry, the lady's father, was here in Blackfield... I have just encountered him at the inn, you see. The second question is more troubling still."

"And what, pray tell, is this question?" The commanding tone in Blakemore's voice brooked no argument.

"There are certain troublemakers in the village, drunkards in the tavern mostly, that are speaking of witches, the devil, and a woman returned from the dead. While the burning of witches is a dark spot on our history, gentlemen, and is no longer sanctioned by the laws of our nation, I would not put it past certain members of our current society to engage in such brutality. It has not been so very long, after all, that our French counterparts were being paraded through the streets to be guillotined and their heads displayed on pikes," Ambrose answered.

"Nothing will happen to Lady Ramsleigh while she is in our care," Graham insisted.

"Nothing will happen to Lady Ramsleigh at all," Nicholas corrected. "She will be well protected."

If either of the other men thought the vehemence of his response was inappropriate for a casual acquaintance, neither remarked upon it. Instead, Graham merely arched an eyebrow at him and then extended his invitation more formally to Lord Ambrose, "Please join us at Castle Black... we can walk from here since I doubt your borrowed mount could survive the climb."

With his newly-acquired half-brother with them, the trio made their way up the hill to the gates of Castle Black. No one spoke. While the silence was not entirely companionable, it was not overly tense either. Nicholas did find himself curious at what Lord Ambrose might actually want of him, though he couldn't imagine that he had anything of value to offer the man. And as no member of the Garrett family had ever shown the least bit of familial interest in him, he dismissed that possibility out of hand.

As they neared the house, the butler opened the door. He looked askance at having someone else joining their ranks.

"Forgive me, my lord," he said, "I was not aware that we were expecting company."

"That's because we weren't," Graham answered evenly. "It will be no trouble to have an extra place set for dinner, I'm sure. Beatrice will instruct you in all that is required."

"Again, my apologies, my lord. I did not mean to imply that our guest..."

"Lord Ambrose," Nicholas supplied, watching the servant flounder.

"That Lord Ambrose would not be welcome. Perhaps, I should have said 'more' guests. A Mr. Daventry arrived earlier to call upon Lady Ramsleigh and I fear his visit was not a pleasant one. She has taken to her bed and Lady Agatha is quite overwrought."

Nicholas glanced back at Lord Ambrose. "Welcome to bedlam."

"At least it's interesting," he replied, and followed them into the house.

Chapter Eight

THE EPISODE WITH her father had left Viola more shaken than she cared to admit. It had also exhausted her entirely. Her energy level had not yet returned fully though most of her injuries were, if not entirely healed, certainly beyond the point of any real concern. Of course, it was possible that her exhaustion had nothing to do with her physical state and everything to do with the soul-deep weariness that her father's coldness and contempt of her induced.

Having retreated to her room, Viola sat at her dressing table, her palms sweaty and her hands trembling. Why it should matter after so long, when he'd done nothing save prove her worst suspicions of him, she could not say. Perhaps, it was the permanency of having him deny her face to face. Regardless, she was in an ill humor and fit company for no one. It was that feeling which prompted her heavy sigh when a knock sounded on her door. No doubt, it was Lady Agatha there to fuss over her once more or, perhaps, Lady Beatrice to inquire politely if she needed anything. Either way, she found her nerves less then settled at the prospect of entertaining anyone.

"I'm fine, Lady Agatha. I'm only tired from the excitement," she called out. It was impossibly rude but she didn't have it in her to be anything else.

The door swung inward and Nicholas stood there, leaning nonchalantly against the frame. *When did I begin to think of him as Nicholas rather than Dr. Warner?* Recognizing just what a terrible sign that was in regards to her own mindset and ability to resist temptation, Viola stiffened her spine and prepared to give him a set down. Lady Agatha's assurances aside, she would not risk denying her son his birthright just to indulge her own base nature.

"You're making yourself quite free with my private chamber, *Dr. Warner.*"

"So I am. I understand you had an unexpected and decidedly unpleasant visitor today," he stated, not even bothering to couch it as a question.

"I see I have been the topic of much conversation already. Yes, my father came to call. Yes, he was unpleasant. No, I had not anticipated his visit or that should he choose to make one, it would be a pleasant affair. He was precisely as he has always been—cold, cruel, and self-serving."

He entered the room fully then, closing the door behind him. She was no longer his patient. It was decidedly improper. And against her better judgement and reason, it was impossibly exciting. "What do you think you are doing?" Viola demanded, more for show than out of any real protest.

"I am hiding," he said succinctly. "You are not the only person who has unwanted family dropping by."

She frowned at that. "I thought you did not have a family."

"Oddly enough, I had thought much the same. It appears my father—producer of many bastards, I fear—has shuffled off his mortal coil. Now, my half-brother feels compelled to hunt us all down and try to have relationships with us. God forbid!"

Viola found his answer very strange, indeed. Having been an only child herself, she had longed for siblings. "Unless he is unkind, why would you not wish to develop a relationship with him? My family has disavowed me entirely. My father only came here to scold me for bothering to return and ruffling the pretty bed of lies he's laid out for everyone. Your family is actually desirous of your company!"

"Now they are. They have never been in the past. When I was a young man, alone in the world, my father bought me a commission in the Royal Navy and sent me off to what was surely supposed to be my death. I survived by mere chance. Afterward, he paid for my medical training. All of this was accomplished without us ever meeting face to face. I find it difficult to account that my half-brother never knew I existed... and even so, we are grown men now. The time for filial bonding has passed, I think."

Viola took note of several things. His easy manner was not so easy now. Oh, he lounged in his chair as if he hadn't a care in the world. But there was a tension in him, a tightness about his eyes and a firmness in his jaw that she had not seen previously. As she'd made a rather particular study of his face over the past few days, even such slight changes were more than obvious to her.

"It hurt you that he never bothered to know you or to see all you had accomplished," she surmised.

He scoffed at that, offering a sharp bark of laughter. "I had never expected any better from him. How could it hurt? He has never hurt me, but he did hurt my mother very gravely, indeed, I think."

"How so?" she asked, curious at this side of him. She had sensed from the beginning that there were hidden depths to the good doctor, concealed beneath his charming facade and easy manner. But this was her first glimpse of them.

"My mother was an actress, at best. At the very least, that is what she called herself. It might have been true, I suppose, or had been at one point. However it began, when her life ended she was a demirep. Of course, I did not bear witness to this. I learned it from the family who raised me, chosen by my father and tenants on his lands. Is it my turn to have shocked you, Viola?"

"No. I am not shocked. But I am to assume that you meant for me to be?" Nicholas did not answer that accusation. So she continued, "I have inferred from the way you speak of her that your mother met a tragic end?"

He shrugged. "It doesn't hurt that he wanted nothing to do with me. It did hurt, however, to learn the truth about her. According to those acquaintances of hers I could track down, she mourned for him and his negligence until the day she died. A paltry list of protectors, if that is what they were, filled the years for her in between her liaison with my father and her untimely death. But she never loved them, as I was told."

"But she did love him?"

He grew quiet, thoughtful, and answered softly. "No. One of her friends had kept a box of my mother's letters and journals. I read them, much to my own discomfort. She obsessed about him. She constantly ruminated over his rejection of her. He ruined her life, but only because she permitted him to."

"Then why are you avoiding a brother who clearly wishes to lay the past to rest? What possible harm could come from at least ascertaining why he has sought you out?"

Nicholas frowned thoughtfully for a moment, and when he met her gaze again, it was with a challenging proposition. "I will entertain my half-brother and determine why he has come here, if you will dress and join us for dinner below stairs instead of hiding up here like a whipped dog because your father dared show his face."

"You mistake me, Dr. Warner. That is not what I am doing at all!" The denial was hot on her lips. It was also a blatant lie. "But if that is what is required to compel you to stop behaving like a petulant child, I will gladly do so!"

"Let us both dress for dinner and I will see you downstairs," he offered, his tone no less challenging than before although he had already secured her agreement.

"Very well. I shall see you at dinner… and not a moment before."

NICHOLAS HAD DRESSED for dinner as they agreed. As he approached the drawing room, he heard voices inside and knew that his half-brother was charming Lady Agatha handily if her peals of laughter were any indication.

He would admit, to himself at least, that there had been some truth to Viola's accusations. He was hiding from his half-brother and there might be some degree of petulance involved. Where had his family been for all of his life after all, aside from noticeably absent? There had never been any hint of familial concern from his father. The man had, at best, ensured Nicholas' ability to support himself and nothing more. It was hardly a ringing endorsement of his paternal nature though even Nicholas would admit that it was far more than many men did for their bastard children.

Taking a deep and fortifying breath, he entered the drawing room and noted that conversation stopped immediately. It was all curious stares and expectation.

"I'm glad you could join us, Doctor," Lady Agatha said after a long pause. "You are always such delightful company."

"It appears someone is already providing delightful company for you, Lady Agatha. You are positively radiant with it... I'll allow him to continue entertaining you until you grow tired of his company and break his heart as you do all young men's," he answered smoothly.

"If you'd forgive me, Lady Agatha, for deserting you so quickly... I'd like to have a private word with Dr. Warner," Lord Ambrose stated. His tone was mild and his expression inscrutable, leaving Nicholas to wonder what on earth their private conversation could be about.

"Certainly, Lord Ambrose. The morning room is just at the back of the corridor," Lady Agatha offered. "I'm certain it will suffice for your needs if you are agreeable."

"Quite agreeable, Lady Agatha," Ambrose replied as he rose from the settee he had been occupying next to her. "Dr. Warner, you are more familiar with the house than I am. If you'd be so kind as to lead the way?"

"Follow me," Nicholas replied. He nodded to Lady Agatha and Christopher. Graham, Beatrice and Viola had yet to come down. Exiting the drawing room, he walked the short distance to the doorway to the morning room and waited there for Lord Ambrose. When the man had neared, Nicholas opened the door and stepped inside.

Once the door closed, Nicholas decided to beard the lion in his den so to speak. "I've no need of familial connections now, nor am I entirely certain I want them. I don't know why it is that you've come, but I think you may be very disappointed in the outcome."

Lord Ambrose cocked his head to one side as if considering Nicholas' words carefully. When he finally spoke, his tone was mild and his words well measured. "I did not seek you out, Doctor, because I thought I might have something you needed. I sought you out because I thought, perhaps, I needed a connection to what was left of my family... even if they were strangers. You are not my father's only by-blow. And I apologize for the use of that term as I myself find it offensive, but there are only so many terms available and many of them are much worse."

"Bastard you mean?" Nicholas queried.

"Just so. Regardless of the marital status of your parents at birth, we do share blood, Dr. Warner... I find myself, having lost our father—worthless as he was—feeling somewhat adrift with no other family to call my own. I am slowly searching out all of the siblings that I can. There are others still that we may never know of," Ambrose admitted. "Father enjoyed women, but to my knowledge never loved any of them. To that end, fidelity was not to be found in either his nature or his behavior."

"And you elected to start with me first? To what do I owe that dubious honor?" Nicholas asked caustically.

Lord Ambrose walked to the window and looked out at the sea beyond the cliffs. There was just enough light left for it to be a truly beautiful sight. "Father made note of your accomplishments. While he might not have been attentive and certainly could not be considered a worthy parent, he did take a measure of pride in how well you availed yourself during your time in the military and your accomplishments since. I suppose you were the easiest to locate. I found your direction without difficulty."

"What is it that you really want? Other than to say you've done your familial duty?"

Lord Ambrose turned back to him. "Is it so difficult to imagine that

I might simply want to know my half-brother?"

"Yes," Nicholas replied. "It is. For over three decades, not a single member of my father's family, my father included, could be bothered with me. To say that your decision to approach the matter of my somewhat embarrassing birth in an entirely different manner is surprising would be the understatement of the century."

Lord Ambrose shrugged. "Father died in a somewhat scandalous manner. We are not impoverished, but our coffers are certainly not as plump as they once were. He gambled heavily, whored with abandon, and ultimately lost his life in a duel with another gentleman whose wife he had not only seduced, but left to bear a child that clearly could not belong to her husband who was in the East Indies for more than a year prior to the birth. He killed the poor bastard, then had the decency to kill himself rather than face the ruin he'd wrought. His actions have left me a social pariah. An object of scandal and ridicule. There is nothing in the edicts of society so unforgivable as to allow oneself to fall into poverty and behave so recklessly in the doing."

"Invite a passel of ill-born bastards into that lovely townhouse in Mayfair and you may find out that there are things more unforgivable," Nicholas replied snappily. "So you have nothing to lose?"

"And a family to gain. Why shouldn't I?" Lord Ambrose asked, his tone challenging. "Our youngest sibling, a sister by the way... is tucked away at one of the few remaining country estates, being tended by a governess as her own mother has no interest in seeing to the child."

Nicholas shook his head. "Have you considered that perhaps you might be better off not finding some of these wayward siblings? Infants aside, of course, a good number of them will likely be reprobates as our illustrious father was... and if you're as impoverished as you say, what on earth can you do for them other than to give them expectations of improved standing that cannot be delivered upon?"

"I can help them to find positions, I can write letters of recommendation... there are a great many things that having a title and connections can offer that even money cannot. And you can help, Dr.

Warner. After all, you are proof that it is possible to escape the wastrel tendencies and the taint of self-indulgence that most believe is in our blood."

"You want me to help you with this... this impossibly foolish pursuit?"

Lord Ambrose shrugged. "I want to get to know you as my brother and vice versa. That is all. If you elect to go on this journey with me to locate the other siblings we may have, so be it. But an opportunity to establish a relationship as brothers is all I ask."

Nicholas was skeptical to say the least, but while his feelings toward his father were complicated, he had no quarrel with the current Lord Ambrose. It would be petty and churlish to refuse the man's acquaintance, regardless of what sort of relationship they might actually develop. Sibling relationships were forged in the fires of childhood, in shared play and escapades. It was something they were both far beyond. But he needed allies. More importantly, Viola needed allies. Ambrose provided an entry into that world, scandal ridden though he might be. Graham had a title but he did not have the connections in society that would allow Viola to resume her rightful place and effectively challenge her late husband's fraudulent report of her death. So he would refrain from judgment for the time being and would tolerate Ambrose's attempts to build familial bonds.

"What do you know of Lord Ramsleigh?" Nicholas asked.

"Current or former?" Ambrose replied. "Though to be fair, most of what I know could easily be applied to either. Bounders through and through. Debauched reprobates that caused even our father to raise an eyebrow."

"How much of a threat is he to Lady Ramsleigh?"

Ambrose shrugged again. "A better question might be how much of a threat Lady Ramsleigh poses to him. If her return jeopardizes his fortunes, then I would say there is very little he would not do to mitigate that threat."

"And her father? Daventry? What of him?"

Ambrose considered the question for a moment. "He's a bit of a mystery to be sure. But the man is cold... not just aloof or distant, but cold to the bone. I doubt he'd dirty his hands to harm her himself, but I would not expect him to intervene on her behalf. Ever."

Nicholas nodded. "It's all rather as I thought then."

"What, precisely, is your relationship with the recently resurrected Lady Ramsleigh? I would hazard that you are going above and beyond your duties as her physician."

"We are friends," Nicholas answered.

"If I recall, she is quite beautiful. Just friends, you say?"

"Do not," Nicholas warned. "We are friends because that is all the lady desires at this time. You'll keep your hands and your flirtations to yourself."

"Or?"

"Or we'll do what brothers have done since the dawn of time... fight." The warning was uttered more fiercely than was necessary. But it was his half-brother's answering grin that told him precisely how much he'd given away. Nicholas cursed under his breath. "This is a delicate situation."

"Is there another kind when beautiful women are involved?"

Chapter Nine

RAMSLEIGH REFILLED HIS glass and drank deeply. The brandy had ceased to burn ages ago. Its purpose was to maintain the liquid languor in his limbs and the soft buzzing in his mind. On the bed, the woman stirred. She wasn't his usual sort at all. Rather than a frightened maid or the hardened prostitutes that worked at his brothels of choice, she was a widow. Fairly respected in the community, she'd never have dared speak to him in public. But they'd reached an understanding at a house party not long ago. The arrangement suited them. They'd take their pleasure with one another, though it was a more tame pursuit for him than for her. Still, he'd pushed her that night, been far rougher with her than he had in the past. More to the point, she hadn't minded. The harsher he'd been the harder her nails had dug into his shoulders and the tighter her thighs had gripped him. In all, it served to underscore the tenet he'd lived by—at their heart, all women were little better than whores.

A knock on the door had her stirring. Ramsleigh frowned. His staff knew better than to disturb him when he was entertaining. Opening the door, he met the dour face of his butler. "What is it?"

"Forgive me, my lord. Mr. Daventry is below and is quite insistent that he see you immediately."

"I'm not at his beck and call, am I?" Ramsleigh snapped.

"Randall, is something wrong, darling?"

He looked back at the gloriously naked woman sitting up in his bed. Her full breasts still bore the red marks from his beard and, no doubt, a few bite marks would bloom on her fair skin before the night was through. She was heedless of her nudity even as the butler averted his gaze. Randall watched her lips quirk at the servant's discomfiture. Despite her demure public persona, she was every bit as perverse a creature as he. "Everything is fine, my dear. Just a matter I have to attend to... a brief matter. I'll return to you shortly."

"Very shortly... I have need of you," she cooed.

He walked over to the bed, gripped her chin roughly in his hand and kissed her. It wasn't soft or tender. It was bruising, punishing, and when he bit her lip, she gasped softly. "You'll wait here... and you'll not touch yourself till I return. Is that clear, my pet?"

She shivered but her eyes gleamed with pleasure at the challenge. "Will I be punished if I disobey?"

"Most assuredly," he replied.

"Then I understand perfectly what is required of me, my lord."

Randall smiled and stroked her hair gently. "I'll return shortly." With his free hand, he snagged his dressing gown from the edge of the bed and donned it quickly. He didn't wait for the butler, but strode ahead of him, down the stairs and toward the pacing figure of Daventry.

At his approach, Daventry looked up and said, "She'll have to be killed."

Cold fury swept through him. Gripping the other man's arm, he shoved him into the nearest room and closed the door. "By all means, announce every crime we might commit to a houseful of underpaid servants."

"It's hardly my fault that your help isn't loyal to you!" Daventry snapped.

"Loyalty is either earned or purchased, Daventry. I've not been lord of this castle long enough for the former and your daughter's paltry inheritance has not allowed for the latter!"

"Paltry? It was a fortune... if you'd spend less time concerning yourself with where to put your cock and more time working to make your estate profitable, her inheritance would have done you up quite well!"

"Perhaps if I'd gotten the entirety of it rather than the half you granted me. Why are you here?" Randall demanded.

"The bitch won't go back to Scotland. Adamantly refused, as a matter of fact. Unless you want to give back that paltry sum you mentioned, you'll need to do something about it," Daventry said. "I sent a letter, but then thought I should see you in person to be certain you understood what was intended."

"What a loving father you are! Are you certain you don't want to at least pretend to beg for her life?" Randall sneered.

"We both know I couldn't care less for the chit aside from the purpose she already fulfilled, to marry your uncle. Her return from the dead is a complication neither of us can afford. You have a plan, I assume?"

Randall smiled. "It's already underway. The villagers here can be a superstitious lot. We're not so very far removed from the witch trials presided over only half a century ago."

"You mean to accuse her of witchcraft?" Daventry asked incredulously. "That's your bloody plan?"

"I don't mean to accuse her of anything. There are already whispers in the village, those who have begun to question whether or not she is who she claims to be... perhaps, she's a changeling or, perhaps she's a witch and the devil sent her back to torment them. One loud voice can set them all to screaming. It's best you return to London and deny you ever visited here. It is best, after all, if you can plead ignorance of all this."

"There's more... apparently in her absence, she birthed a bastard she means to pawn off as a Grantham," Daventry hissed.

Randall felt his blood run cold. "She did what?"

"She has a son. She claims he is the rightful heir to the Ramsleigh title. It isn't just the money you might have to let go of. Are you prepared for that?"

Randall crossed to the desk and sat down. So that was why she'd run when she did. How many nights had he gone to her chamber, rutting on her in his withered uncle's stead, trying to get a bastard on her that he'd never let draw its first breath. The first time his seed had taken root in her belly, it had been an easy enough thing to shove her down the stairs. She'd run because he'd confessed to it, because in his own drunkenness he'd gloated of it to her that no child of hers would live to claim what was his.

Fury swept through him—at her, at himself, at the child she'd borne who threatened everything he held dear. Rising to his feet in one quick motion, he swept his arms over the desk, sending everything upon it crashing to the floor. As ink pooled on the carpet, dark and thick, Daventry stepped back.

"You're utterly mad," he sneered, clearly repulsed by such a display of emotion.

"Where is this child?"

"I suppose in Aberdeen with her mother's people... that is where she took off to, after all."

"Then we'll be needing to send someone for him, as well. I'll not lose a single sovereign to the bastard!"

"And if he isn't a bastard?" Daventry demanded.

"Oh, he's a bastard. Who do you think planted him in her belly? Do you honestly think my ancient uncle was up to the task? He wanted a brat on her, and to stay in his good graces, I plowed her whenever it was asked of me," Randall confessed the words gleefully, watching Daventry's face pucker with distaste. "Is that too coarse for your delicate sensibilities? You shouldn't have auctioned her off to an old goat like him if you'd wanted better than that for her!"

"I couldn't care less, but my God, you are a disgusting creature... foul and low as any wretch in the gutter. You're not deserving of a title."

"Deserving or not... I earned it. By fair means and foul. And you'll do what's necessary to help me keep it or pay the price for your own perfidy. You think I don't know that you helped dear old uncle shuffle off the mortal coil? He was a threat to you, Daventry, because declared dead or not, he wanted his pretty wife back in his reach, close enough to feel the weight of his fists! How strange it was that the bottle of brandy you gifted him arrived just days before his death… and that the man who despised garlic reeked of it. Arsenic is an obvious choice, of course, but still an effective one."

"You can't prove it," Daventry insisted.

Randall unlocked the desk drawer and produced a bottle, placing it on the desk. "I kept it. Just in case proof was ever required. You'll do what you're told in this, you arse, or you'll pay for it. You don't have a title to keep you from the hangman's noose!"

Daventry frowned. "Fine. I'll cooperate, and you'll keep my name out of all of it. There is another complication, however. I had the misfortune to run into Lord Ambrose at the inn. What the devil he's doing here I'll never know!"

Randall sighed and rolled his eyes. "You're a damned nuisance. I'll take care of Ambrose, too. Now get gone and stay gone. Leave all this to me."

"You'll let me know when it's done?"

"Oh, you'll know. I imagine it will be quite newsworthy when a resurrected noblewoman is hanged for a witch by a mob of angry villagers. It's a little too French for the comfort of our peers, after all."

"And the child?"

"No one will ever know he existed," Randall vowed.

Daventry frowned but nodded in agreement. "This had better work, Ramsleigh. Neither of us can afford for it not to."

"One way or another, your nuisance of a daughter will cease to be a problem for either of us," Randall assured him. "Now, I have a naked and randy woman waiting for me in my bed. I'd far rather spend the evening in her company than yours."

Daventry grimaced. "You're worthless, Ramsleigh. Worse than your damned uncle even!"

Randall laughed, calling out as he walked away, "I certainly hope so!"

DINNER HAD BEEN an unusual affair. Viola watched the interplay between Nicholas—Dr. Warner—and his half-brother, Lord Ambrose, with more curiosity than she cared to admit. She could see the similarities between them, more so than either of them would likely care to admit. They were stiff and overly formal with one another, the end result being that everyone else felt just as awkward. Ultimately, it was a relief when the meal ended and the men retreated to brandy and cigars in the library while she and the Ladies Blakemore made their way to the small drawing room.

"He's quite handsome, isn't he?" Lady Agatha said.

"Lord Ambrose?" Lady Beatrice asked.

"Yes. I must say, it's quite apparent to anyone viewing them together that he and Dr. Warner must be blood. If only we were in society, my dear! We'd be the toast of the ton with gossip such as this."

Beatrice shuddered delicately. "I'm quite relieved to not be in society. I cannot begin to imagine the gossip that would beset all of us! Far better to rusticate here in the countryside with clean, sea air and the company of friends."

The gentle smile in Viola's direction was testament to the fact that Lady Beatrice counted her in that number. Viola felt a pang at the thought. How long had it been since she'd had a friend? In truth, never. Her father never encouraged her to socialize with other children and with her marriage to Ramsleigh arranged before she was even out of the school room, there had been no bosom friendships formed at balls and musicales. She'd gone from one isolated household to another. It was only in Aberdeen, where she'd enjoyed the company of the women who often helped her aunt on the farm, that Viola had come to appreciate how good it could feel to be in the company of other women. Even then, they'd been somewhat reserved with her due to the difference in their social standing.

"It is very good to be amongst friends," she agreed softly. "I always regretted that we could not visit and come to know one another better while I was at Ramsgate."

"And I," Beatrice agreed heartily. "But alas, that is rectified. You must tell me of your son. I daresay he must be a remarkably beautiful child."

He was. Dark-haired, with perfectly cherubic features and a hint of mischief in his dark eyes, her son was her greatest joy and she missed him so fiercely it was like she'd lost a limb. "He's a very willful little boy," she said as the sherry was poured. "He insists on doing things for himself when it isn't possible for him to achieve them yet. But I am very proud of him for trying, for wanting to be independent. I cannot help but feel his independence and strong will as a child will carry him well into his adult life."

Beatrice smiled in that coy way that so many expectant mothers had, as if they carried the very secrets to the universe within them. Perhaps they did, Viola thought.

"I cannot help but wonder what our child will be like," she admitted. "Fierce and strong-willed like Graham or more even tempered as I am?"

Lady Agatha chuckled. "My dear, your husband would likely challenge that description. Even tempered! At one time, perhaps, but not after his return. I daresay, he was the spark who lit the fire in you. You've been quite different since then, have you not?"

Lady Beatrice looked rather chagrined. "I suppose that is true. But those were certainly unusual circumstances that we found ourselves in! How rude we are being, Lady Agatha, discussing these things when poor Lady Ramsleigh has no notion of what we speak!"

Lady Agatha smiled. "I think Lady Ramsleigh understands precisely what it is like to meet a man who ignites one's passionate nature. Isn't that so?"

Viola blushed. "Lady Agatha, you are being quite scandalous."

Lady Agatha waved her hand dismissively. "Scandalous! Ha! There's no one to hear it but us. As we are the only society one another keeps, it matters little enough. I do believe, Beatrice," she said, turning her attention back to her daughter-in-law, "that Lady Ramsleigh has caught the good doctor's eye. And he hers!"

"I suspected as much! But you really must stop," Beatrice admonished. "If and when Lady Ramsleigh feels compelled to share the details of her flirtation with Dr. Warner, she will likely tell us all about it!"

Viola raised her hands in mock surrender. "There is no flirtation! We are friends. That is all. My life is far too complicated to be anything more than that with any man... I am dead, after all!"

"He's handsome enough to raise the dead, dear," Lady Agatha said. "And if not him, then Lord Ambrose! What a fine figure of a man he is!"

"Then perhaps you should pursue him."

The rejoinder had been uttered in a deep, low voice from the doorway. Dr. Warner had entered without them being the wiser.

Lady Agatha fell into fits of giggles and Lady Beatrice pursed her lips to keep from laughing with her. Viola, meanwhile, wanted the earth to open up and swallow her whole.

"I'm much too old for him, dear boy," Lady Agatha called out. "And too old for you to be sneaking up on! It's a wonder my poor heart didn't simply give out!"

"Nonsense," Nicholas said, stepping deeper into the room. "You are fit as a fiddle."

"And is that why you're here... to discuss how fit I am?" Lady Agatha asked with an arched eyebrow and a knowing look.

"No," he replied. "I had come to ask Lady Ramsleigh to walk with me. The night is cool but quite clear and there is a full moon rising above the sea. It's quite a sight to behold."

Viola knew she should decline. Walking with him in the moonlight was more temptation than any woman could resist, and she'd already admitted her weakness when it came to him. But as she opened her mouth to utter her refusal, something else entirely escaped it. "I'll fetch my wrap." It appeared her mind and heart were not of one accord. *It isn't your heart*, her conscience corrected.

"No need, my dear," Lady Agatha said and removed her shawl. "Take mine."

Accepting the intricately woven paisley shawl from Lady Agatha, she draped it about her shoulders and accepted Nicholas' proffered arm. Nothing was said, but she could feel the weight of both Lady Agatha's and Beatrice's stares as they exited the room. His interest had been marked and her all too eager acceptance of it had not gone unnoticed.

"Are you attempting to ruin my reputation, Doctor?" She asked the question softly once they were in the corridor.

"You are a widow, Viola, not some innocent deb. It's hardly of consequence if you walk with a man in a garden. If it makes you feel any better, I have no designs upon your virtue."

"I'm a widow, as you pointed out. I have no virtue for you to have designs upon," she reminded him, recalling one of their earlier conversations.

He smiled. She could see the faint curving of his lips in the shadows of the hall. "How lucky for us both then that virtue is not what I desire."

It was a double entendre, one that even she with her limited experience could grasp. More surprising was the heat that suffused her at the thought. Had she been a more morally upstanding woman, she would have slapped his face for such offense. Instead, she pursed her lips in disapproval, disengaged her arm from his and stepped out onto the small terrace.

"Don't feign displeasure because you think you ought to. If I offend you, tell me… if I intrigue you, Viola, do not deny us what we both clearly desire," he chided softly.

"And what is it that we desire, Dr. Warner? A walk in the garden? A stolen kiss? Or more? I cannot afford to indulge in such flirtations! My life and my son's future hang in the balance!"

"Your son's future will be secured. You have the full support of Lord Blakemore and, now, Lord Ambrose to ensure it," he replied. "And I've no doubt that you had his birth properly documented in Aberdeen, did you not? So that the date of it and his legal paternity could never be challenged?"

She had, of course. The Bishop of Aberdeen had been called upon to record Tristan's birth in the church's registry. It had taken some persuading but the man had agreed finally, given her title and the last of the money she'd managed to escape with. "There is documentation, of course. But we both know that Randall will contest it as viciously as possible. I cannot indulge myself with whatever this is between us, Dr. Warner."

"But you do admit that what is between us exceeds the bounds of platonic friendship?" he challenged.

Viola felt her blush deepen. "I concede that it could, but I cannot allow it. Not with the risks involved! Can't you see that?"

"What I see," he said, stepping closer to her, "is a woman that I admire, that I am drawn to for far more than her exceptional beauty. Smart as a whip, daring and braver than most men would have been, willing to risk everything for the safety of her child... what is it that you think I want from you, Viola?"

"More than I can give," she answered.

"Perhaps. But let me tell you what I will accept from you... at this moment, alone in this garden, all I ask is a kiss."

"A kiss is never just a kiss, Dr. Warner," she refuted. "For an innocent young girl, it might be. But I am neither of those things and we both know that a kiss is simply a prelude to something else."

"One can hope," he replied with a boyish grin. "But a kiss, whether it is a prelude or the extent, can still be savored on its own merit."

Viola shook her head. "I should go back. This conversation has done little but muddy the waters further. I think under the circumstances, Dr. Warner, that our friendship should be—well not suspended—but strictly limited for the time being."

<hr />

NICHOLAS WATCHED HER turn, watched her take a single step toward the house. It was only a second, a minuscule amount of time, really. But in it, he weighed his options very carefully. Part of him thought he should simply let her go. She was entitled to make her own choices, after all. Too many men had made decisions in her life already and she had suffered the consequences for them. But there was a difference between him and those other men in her life. He cared. At the end of it all, he wanted her to be happy. He wanted her to have the security and the confidence that a woman of her position should have. At the same time, he knew that there was something else inside him—something jealous, possessive, selfish—and that part of him would not simply give ground. Not when they could have something glorious.

So that single step, slow and torturous, toward the house was all he permitted her to take. One hand snaked out to grasp her wrist and tug her back to him. Her back was pressed against his chest, the curve of her bottom pressed into the notch of his hips, and his arms circled around her. He could feel the weight of her breasts against his forearm. "Don't walk away... not yet."

She shuddered softly. "I should. We both know that."

"Did you ever love your husband, Viola? Did you ever long for him?" he whispered against her ear.

"Never."

"And do you long for me?" It was a question that her body had already answered for her. He could see the pounding pulse at the base of her throat, feel the shiver that arced through her.

"God help me, I do," she admitted softly.

That breathless confession was all the prompting he needed. Slowly, deliberately, Nicholas pressed his lips to her neck just below her ear. Her skin was scented with the rose oil that had been added to her bath. Kissing her there, feeling the warmth of her skin beneath his lips as she let out a startled gasp, he knew that it would not be enough. He imagined that where Viola Grantham was concerned, the idea of "enough" was a myth. She was the type of woman who invaded a man's very soul. In all likelihood, he would crave her till the day he died.

When she sagged against him, her head dropping back to rest against his shoulder, it bared her neck more fully to him and provided him a delectable view of her breasts in her borrowed evening gown. But they were a temptation he would resist for now, because a wise man knew his limits. He contented himself with kissing her neck, teasing the delicate skin there with his lips and tongue until she was pliant against him. Only then did he scrape that same sensitive spot with his teeth. It was a gentle nip, one that would not leave a mark. But he wanted to mark her. It was a primal urge in him, to show his possession of her.

A sound escaped her, soft and breathy, but filled with the same longing that he felt for her. "You said a kiss," she admonished.

"And have I not kissed you?" He asked.

"Not as I anticipated," she replied.

"Is that what you want, Viola? To feel my lips on yours?"

"Yes," she admitted. "It's foolish and unwise beyond measure, but yes."

Nicholas shifted slightly, turning her to face him. "I wouldn't call it foolish... not when it's as necessary as the breath we draw."

Rather than wait for her to reply or to come to her senses, Nicholas lowered his lips to hers. The fullness of her lips was soft and pliant beneath his and when her lips parted softly, welcoming him to deepen that kiss, he did so without hesitation. She tasted of sherry and the sugared fruit that had been served for dessert. But it wasn't that which made the kiss so sweet. It was her.

Desire unlike anything he'd ever known threatened to consume him. It tested the limits of his willpower and called upon every last shred of control that he possessed. He'd pushed, prodded and challenged her, but he would not take more than she was willing to give. When she came to his bed, it would be of her own choosing and wouldn't be because he'd lured her there. If he'd any doubts about that course of action, the gentle and tentative manner in which she responded to his kiss would have quelled them.

Soft, hesitant but oh-so eager, she was a study in contradiction. A widow with a child and yet her innocence was undeniable. She had taken a man into her bed, but it was clear to him from her untutored touch that she had never been made love to. He would rectify that, but only when she was ready.

Easing back from her, he paused to press one more gentle kiss to her softly parted lips, before stepping back entirely. "A kiss can be a dangerous thing even if it leads to nothing else."

"I thought you'd be more smug," she said. "As it's clear I have no will where you are concerned."

He grinned. "I might be smug later... for now, I'll send you back inside and allow the crisp night air to cool the fire in my blood."

"And if there is a fire in mine?" she queried.

"Then I hope it never cools. It is my fondest wish that the kiss we shared lingers in your mind and upon your lips—that it teases you with the fantasies of what might follow. At least until our lips can meet again."

She shook her head and started to walk away. As she neared the terrace doors, she turned back to him. "My husband never kissed me. Not even on our wedding day."

"And you said you had no virtue left to give."

Viola ducked her head, and it was easy to surmise that she blushed. "That hardly makes me virginal."

It was, to his mind, worse than being virginal. He hadn't forgotten his earlier assessment that Viola had suffered at the hands of her husband. Her admission only confirmed the suspicion. Ramsleigh had used her body, abused it no doubt, with no thought whatsoever to tenderness, passion, or the pleasure that it was a man's duty to give his partner. "A virgin fears the unknown. You may know the details of the act, and have likely experienced them in their most brutal reality. Your fear is, therefore, more intense and even more well founded... but in this case, it is unnecessary."

"I'm not afraid of you," she countered.

"No. But you're afraid of him still... the specter of your husband's cruelty will cast a long shadow I think. But I am a patient man. I understand the value of waiting for one's reward. In the meantime, I'll steal kisses where I can and whisper shocking and improper things in your ears when you least expect it."

"You mean you'll seduce me."

"No, Viola. I mean to instruct you on what it means to share a passion with someone, to know desire and all the pleasures of the flesh. Once you have that knowledge, I will let you seduce me," he offered.

She gaped at him for a moment, before managing to say, "You are certainly very sure of yourself, Doctor."

"Not in the least. But I am hopeful."

Nicholas watched as she turned once more and walked away from him. At the door, she paused, glanced back, and then rushed inside. He did not. He needed to let his blood cool and to let the raging evidence of his desire for her subside before making his way inside. It might come to naught. She could very well decide that it was too great a risk and if she did, he could not and would not fault her for it. But with everything in him, he wished for a different outcome.

Chapter Ten

Vivid dreams, sometimes highly erotic and at others terrifying, had robbed Viola of any true rest. Haunted by the kiss she'd shared with Dr. Warner, *Nicholas,* she'd plead fatigue after their walk and sought the solace of her bedroom. Isolation had not been the answer. Rather than offering her peace, it had instead prompted her to relive those moments again and again. When she had finally sought her bed, she'd lain awake for hours, her heart still racing and the only faintly familiar stirrings of desire flaring within her.

In spite of the very businesslike arrangement of her marriage, in the beginning, she had not been repulsed by her husband. Though older than her by more than two decades, Percival had not been an unattractive man. There had been times, at the outset of their marriage that she had welcomed his touch and found that he'd incited some desire in her, as well. But as the union progressed and his cruelty began to show more frequently, her response to him had shifted entirely.

It wasn't until Nicholas had kissed her, until she'd felt that strange warmth suffusing her once more, that she even recalled the feeling enough to identify it. Percival had said kissing was for mistresses and not for wives, that women of her stature were not supposed to enjoy the physical aspects of marriage. He'd denied her the right to take pleasure in her own body. But Nicholas was another matter altogether. He'd seemed to glory in the fact that she responded to him thusly, instead of shaming her for it.

Shaking off thoughts of Dr. Warner and her late husband, Viola rose from her bed and moved toward the dressing table. After unbraiding her hair, she combed the dark tresses and then pinned them up in a loose chignon. It was a simple style, one that she'd often employed because it kept her from requiring the attendance of her maid who would cluck in disapproval at the bruises Percival had often left on her.

With her hair done, she dressed in one of the borrowed morning gowns that Beatrice had provided for her. She'd only just made her way to the top of the stairs when she heard a commotion followed by a familiar cry.

"Tristan," Viola whispered.

The cry echoed again, growing louder. She didn't hesitate but nearly flew down the stairs to see her harried nurse and her very fussy baby standing in the great hall next to a very flustered butler.

"Oh, my lady! What a trip we've had! He's fussed all the way here," the nurse said.

Viola opened her arms and the little boy flew into them. She hugged him closely, the weight of his body against her a welcome burden as she smoothed his silky, brown hair. For that moment, with her child once more safely in her arms, it didn't matter that she hadn't slept more than a couple of hours or that her entire life was in upheaval. All that mattered was that he was there, he was safe, and they were together again.

"Oh, my sweet boy!" she whispered, kissing his cheeks, his forehead, inhaling the sweet scent of him. "How I have missed you, my little man!"

The nurse clucked her tongue. "And there he is again, the angel we normally see. All it took was setting eyes upon his mother once more. He's been miserable since you left, my lady. Awful to say that to you, I know, but it's true. Fair broke that baby's heart, it did!"

"It very nearly broke mine, as well," Viola said, cuddling him again as he simply laid his head against her, one hand fisted in the neckline of her dress and the other tugging at a stubborn curl that had escaped her chignon. "I'm so happy Lord Blakemore sent for you. I don't think I could have waited for spring!"

"Well, now you won't have to. The dear boy is where he belongs again... at his mother's side!" the nurse said emphatically.

"Oh, dear heavens! Look at this handsome little fellow!"

The exclamation had come from Lady Agatha who had just emerged from the breakfast room. Viola smiled with pride. He was a beautiful boy, smart, independent, willful, and so very dear to her that her heart ached with it. "He is handsome... and quite the little rogue, as well. Be mindful, Lady Agatha, or he'll soon have you as wrapped around his chubby little fingers as I am."

Lady Agatha stepped forward, placed one hand on the child's back and patted him gently. "Oh, it has been so very long since we've had a child in this house. It will be a delight to hear such innocent laughter here again."

Tristan turned his head, pressing his face into the curve of Viola's neck and held on to her even more fiercely. Playing shy, he still kept his gaze locked on Lady Agatha. Viola patted his back soothingly, marveling at how even in the few short weeks she'd been away from him he had grown so much. He'd grown and she had missed it. That thought caused her immeasurable pain and she vowed that she would let nothing else separate her from her child, ever again.

"He doesn't appear to be in a good humor at the moment, Lady Agatha. It might be some time before you hear any laughter from him. The stress of travel appears to have taken a toll on him," Viola said.

Lady Agatha laughed softly, "Of course, it has! Why don't you and your servant see him to the nursery? The footmen will bring his bags up. Get the child bathed and dressed in clean clothes. Tuck him in for a nap and appease your own wounded spirit by watching him sleep for at least an hour."

Viola laughed then. "I think that sounds like a fine idea. I plan to do just that."

At that point, Lord Blakemore and Dr. Warner entered, along with Lord Ambrose. The three of them were dressed for riding, their boots dusty and their dark hair windblown. Together, they presented a shockingly attractive trio, but it was Nicholas who held her attention. Her gaze was drawn to him immediately and made her breath hitch. He was looking back at her, his gaze locked on Tristan's small form as the small boy uttered a broken, hiccupping sigh—evidence of his recent bout of tears. Nicholas' lips curved in a slight smile.

"It appears that the Ramsleigh heir has arrived safely, if not in the best of moods."

"It was a trying journey, Dr. Warner," Viola agreed. "I'm going to take him upstairs and get him settled."

"Have you had breakfast yet?" He arched one eyebrow with the question. "You are not so far from injury yourself that you can afford to skip meals."

"I have not."

"Then take him on. I will bring something up for you and help you attend him," he offered.

She wanted to protest that she could handle it alone, that she could care for Tristan without help. But selfishly, she wanted his company. And with her son present to act as a buffer, she might actually manage being in his presence without losing all sense. She nodded her head in acknowledgement and gratitude. "Thank you, Doctor."

Turning away, she carried Tristan securely on her hip as she made her way back up the stairs. Nicholas would follow soon enough.

IT WAS EARLY for Randall to be up and about, especially given his exertions of the night before. His widow was quite greedy for all the pleasures, and the pain, that he could provide her. As much as he'd been enjoying her company, there was something missing from their encounters. He had no plans on halting their arrangement but there was something vaguely unsatisfying about inflicting pain on one who was not only willing but eager for it. An unfeigned protest, a struggle that he would always ultimately win—that was what he longed for. Thinking of Viola and the way she'd battled him at every turn, he felt a pang of regret that he wouldn't get to sample her charms once more before she shuffled off the mortal coil for real.

Stifling a yawn, he halted his mount in a stand of trees at the edge of the woods that bordered his property and spilled over onto the Blakemore estate. Timothy Cobb stood waiting for him beneath the shadows of a large oak tree. The man reeked of cheap ale and the stench of being unwashed. Snarling his lip in distaste, Randall said, "You're prepared to do what has been asked of you, Cobb?"

"Aye, m'lord. I've already talked to some folks in the village, and some others what live just outside it. It makes people rightly uncomfortable when folks come back from the dead. It won't be hard to convince 'em to send her back to hell once and for all," the man chortled.

Randall pulled a small pouch of coins from his pocket and tossed it to the filthy urchin. "See that you do. That's half the payment. You get the other half when they march through the village with her head on a pike."

Cobb opened the pouch, counted the coins, and then in a crass manner, removed one and bit into it to test its worth. He grinned, showing great gaps in his blackened teeth. "Fair enough... I'll see her dead. Whether drowned, burned, or beheaded will be up to the mob you're after, now won't it?"

"So it will. This is the last time we speak until it's done," Randall warned. "It's too much of a risk being seen in your company."

"Oh, I ken it's a risk all right... and I ken I might not be up to snuff for the likes of you, my lord. I'll do your dirty work and be well paid for it," Cobb said, his voice gruff with barely contained hostility. "But you take heed, Lord Ramsleigh, I'll not be crossed. Not by you or anyone else!"

"Fair enough... and you be warned as well, Cobb. If you utter a word of our agreement to anyone, you'll lose far more than just the pay!"

Cobb laughed. "We're not so different, my lord. You might be dressed like a gent... but you ain't got the heart of one. Black as mine, it is!"

"Blacker, I'd warrant," Randall agreed. "Get to work, Cobb. I want that mob marching on Castle Black before week's end."

"And what about Lord Blakemore and all them gents? He's got the doctor and a Lord Ambrose up there, as well. Might pose a threat... I wager they'd be more than willing to protect the lady."

Randall smiled. "It's called distraction, Cobb. Divide and conquer. Create some hullabaloo that will warrant they must all leave the castle along with a bevy of their servants. Fire, for examples. Fires always require an all hands on deck response, do they not?"

"There's an old mill on the estate," Cobb suggested. "Lord Blakemore's been working on it something fierce... seems to think that if the tenants can mill their own grain, their farms will be more profitable."

"Then it's of great value to him and to everyone else, is it not?" Ramsleigh said. "You have your target."

"Aye, m'lord, I do. And I took care of our other target... William Wells, won't be telling any tall tales about the good doctor's heroics no more. As for them ladies what heard it, who they'll repeat it to is unknown."

"We'll deal with that when we have to. Set the fire and make sure it catches well. It needs to be discovered quickly and the whole of the estate called out to battle it. That way we can be certain they are well away and she is left with nothing but an aging woman, a pregnant cow and a household full of worthless servants... I doubt any of them would be willing to risk life and limb for a veritable stranger."

"Then we've a plan, my lord. I'll hold up my end and you hold up yours!"

Randall nodded, wheeled his mount and rode back toward Ramsgate Hall. He intended to sleep the better part of the day away and then drink himself into oblivion. Then, he'd start working on Daventry. The man might be cold through and through, but he had his vices just as all men did. There would be something to hold over his head, some way to get a larger share of the money than had been given so far. He would not give up the lovely inheritance she'd brought with her as a bride. His only consolation was that she posed no threat to the title. Thankfully, she'd never managed to produce a brat for his uncle despite the man's near incessant attempts to impregnate his young bride by assaulting her with his withered old cock.

Chapter Eleven

NICHOLAS APPROACHED THE nursery but paused just outside the door. He could hear splashing and the tinkling peal of childish giggles. As he listened, Viola began making kissing noises and talking nonsense to the baby who then laughed even harder. He was smiling as he pushed the door open and observed them. The boy was standing naked in the tub, splashing water on himself, his mother and the surrounding carpets.

"You must stop," Viola scolded. It was less than effective as she was giggling herself.

"I daresay, the floors have survived worse," Nicholas murmured. "Your gown may not recover, however."

She turned and glanced back at him. "He's always loved his bath time. Any body of water, in fact. He'd be splashing in the waves on the beach right now if he could get to them."

"Then when the weather warms, we shall take him," Nicholas offered.

"You needn't do that," she said. "I understand your interest in me, Nicholas. And obviously your interest is returned—I have not yet decided whether or not to act upon that interest," she warned, "but you needn't play nursemaid to my son in order to court my favor. I do owe you my life, after all."

"You owe me nothing. As for playing nursemaid to curry your favor, that is an insult to all of us. I like children, Viola. I find their company and their exuberance in all things to be rather refreshing. They are so much more honest than the rest of us."

"I've offended you and that was not my intent," she offered apologetically.

"No. You haven't. You have, however, underscored for me just how utterly deplorable most of the men of your acquaintance must have been. Rest assured, there are men who are capable of honesty and action free of ulterior motives."

At that moment, Tristan showed his displeasure at having to share his mother's attention and let out a viciously shrill screech, accompanied by a healthy splash of his bath water which thoroughly drenched Viola.

She sighed and turned back to the boy, lifting him from the tub and wrapping a towel about him. He kicked in protest and screamed again. Both of which were dealt with in a patient and unfailingly kind manner. She distracted the boy with tickles and funny faces as she dried him and fastened a nappy over his bottom and dressed him in a simply-embroidered gown.

"Perhaps we can court his good humor with some of the scones I bribed from the cook?" Nicholas suggested, and pulled back the serviette that covered the small platter he carried. It was piled with cold meats, cheeses, breads, and the aforementioned scones drizzled with a still warm sugary glaze. There was also a serving of mashed vegetables for Tristan.

"Oh, that looks divine," Viola admitted. "I didn't realize I was hungry!"

Tristan certainly knew. He was already eagerly reaching for the treat. "Real food first or the sweets?" Nicholas asked.

"I ought to say real food, but clearly he knows what he wants. I've missed him so terribly, I'm inclined to indulge him at the moment," she admitted ruefully.

Nicholas laughed as he gave the boy a small bite of one of the scones. "I suspected as much." Watching the child tear into the sticky treat, he added, "It might have been wiser to bathe him after breakfast."

Viola sighed. "We'll wash his face and hands again and change his gown... yet again."

Nicholas seated himself on the floor, crossed his legs and absent-mindedly chose a small bit of cheese and bread from the plate. Casually, as if he weren't admitting something of great importance, he said, "I think I rather like Lord Ambrose. He's not at all as I had expected him to be."

He saw her smile, the soft curving of her lips in that knowing way that all women seemed to have mastered from the cradle.

"I thought you might," she said softly.

"Oh, really? And how did you know so much of Lord Ambrose?"

"I don't," she replied. "What I do know is that my late husband sometimes entertained his father—your father—and that while he was never anything but pleasant to me, the late Lord Ambrose often bemoaned just how much of a prude his heir was."

Nicholas considered that. "I wouldn't call him a prude... he simply isn't a libertine."

"One man's good behavior is another man's prudishness," she mused as she sat back on her heels and tore off a small bit of the scone for Tristan. "There are those who would have considered my late husband a good man... because he did treat other men with courtesy and respect. It was women, servants, those poorer than himself that faced his wrath and ill temper. When you haven't the means to fight back or a voice to be heard, it matters little enough what you say of someone."

It was a phenomenon he was familiar with. He'd been enrolled at a small, private school, not as prestigious as Eton or Harrow, but still well respected and attended by the sons of gentry and less well-heeled nobility. As the bastard of a profligate rake, he'd often been accused of infractions he had not committed or singled out to take the blame for the bad behavior of other boys. No amount of protest on his part would have made a bit of difference and, instead, often made his punishment worse. He'd learned simply to accept it and be done with it.

"That is true enough," he agreed. "I think I may help him in his endeavor to locate any other siblings we may have."

"Is that what you want or what he wants?" Viola asked.

"It is what he wants, but I find myself inclined to indulge him. I also feel that I may be a bit more well-versed in the ways of the world than Lord Ambrose. Without someone to guide him, I fear he may come to a great deal of trouble in his pursuits," Nicholas admitted. Lord Ambrose was not necessarily naive, but he'd been far more sheltered from the ugliness of the world than Nicholas had. That fact was glaringly apparent.

"Will you go with him then?" Viola asked.

Her tone was odd. When he looked up, he could see that she appeared somewhat crestfallen. "Will you miss me if I do?" he asked.

"Of course, I would. We are friends, are we not?" she asked evasively.

"We are at least friends... I would that we were much more. But then you're aware of that, Viola. You want more as well, I think. You must simply be brave enough to pursue it," he reminded her gently.

"There is a great deal at stake."

"There is," he agreed. "But that is true regardless of which direction you decide."

At that moment, Tristan approached him, not the least bit shy and attempted to feed Nicholas the bite of scone his mother had just handed him. Dutifully, Nicholas took it and made all the appropriate noises to indicate his enjoyment of the treat. The little boy giggled and clapped his hands delightedly.

WATCHING THE WAY Nicholas interacted with her son, his clear enjoyment of the boy and the ease he seemed to have with him, Viola knew that her decision was made. Had there ever been any doubt that she would succumb to his charms?

"You are very good with him," she commented.

"I like children. That certainly helps when treating them while they are at their worst," he said. "Though it does carry certain risks in and of itself. I hate to lose any of my patients, but the younger they are, the more painful the loss."

Viola shuddered at the thought of it. She had been remarkably lucky. Tristan was a very healthy child and had suffered only the most minor of illnesses. Her aunt had insisted that it was the sea air that kept his lungs clear and protected him from the putrid throat infection that so many children perished from. It also helped, Viola thought, they'd she'd kept them so isolated on the small farm. Having no notion that Percival had fabricated her death, she'd attempted to be as discreet as possible about her whereabouts. The last thing she'd wanted was for her husband to come and drag her back to Ramsgate Hall before Tristan was old enough to travel safely.

"I can't imagine how awful that must be… for you and for their poor parents. Thank goodness, Tristan has always enjoyed remarkable health!"

Nicholas smiled at that. "Considering that you've cheated death twice now, I would say he comes from remarkably hardy stock."

She grimaced. "Only once… and only because you risked life and limb yourself to haul me from the water."

"I'd do it again in a heartbeat. Every day if need be," he said solemnly.

"Let's hope it never comes to that," she said and offered Tristan a bit of the cold ham to offset the sweetness of the scone. He took it, but with noticeably less enthusiasm. "You should know that I've reached a decision."

"About what?"

"About the nature of our friendship," she said softly.

He paused in the act of tickling her son's ribs to glance over at her. "More quickly than I had anticipated, it would seem."

"Come to my room tonight," she said softly.

"Viola, I am in no way trying to dissuade you, but I do want you to be certain," he said solemnly.

"I am quite certain. I think that I was always certain, if the truth were known. It feels rather inevitable, doesn't it?"

"For me, yes," he agreed. "I was drawn to you from the moment I first laid eyes on you. Now, I have to go. If I stay, knowing your current mindset, I don't know that I would be able to continue behaving as a gentleman ought to, and oddly enough, behaving as a gentleman is rather important to me where you are concerned."

Viola watched him leave, pausing only long enough to ruffle Tristan's damp curls before exiting the nursery. She looked at her son and said, "I do hope that he does not break my heart... and I hope that when the time comes when your heart is vulnerable to members of the opposite sex, that you find your heart and mind engaged by someone who can challenge both and return your affections. If not, it's a terrible muddle to be in."

The nurse entered then, her eyebrows raised in shock. "What on earth was the doctor doing in here? Our little angel hasn't taken ill from the journey, has he?"

"No, Belinda," Viola answered. "Dr. Warner was here to visit... he has become a particular friend since I arrived here."

The nurse cackled. More than twice Viola's age, she'd been a maternal figure when acting as Viola's maid and doted on Tristan as a grandmother might. "A particular friend, is he now? Women are not friends with men that handsome! And as you're a widow now, who's to say anything about who you choose to keep company with?"

"I'm also apparently dead," Viola said, hoping to change the subject. "Percival and my father cooked up a scheme to fake my death, likely to claim the inheritance left to me by my grandfather. The entirety of the village and all of London society believes that I perished. Needless to say, washing up on the beaches here from a shipwreck came as something of a surprise to everyone. Naturally, Randall is being difficult about the entire thing."

Belinda's lip curled with distaste. "Unpleasant my eye! He's a bully. Never in my life have I ever seen a boy that took such pleasure in the pain of others! He'll not make it easy on you, especially not with what your late husband did. But you will prevail, my lady. I've no doubt.

And little Tristan will take his rightful place at Ramsgate Hall."

"What if he doesn't?" Viola asked. "Would it be so awful for him to not be acknowledged as the Ramsleigh heir? We both know the truth of his parentage, Belinda. He's a Grantham, but he isn't Percival's!"

"He is by law... and if that man wishes to challenge it, then his own actions will be brought under scrutiny. He's not well liked enough to risk it, I think."

That was true enough, but Viola also knew that his spite was boundless. He'd see her and Tristan both ruined even at a cost to himself. "If I agreed to disappear again, to take Tristan away and never challenge him for the title, he might release enough of the funds for us to make an escape. We could live a quiet life somewhere without Tristan ever being touched by the inherent corruption of that place or the family he hails from."

"He'd never permit it," Belinda said softly. "He's a man without honor and so that is how he views others. He'd never trust you to keep your word because he's incapable of keeping his own. You'd be hunted for the rest of your days and so would that dear boy. Best to make a stand here while you have the support of others just as powerful as Randall Grantham!"

Viola sighed wearily. "I hate to pull them into this, Belinda... they don't deserve it. They are good people and will be embroiled in this ugly process for too long."

"Including the good doctor?" Belinda asked with a knowing smirk. "You thought to change the subject, but I'm like an old dog with its favorite bone. He's very handsome. He also appears quite taken with you, as you are with him."

"I am," Viola admitted. She had no secrets from Belinda. Even the shameful abuses of her husband and his nephew were known to the other woman as it had been Belinda who had tended her in the aftermath of their cruelty. "I've decided to take him as my lover."

Belinda nodded. "I suspected you might one day wish to know a man's touch by choice rather than force. There's no shame in it."

"No, there isn't," Viola agreed. "He's a rarity, Belinda... a genuinely good man."

"Then why are you afraid?"

Viola shrugged and glanced at Tristan who was occupied with a small toy he'd found. She smiled as he turned the simple, wooden horse over and over in his chubby hands. "Because even a good man can break your heart."

"Then let us hope it is worth the risk," the nurse answered.

Chapter Twelve

TIMOTHY COBB WAS on his third pint of ale. His speech was still crisp and he wasn't even close to being in his cups yet. That was well enough, though. He might be drinking on the job, but as long as he was drinking Tarley couldn't throw him out of the tavern. There was no better place to sow the seeds of discontent.

"It ain't right, I tell you. It ain't natural," he whispered to the man next to him.

"It ain't right, but it ain't got nothing to do with me," the man answered.

"Is that right, John Alberts? Nothing to do with you, does it? Didn't you lose two lambs last week alone? And ain't your dear wife developed a cough she can't get rid of?" Cobb pointed out.

The other man looked decidedly uncomfortable. "That don't mean nothin'!"

"Oh, and your neighbor, old Farnsworth... his well went dry, didn't it?"

"I ain't got no quarrel with her and I won't be making an enemy of the new Lord Blakemore," Alberts replied. "You can stop your wheedling, Timothy Cobb."

"I don't think he should!"

The protest came from a neighboring table. An ancient, dirty, raggedly-dressed man with blackened teeth and a cloudy eye was the source. "What say you, Ned Chambers? You were here the last time a witch was found in Blackfield, were you not?"

"Aye, I was. Old Fanny Eddington, it was... hung her in the square for cavorting with the devil on the full moon!" Chambers replied. "It was just like it is now! Lambs dying off left and right, wells drying up, cows going mad and charging their owners in the fields! That Osbourne boy was trampled by one and died after three days of talking out of his head, gibberish about the devil. Cursed by Old Fanny, he was!"

"It's all nonsense!" John Alberts protested. "You say she's come back from the dead and I say that not a single person ever saw her body. For all we know, she left that blackguard Ramsleigh and rightly so, from what I heard of him. He could well have buried a box of stones in that churchyard and we'd never know the difference!"

"I know the difference," Chambers said. "I dug the grave and I filled it in. Thought I heard a noise from that coffin. Wouldn't be the first time we've made a mistake and buried someone alive... I looked inside it. Saw her laid out there plain as day, I did. Black hair shining and looking fresh as a girl at her first dance! Gave me cold chills then, just as it does now." The old man shoved the sleeve of his coat up to reveal the gooseflesh on his dirty skin. "Even then, I knew it weren't natural. Something was off about the whole thing. And now I know why. I could feel the evil, I tell you. I could feel it!"

Cobb concealed his smile behind his tankard. The old man had given a performance worthy of even the finest London theaters. For the promise of a pint and coin enough to purchase the company of his favorite whore, the man had lied with the conviction of a saint. The other patrons began to whisper, some of them making signs to ward off the evil eye and other superstitious nonsense. Ned Chambers had earned every shilling that Tim had promised him and then some.

"And what about poor William Wells?" someone asked from a darkened corner. "Talked about her, about how the doctor saved her... and he's not been seen or heard from since!"

"What'll it take, Alberts?" Cobb asked, quickly averting the topic of Wells. "Will your wife have to die first? Or your children? You think the devil let her come back here without a bargain to sacrifice the lot of us? Maybe she did escape her husband and maybe he was a cruel bastard... but that doesn't mean she's any better."

"Do what you will, Timothy Cobb, but I'll not be a party to it," the farmer said and rose from the table to leave.

"What should we do then?" another voice called out from near the hearth. The cry was followed by a chorus of "ayes".

"The good book says... 'suffer not a witch to live'," Chambers intoned melodramatically.

"There you have it," Cobb said. "The answer is plain as day to me even if there's some what don't want to see it."

"We'll march up to Castle Black and take her by force if need be!" one man said, rising to his feet.

"It won't be quite that easy. We'll need to be certain Lord Blakemore and Dr. Warner are well away," Cobb replied reasonably. "It's one thing to hang a witch that's already dead. It's another to kill a titled lord. We'd all hang for it."

"What do you suggest?" the man demanded.

"Let the ground dry up a bit... and then we'll set a fire on the estate. Just large enough to draw them away from the house," Cobb offered. "When they've gone, we'll take her and see that God's work is done."

A chorus of agreement went up, but Tarley, the innkeeper, chose that moment to intervene. "The lot of you are mad... and led like sheep by this charlatan! You'll hang for it. I swear you will. If I have to go to the magistrate myself!"

Cobb rose. "No, Tarley. You won't be going to the magistrate at all. You'll be staying right here. Get him, lads! Get him down to the cellars and tie him up right and good! He's under the she-devil's spell!"

The mob of angry farmers and miners didn't need much in the way of inducement. They charged the bar and the poor innkeeper, kicking him and slapping him as they dragged him down to the cellars.

Cobb moved behind the bar and refilled his tankard, whistling a jaunty tune under his breath. A sound caught his attention and he looked over to see the single, harried and bullied serving girl hiding behind a cask of wine. "Are you of like mind with poor Tarley, then?"

"No," she said, shaking her head. "I heard what you said and I don't want no truck with a witch or the devil."

"Then you'll keep quiet, girl... or pay the price for it."

She nodded, wide eyed and terrified. "I won't say nothing. Not a word."

Cobb smiled. He had a fat purse full of coins and while she wasn't the prettiest of girls, she was clean and had a generous pair of tits. "Tell me, girlie, do you ever take on any extra duties for old Tarley?"

She understood his meaning immediately and began to cry. "I'm a good girl. I only serve ale and food to the patrons... I've never done nothing like what you think! I'm not a harlot!"

Cobb shook his head and waved his hand at her to go. He'd never much cared for crying women that hadn't an ounce of spunk or fight in them. "Go on home to your family, girl. But breathe a word of what you heard here and it won't just be the devil you have to fear. You ken?"

She nodded again. "I understand."

Cobb watched her go, running out the door and through the narrow streets of the village. It was probably a mistake, but he reasoned that Ramsleigh hadn't been nearly as generous as he'd expected.

VIOLA MADE HER excuses after dinner rather than joining Lady Agatha and Lady Beatrice in the drawing room. She'd taken a small detour to look in on Tristan. He was sleeping soundly, no doubt still exhausted from the journey. Belinda had fared no better. The nurse was lying on a cot, snoring louder than a swarm of bees.

After exiting the small nursery, she made her way to her room and stepped inside. She didn't know when Nicholas would arrive, but her vanity demanded that she make some preparation. Removing her gown, she stripped down only to her chemise and then donned the dressing gown Lady Agatha had lent her. She removed the pins from her hair and brushed it till it shone, the dark waves cascading down her back and over her shoulders. Nicholas had made no secret that he admired it and it was beyond important to her that he find her pleasing.

She was, oddly enough, more nervous about receiving him than she had been about receiving her husband on her wedding night. Of course, she had infinitely more knowledge than she had then as an innocent bride, and none of it did anything to dispel her nerves. In truth, she didn't anticipate that welcoming Nicholas Warner into her bed would be even remotely similar to the experiences she'd had with Percival. More often than not, he'd been perfunctory. But on occasion, when he'd been too much in his cups, he'd been intentionally cruel, seeking to cause her as much pain and humiliation as possible. Even thinking of it made her hands tremble and her palms sweat.

Forcing herself to think of anything else, Viola surveyed her reflection critically. Would he be pleased with what he saw?

There was a soft knock upon the door and Viola's hand flew to her heart as she bit back a nervous shriek. It appeared that while she might have succeeded in pushing thoughts of her late husband aside, she had not managed to adequately ease the fear they had elicited. Trying to calm her heart which raced for all the wrong reasons, she took one final glance at her reflection before crossing to the door.

With a last steadying breath, she opened it and found herself face to face with the man who had created such anticipation and such turmoil in her. Nicholas had discarded his coat and his cravat. Wearing a simple waistcoat, his shirt open at the neck revealing a glimpse of bronzed skin and crisp, dark hair, and his breeches, he looked far more appealing than he should have.

"Are you going to invite me in?" he asked.

Realizing that she'd stood there, gawking at him, for far longer than was either necessary or appropriate, Viola stepped back. "Forgive me," she said softly. "My mind was elsewhere."

He entered the room and seated himself on the small settee at the foot of the bed. "You invited me to your room, ostensibly to become your lover. But nothing will happen here tonight that you do not wish for. This goes only as far as you want it to."

"And if I don't know the answer to that?" Viola challenged. "What I think I want and what my overactive nerves will permit may be very different."

"You have only to say stop and I will. I am not your late husband, Viola. If you cannot trust that, then I should not be here," he replied.

"I do not in any way see you as being remotely similar to Percival. But the fear I have isn't a rational thing... my mind says one thing and yet my body responds in an entirely different manner. Even now, my pulse is pounding and I want to run."

"To me or away from me?" The question was voiced gently, but there was a challenge in his voice despite the mild tone.

"I don't know," she answered honestly. "Is it very unfair of me to say both?"

He held out his hand to her, a simple gesture of invitation. "Then let us start with something simple... let us begin with a kiss. Then you may decide."

Nervously, Viola moved toward him, allowed him to take her hand. But he didn't simply pull her close. Instead, he tugged her down so that she sprawled on his lap and could feel the hard press of his chest against her as his strong arms enveloped her completely. Strangely, she did not feel confined or trapped, but sheltered.

She wasn't caught unawares by the kiss as she had been on the terrace. The memory of that kiss had nearly driven her mad. But she knew what to expect, could anticipate the rush of sensation and yearning that would follow in its wake. As his lips moved over hers, commanding but gentle, fierce and yet achingly tender, she found that her fears were simply melting away. Never was she more aware of how different he was from her late husband than when he touched her—even more so, she became aware of one undeniable fact. She was different with him. Tension and anxiety melted away. With him, she felt normal, as if all the ugliness of her past had not occurred.

Her body grew lax, molding to his, as she returned his kiss. Savoring the scrape of his whiskers against her skin, the gentle nips of his teeth at her lower lip, she felt the heat spark within her, fanning out until every limb was suffused with it.

As his fingers tangled in her hair, tugging her head back to deepen the kiss, Viola shivered, but not with fear. It was glorious anticipation. The fear had been beaten back by curiosity. If he could create such a feeling with only a kiss, what on earth would it be like when he did even more?

He pulled his lips from hers, skimming them along the line of her jaw and then the curve where her neck and shoulder met. As he bit her there, his teeth gently scraped over her skin in such a way that she couldn't hold back the soft moan that built within her.

"I doubt I'll be changing my mind," she admitted, breathlessly.

"I had really hoped you would say that," he answered.

Before Viola could say anything, he'd risen with her in his arms and turned to place her on the bed. Spread out before him, her hair mussed and her gown askew, she knew precisely what she looked like. Wanton, wild, wicked. And she found that she reveled in it. It was so much better than being timid and afraid.

"I've never been one for flowery praise, but then I don't need to tell you that you're beautiful," Nicholas stated. "You know that. What I can tell you is that, beautiful as you are, it's the least captivating thing about you."

Viola had been complimented on her looks since birth. With her black hair and her violet eyes, the striking combination had always invited comment. It was a heady thing not only to be recognized for something else but also valued for it.

"Be very careful, Dr. Warner, or you will turn my head," she said coyly.

He reached for the buttons of his waistcoat, releasing them one at a time until the garment fell loose about him and was shrugged off with ease. "I intend to turn a great deal more than that, my dear."

NICHOLAS WATCHED THE blush creep over her cheeks. From the heat in her gaze, he knew it was more than embarrassment or shyness. She wanted him, just as he wanted her. That a woman married for so many years could still be so innocent of lovemaking and yet so versed in the cruelty of men was both a crime and a shame. But he intended to rectify both, to teach her not only the ways of passion, but that a man was capable of tenderness.

He also had no intention of taking all that she offered. The desire was there, of course. He wanted her more desperately than he'd ever wanted a woman in his life. But for that night, he wanted only to show her pleasure, to let her reach those soaring heights without taking anything for himself. Part of that was to build trust between them, another part of it was that he wanted her to yearn for him just a bit more, he wanted her to reach such a state of desire that fear never entered the equation. For him, it was about evening the pitch a bit. It was a terrifying thing to recognize in himself, that for the first time in his life, he was in the presence of a woman he could not simply walk away from.

Viola, from the first moment he'd laid eyes on her, had been something unknown to him. There was a connection between them, an intimacy that went beyond simply physical and had been there from the start.

Reaching out, he touched the delicately embroidered hem of her nightrail before allowing his hand to slip beneath it. His fingertips skimmed over the delicate bones of her ankle, along the silken skin of her calf, up to the tender curve at the back of her knee. She shivered then and he felt the gooseflesh on her as every nerve in her body heightened to a point of aching awareness. He knew it, because it was what he felt himself. Anticipation was its own kind of torment.

"Is this what it's like for others?" Viola queried.

"How do you mean?" Even as he urged her to explain, his hands were drifting further, coasting along her thighs and pushing the fabric of her nightrail upward until it bunched at her waist and barely concealed the tantalizing flesh at the juncture of her thighs.

"This slow and deliberate seduction... I always imagined that this is what it would feel like. Tremulous, to be sure, but not at all lacking in certainty," she admitted.

"If not, it should be." No longer content to simply stand beside the bed and tease her, Nicholas hastily removed his boots and then climbed onto the bed beside her. He kissed her then, covering her softly-parted lips with his own. The taste of her was as intoxicating as the strong rum that had been swilled in great quantities while he'd lived in Jamaica.

Mapping every curve and contour of her lips, nipping gently at the fullest part of her lower lip, he was rewarded when she opened for him, inviting him inside. Nicholas didn't crow with triumph but the urge was there. Instead, he doubled his efforts in kissing her so intently and so passionately that she would lose all sense of reason and, with it, any lingering fears she might have.

Her hands lifted to his shoulders, sliding over them not to push him away but to cup the back of his neck and hold him close. She kissed him back with equal fervor, her lips moving against his, her tongue sliding against his own in an intricate and sensual dance.

They kissed until they were both breathless, until she was pressing herself against him with abandon. But when the kiss broke and he eased back, he saw doubt in her gaze.

"You aren't fearful of me or what will pass between us. So, what is it that holds you so completely in its sway, Viola?"

The question hung between them, weighted and heavy as it seemed to rob them both of air. She looked away from him, her gaze fixating on a point beyond his shoulder. "I haven't lied to you, but I haven't been entirely truthful either."

"Does continuing our planned activities for this evening necessitate you telling the whole truth?" Nicholas asked. "Because you must know that nothing you could say or confess will change my feelings or my desire for you."

She looked back to him, her violet eyes filled with an agony that nearly undid him. "I told you that Tristan was a Grantham. And he is.

But he is not Percival's son… Randall is his father."

He didn't move, didn't draw back from her or accuse. Instead, he kissed her cheek softly. "He is Tristan's father, but he was not your lover. Was he, Viola? He was simply another element of your husband's cruelty."

Chapter Thirteen

VIOLA HAD THOUGHT the shame of that admission would break her, and yet it didn't. It was his tender kiss and the softly voiced question that showed her how much he understood of her life at Ramsgate Hall. Battling back the tears that threatened to consume her, she pushed him away and rose from the bed. Crossing to the window, she peered out into the darkness. "I had thought it didn't matter. That I could simply set it aside and pretend it had never happened… that was what Percival planned to do, you see? He'd never conceived a child. Not with either of his previous wives and after three years together, I'd also failed to conceive. In spite of his tremendous conceit, even he had to acknowledge, at that point, that the failure was likely his own."

"And he wanted Randall to step into his shoes, as it were," Nicholas surmised.

"Something to that effect. Naturally, I refused. Then I learned in a very difficult and humiliating manner that refusal was not an option for me."

He was silent for the longest time. So long, that Viola was afraid to look back at him, afraid to see the disgust on his face or, worse, to see the door closing on his departing back. What man would want her after such an admission, after all? Randall was the most despicable of men and he'd used and abused her horrendously, not simply with her husband's consent but at his behest.

"How many times?"

Dropping her chin to her chest, Viola closed her eyes tightly.

"Does it matter? Whether it was one or a dozen... how could it possible matter?"

"Because I'd like to know how many times I must beat him to the point of death, allow him to recover, and then repeat the process. I won't kill him. I won't give him the satisfaction of hanging for it... but I will see that he pays."

She shook her head. "To what end? It won't undo what was done to me. It will not change Tristan's true parentage and, in truth, would only make people question it. I cannot afford to antagonize Randall and have him announce to the world that the child I bore while in exile was not my husband's but his! Tristan's future depends on it... I suppose I ought to feel somewhat guilty. I am perpetuating the lie only to take back the estate. But it was what Percival had planned all along, after all! If I had to suffer for it, then I'd rather it not be all for naught."

"Why did you run? If Percival had gone to such lengths to have an heir, then while you were carrying his child... you should have been safer than ever before," Nicholas pointed out. "What other secrets are you keeping, Viola?"

"I had conceived once before... of course, it was Randall's child. When it became known, within days, I suffered a terrible accident—a tumble down the stairs. I lay there at the foot of them, bleeding, knowing that my child was dying within me. And I knew something else... Randall had done it. I could see him standing at the top of the landing, looking down on me. Then I saw him walk away. He was perfectly willing to play stud at his uncle's behest, but he would never let the child be born. To do so would have been to seal his own fate as the poor relation."

She'd never been able to prove it. Even when she'd tearfully confessed it all to Percival, he'd dismissed it as feminine hysterics. It hadn't been his unwavering faith in Randall that had prompted his denial. It had been his own ego, his own belief that no one would dare defy him.

Only Belinda knew the truth, only her maid who'd helped her, nursed her afterward, had been privy to the ugly details. Having finally given voice to it, she felt as if a weight had been lifted from her. But she also knew the admission might cost her. Disclosing such things, her own slightly warped morality in passing off Randall's illegitimate child as the heir, the depth of the depravity that she'd been forced to endure—any of those things could change the way he looked at her. But it was better, she thought, to have the entirety of the ugliness out there now than to give herself to him completely and then have him turn from her. The very thought of it was unbearable.

Continuing her tale, she added, "When I discovered that I was once more with child, I knew what I had to do. As terrifying as it was, and with all it might cost me, escape was the only option."

She heard the rustling of fabric as he rose from the bed, the soft footfalls as he walked toward her. When his hands closed over her upper arms and pulled her back to rest her head against the firm wall of his chest, she wanted to weep.

"I'm sorry, Viola."

"I understand, Nicholas," she whispered.

She felt him smile, felt the curving of his lips against the top of her head where he placed a gentle kiss. "I'm not leaving, you halfwit."

"Halfwit?" The word squeaked out of her, her tone sharp with annoyance.

"Yes," he said. "Halfwitted if you think telling me how badly you were abused at the hands of the monster your parents sold you to—and that's what it was, no better or worse than the slave trade I witnessed while in the West Indies—would make you less desirable to me! Nothing, Viola, could change what I feel for you... or how much I want you."

She swallowed convulsively. "What is it that you feel for me then?"

"More than I care to admit and far more than you are ready to hear," he answered.

"I ruined everything, didn't I? This was certainly not what you wanted to hear me say prior to... I'm not even certain what to call what we were about to do. The consummation of our affair?"

He laughed softly. "If it's any consolation, I hadn't intended to consummate anything tonight. I had thought I would introduce you to just a few of the many ways in which I can bring you pleasure. And I mean to do that still."

Before Viola could even process what had been said, Nicholas scooped her up in his arms and carried her back to the bed. When he kissed her this time, he didn't stop. His lips moved from hers after a moment, but remained on her skin, pressing hot, open-mouthed kisses against the tender column of her throat. When he licked that same spot, and then grazed it with his teeth, she couldn't stop the soft sigh of pleasure that escaped her. It was a marvel to her that he could touch her in one place and incite such a response in others. Heat flooded her belly, suffused her limbs, and her pulse raced with it.

Consumed as she was with the wicked skill of his mouth, she hadn't even realized he'd freed the ties of her nightrail until she felt the brush of his palm on her naked breast. The heat of it, the rough and callused texture of his skin against hers, was shocking, but also intensely pleasurable. That gentle caress was about discovery, about letting her get used to the sensation of his hands on her. She knew that. But she wasn't prepared for the sensations that would follow or the hot rush of desire that it prompted.

"I'm not fragile or delicate," she said. "And I'm not afraid... not of you. You needn't treat me as if I might collapse in a fit of the vapors at any moment."

NICHOLAS LOOKED DOWN at her, taking in the fall of her dark hair as it spread over the pillows, the pale, satin-textured flesh of her body bared to him, the dusky-hued peaks of her breasts which tempted him so desperately. Her beauty was simply unparalleled. But physical perfection aside, it was the totality of her that held him enthralled. "I'm not taking my time entirely for your benefit, Viola. I mean to savor this moment, and to draw out the pleasure in it for us both."

Before she could respond, Nicholas dipped his head and claimed one nipple. Closing his lips over that tender flesh, he nipped and laved as she gasped in shock and then delight. He took his time, savoring every moment just as he'd warned her. He didn't simply touch her breasts, but worshipped them with his hands and his mouth until she was writhing beneath him. First it was only his lips, but they were followed by the fiery brand of his tongue, and punctuated with the sharp and yet still pleasurable sting of his teeth on her flesh. Each touch enflamed her, every pass stoked the fire that he'd built inside her to new heights. She was breathless and gasping, writhing beneath him while her hands tangled in his dark hair and held him to her.

"What are you doing to me?" she asked breathlessly. "It's like I'm on fire!"

"Then you know precisely what I am feeling now... what I have felt from the moment I first laid eyes on you. Even on that beach when you were half-dead, I was consumed with the need to make you live, to will the breath back into your body because even without knowing you, I knew that I needed you," he confessed.

"Make love to me, Nicholas," she pleaded softly. "Not as if I were some broken thing that needs to be healed, but as if I have no past, no ugly history looming over us."

"Soon enough," he chided. "But for tonight, let me just glory in giving you something no man ever has."

Before Viola could question him, he pressed a series of soft kisses along her rib cage, down her belly. She hated the faint silvery marks on her belly from where it had grown round with Tristan, the skin stretched far beyond what it could reasonably bear without scarring. But Nicholas did not share her aversion. He kissed each one and then moved lower. When she felt the hot rush of his breath ruffling the dark curls at the juncture of her thighs, Viola's breath caught. *Surely he would not.* She wasn't an innocent, of course. She had heard of such things. But as her pleasure had never been something that Percival had been concerned with, she had no experience with the act. Other than ribald comments passed between her husband and the uncouth gentlemen he'd entertained, she was ignorant.

When he kissed her there, softly and then more fervently, she shuddered. Whether it was anticipation or fear, she couldn't quite be sure. But then he parted the folds of her sex and kissed her more intimately still. The gentle pressure of his lips, followed by the sweep of his tongue over tender flesh elicited a gasp from her that quickly faded into a broken moan. Gentle, insistent, and with a skill that was beyond wicked, he drove her mad.

Every pass of his tongue, every soft nibble and kiss, had her shuddering with need. Tension coiled inside her, hot and insistent, growing tighter with each second until she felt as if her entire body would simply snap and fall into nothingness.

"You are supposed to breathe, Viola," he teased softly, before nipping at her inner thigh.

"What?" she squeaked the question, her mind having simply gone altogether.

"Breathe, my darling girl. Take air in, then force it back out... it helps, I'm told," he answered.

Viola somehow did as he instructed, forcing her lungs to expel the breath she hadn't even been aware she was holding. When it was done, she drew in another shuddering breath, filling her lungs once more. But it was futile endeavor. He returned to his previous ministrations but, this time, he pressed his fingers inside her, pressing deep and stroking her as he closed his lips around the small bud that he'd tormented with such skill.

The sensations overwhelmed her, dragging her to the depths just as the sea had threatened to on the fateful day her lover had entered her life. The tension that had strummed inside her, building, released instantly. Her breath hissed out and a soft cry followed as the waves of it ebbed and flowed within her. When at last it receded, she collapsed back against the pillows, unaware that her body had even bowed to such an extent. Her limbs trembled still and her breathing was ragged as her pulse beat a rapid tattoo.

"What have you done to me?" she queried so softly.

"Only what you wished for me to," he replied, levering himself up to lie next to her. His arms closed about her, holding her to him. "I promised you pleasure, Viola. And I delivered on that promise."

"And took nothing for yourself," she pointed out. "I cannot fathom what manner of man you are."

He looked up at the ceiling. "If you think I took no pleasure in watching you climax, in knowing that I was the man who brought you to such quivering release, then you simply couldn't be more wrong. Physically? Yes, I am in an agony of wanting you. But my pride and my ego are infinitely satisfied with what I have wrought here."

Viola couldn't stop her gaze from traveling the length of his body, to the unmistakable ridge of his arousal straining against the fall of his trousers. "How is it that I might offer you some relief from your current agony?"

"You needn't. I am content to wait," he said.

"But I'm not. It isn't in my nature to simply take, Nicholas. And I've taken from you tonight... I've reveled in what you offered for me, and I would gladly offer you the same pleasures you have shown me, but I'm at a loss as to where I should begin," she stated.

He looked at her, meeting her gaze steadily. After a long, aching moment, he shifted slightly and released the buttons of his trousers, releasing his rigid member. "Touch me then... take me in your hand," he urged.

Tentatively, Viola did as he asked. Her fingers closed around him. It was a revelation. She was shocked by the silken texture of his skin, by the heat and firm resilience of the flesh beneath. But he didn't move or say anything at all. He simply waited patiently and endured her exploration. Touching the rounded head and the veined ridges, she then reached the soft pouch at the base and cupped it gently. The shaft jerked against her arm and a rumbling sound escaped his throat, almost like a growl. She glanced up, meeting his darkened gaze and the truth of his desire was plainly evident in that heated look. But it was his control that she marveled at. His jaw was clenched, the muscles locked tight as he reined in his most basic of instincts.

"You would let me touch you this way all night, without ever offering instruction on what it is that you prefer," she accused gently.

"I want you to know my body... to be comfortable with it and with me. If that means I must endure this torturous need for you, so be it."

"I am comfortable with you," she admitted. "I am not embarrassed or afraid. I am not at all regretful for the vast number of sins we have just committed in this bed. Show me how to touch you, to ease your suffering."

His hand closed over hers, once more wrapping her fingers around the thick shaft of his manhood. He guided her at first, moving her fist over him, setting an easy rhythm.

Viola watched him closely, noting when his eyes closed with pleasure, when his breathing grew more ragged. Perhaps it was instinct, or perhaps it was some intuition shared only by lovers, but she quickened her strokes, tightening her hand slightly. He gasped and ground out a harsh curse. He grew more rigid still, his flesh tightening against her palm as his thighs tensed. She was lying close to him, face to face. Then she felt the first drop of his essence, hot against the skin of her thighs. He grasped her wrist, stilling her hand over him as his hips thrust against her and his seed spilled over her flesh and onto the discarded fabric of her nightrail.

"That was rather embarrassingly quick," he admitted, his voice gruff and deep, his breathing ragged. "When I make love to you completely, I promise not to lose my head like some untried boy."

Viola said nothing in response to that as he picked up the nightrail and cleaned away any traces of what had just passed between them. But when he wrapped her once more in his arms, her head nestled against his shoulder and the heat of his body warming her, she realized that there was very little to be said. In his arms, she'd discovered pleasure, sensuality, what it meant to actually desire the touch of another. The giving and receiving of pleasure had never taken place in her marriage bed. It had been cruelty and humiliation. He'd asked what manner of man she thought he was. The only answer she possessed was a simple one. He was the very best of men and she'd given him far more than her body this night.

Chapter Fourteen

WILLIAM WELLS STAGGERED up the embankment. It was pitch black and he couldn't see his hand in front of his face. Having laid there for hours, he was more sober than he'd been in a decade and hurting enough to regret the fact.

Rivulets of blood had seeped from the wound on his scalp and dried on his face, making his skin feel taut. Every movement, even the blinking, caused him pain. His vision was blurred whether from being bashed on the head or from laying senseless in the elements for days— he couldn't be certain. He wasn't even entirely certain how long he'd been out there. It could have been overnight. It could have been days. As he struggled to climb up the steep slope to the road, he slipped and grabbed on to the rocky outcroppings for support.

"Damn Timothy Cobb," he muttered. The other man was a long acquaintance, a fellow patron of the local tavern. They'd always been friendly, if not friends. When the man had joined him on his walk home from the tavern, he'd thought nothing of it. It was only when they were on a dark stretch of road, nearer to Castle Black than the village and far from any that might overhear that he'd had any inkling of Cobb's nefarious plans.

After multiple false starts, stumbles, falls, and other collapses, William finally reached the road. Unable to go any further, he settled himself against the trees, being sure that he was well concealed. If Cobb came back, he was in no position to fend off another attack when he'd barely survived the first one. "Bashed in the head with a rock and left for dead by a no good wretch of a man," he muttered.

"And I offered to share me brandy with him!"

Still cursing his attacker under his breath, William slipped once more into unconsciousness. His last waking thought was that he needed to warn the good doctor that there was plotting afoot.

Viola awoke alone, but she was not bereft. She had vague recollections of a gentle kiss on her cheek and the blankets being tucked about her before he'd made his getaway just as the first faint rays of dawn had seeped between the curtains. To say that the previous night had been a revelation was to make a vast understatement.

There, in the clear light of the morning, Viola admitted to herself that she had fallen irrevocably in love with Dr. Nicholas Warner. She didn't question that he cared for her deeply and that he desired her. But she had no notion if he wanted a more permanent arrangement between them or if they would simply enjoy one another's company and favor for a short time and part ways. It was a strange thing to find herself desirous of being tied to a man, when from the outset of her marriage to Percival, she'd longed for freedom. There had been times when she'd prayed for death, sometimes his and sometimes her own, just to have an escape.

The door opened and Belinda entered. She took one look at Viola's bare shoulders and mussed hair and gave a soft whoop of joy. "Well, the doctor seems to have cured all that ails you, I think!"

"Shush," Viola said. "I don't need you crowing about it!"

"He's a handsome man and I daresay one that knows how to see to a woman's pleasure," Belinda said as she stepped deeper into the room. "I came with a message from the butler. He says they received word that Lord Blakemore's solicitor is down from London, staying at the inn, and will be here before the noon hour to discuss your 'situation'."

"Will you fetch another nightrail from the wardrobe and help me tame this hair?" Viola asked. "I'll need a bath prepared but I fear poor

Maggie would be quite scandalized to see me in my current state."

Belinda retrieved the garment and brought it to her. "I wouldn't worry too much about scandalizing folks. I have a feeling that the good doctor will come up to snuff soon enough."

Viola wasn't so certain of that, but she didn't mean to barter today's happiness for tomorrow's expectations.

Once more modestly robed and with some semblance of order restored to the mass of her hair, she rang for the maid to begin her morning toilette.

"I'll go and fetch Tristan. He should be up and terrorizing the housemaids by now," Belinda said.

"Do you have the documents from the archbishop?"

"I do," Belinda answered. "A signed and witnessed letter from him that he was present for the boy's birth. The date and location of it and your name and title. Whatever else they can say about it, there'll be no questioning that the child was conceived and born during your marriage to the late Lord Ramsleigh."

Viola nodded. It had been Belinda who, before she'd even left Aberdeen, insisted that she not take those documents with her when traveling by sea. It had been a stroke of luck that she'd listened, trusted the older woman's intuition.

"Let us hope that Lord Blakemore's solicitor shares your certainty on that score. I am hopeful that this can all be handled with a minimal amount of difficulty. Knowing Randall as I do, I recognize it's a fool's hope."

"It'll all work out," Belinda said. "I believe that with all my heart. After what you were made to suffer, I can't accept it would be any other way."

As Maggie entered, Belinda left with a nod in passing and went to see to Tristan.

"Will you be wanting your breakfast first, m'lady, or your bath?" Maggie asked.

Viola found that she was not hungry at all. Her nerves were too fraught with the meeting that was to come to even think of food. "The bath, I think. I'll have some chocolate later."

When a bevy of servants had come and gone, Viola sank into the tub of blissfully hot water and contemplated what was to come. If the solicitor asked her outright if Tristan was Percival's child, she'd have to lie. Would it be so awful for him to not have the title? Yes, because then the world would call him a bastard. Thinking of Nicholas and the hurt that such a word had caused him in his life, she knew she'd do whatever was necessary to spare her son that same sort of pain.

"He will not know," Viola vowed softly, "how he came to be in this world. I will spare him that at any cost."

ON HIS BORROWED mount, Nicholas went for a morning ride. While it was not a favorite pastime, he found himself in need of solitude. He'd needed to be alone with his own thoughts and to determine how he meant to proceed. Viola had become his lover. Some might argue the fact given that the deed itself had not been entirely completed, but the intimacy they'd shared was too great for him to be pedantic about what had passed between them.

While that had been his goal, he'd realized as he held her through the night that it would take much more than that to be satisfied. What he wanted from her was far more permanent. It wasn't simply that she'd claimed his heart. In some ways, he felt that she'd taken a piece of his very soul. There could be no half-measures between them for him to be satisfied. But could he, in good conscience, offer for her when she'd be taking on a much lower station in life? He was a physician in a small, country village and a poor one at that. Paid in chickens and preserves, there was little hope of his fortunes turning. He was also a bastard with no family and no connections save for a half-brother he'd only just met.

If he accepted the bequest from his late father, any hope of keeping his parentage and illegitimacy a secret were forfeit. If he refused it, he'd be damning Viola to a life of penury if they had to subsist only on his earnings. Given what Graham had revealed about the nature of Ramsgate Hall, it appeared that any inheritance she might have had was already squandered.

It wasn't truly his decision to make, Nicholas decided. It was hers. She had to decide for herself and for her son what they needed. He could only hope that he would get to be a part of that.

Turning his mount, he headed through the woods toward the road. He wasn't quite ready to return to the estate yet and taking the longer route would give him time to work up the nerve necessary to have such a soul-searing conversation with her. Letting the horse take the lead, it plodded along at a slow and steady pace, pausing periodically to investigate whatever treats might be growing by the roadside.

As he rounded a bend, Nicholas drew sharply back on the reins. The body lying face down at the roadside was something of a shock. Dismounting, Nicholas crossed the short distance and felt for a pulse. It was faint and erratic, but still present. Carefully rolling the man onto his back, Nicholas cursed.

"William Wells, if this is the result of brandy—"

Wells opened his eyes then. "Cobb. Tim Cobb," he murmured softly.

"He struck you?" Nicholas asked, carefully checking him for other injuries.

"Left the tavern with him… don't know what it's all about."

"Were you robbed?"

"Nothing to rob," the man answered softly and then drifted once more into unconsciousness.

Cursing, Nicholas managed to hoist him up and drape him across the back of the horse. It wasn't an ideal way to transport a patient, but he had little choice in the matter. With his patient as secured as possible, Nicholas mounted the horse once more and sped toward Castle Black. Any thoughts of solitude or further rumination on his possible future with Viola would simply have to wait.

Chapter Fifteen

As Viola descended the stairs, there was quite a bit of chaos. Servants were running to and fro and Lady Agatha appeared quite disturbed. She stood in the foyer, her hands clasped to her breasts and a troubled expression marring her features.

"Has something happened then? Lady Beatrice is well?" Viola asked, immediately concerned for the woman who had become her friend.

"She and my grandchild are well," Lady Agatha answered immediately. "I'm afraid Dr. Warner has discovered a poor man near bludgeoned to death by the roadside. He's a local fellow, a bit of a drunkard, I fear, but quite amiable. He's as poor as a church mouse as I understand it so what reason anyone might have to harm him is simply beyond me!"

"Where is he? Does Dr. Warner need our assistance?" Viola asked.

"They've taken him to a small room just off the kitchen. I'm not certain if he requires assistance, but I am certain he would be glad of your company," Lady Agatha offered. "He appeared quite distressed when he brought the gentleman in. This is so very much like what happened to poor Edmund! But that culprit was found. What violence we've had here!"

Leaving Lady Agatha to her own devices which were just shy of hysterics, Viola made her way toward the kitchen. She could hear Nicholas giving a list of commands to the staff, items he needed. His tone wasn't sharp per se, but it was clipped, indicating that whatever injuries his patient had suffered, they were pressing.

"How can I help?" she asked upon entering.

He paused then, looked at her, gave a brief nod and said, "Come with me."

She followed immediately and without question. Entering the small chamber just off the kitchen, it was equipped with a wash stand, a bed, and two hard-looking chairs. It was clearly a room for working, for tending to the sick, and not for taking one's rest. The spartan quality of it reminded her of the farm in Aberdeen.

"I'm going to turn him over and I need you to hold him while I clean the wound. Don't let him thrash about it. One of the maids will be in here to help," Nicholas said.

Viola did as he asked, holding the injured man by his shoulders after Nicholas turned him on his side. She could see the wealth of dried blood coating his hair and skin. She could also smell ale and perhaps even brandy upon him.

"Lady Agatha says it was an attack, but is it possible he simply fell in his drunkenness?" It was a reasonable question, she felt, but Nicholas' immediately shook his head in response. She hated to imagine that there was such violence so close to them, although she certainly knew first hand of its existence. But this sort of crime, footpads accosting hapless people on the road, was something else altogether.

Nicholas paused in his ministrations and looked up at her. His expression was severe and telling for it. "He was conscious on the road... just long enough to disclose the identity of his attacker. A man named Timothy Cobb."

Viola's blood ran cold at the mere mention of it. She was well acquainted with Cobb. He'd committed any number of dirty deeds that her late husband had considered beneath him and, no doubt, still completed similar tasks for Randall. That thought gave her pause and created a sinking feeling in the pit of her stomach. "Is this man connected to you at all... or to me?"

"He identified you at the beach after I'd pulled you from the water," Nicholas said, not looking up from his task. He was intent upon cleansing the wound.

"Timothy Cobb worked for my husband," Viola admitted haltingly. "He was Percival's henchman for lack of a better word. If a tenant was late with their rent or if he was owed something by someone not of his class, Cobb was his debt collector. And he would collect, by fair means or foul. I also imagine that there were other far less respectable things that Cobb did for him, as well."

Nicholas didn't stop his surprisingly gentle but sure strokes as he swabbed the wound, wiping away the blood and dirt gathered there. Nor did he look up. Yet from the tension that settled about him, she knew that he understood perfectly what she had implied. "You think Cobb acted on Randall's orders?"

"I cannot say. Only that it is a possibility... to what end, I cannot even guess," Viola admitted. "But it seems a rare coincidence that the man who identified me as Lady Ramsleigh would be attacked by a man who worked for my husband unless the two events are connected in some manner."

Nicholas said nothing further, just continued washing blood away from the wound. When at last he'd finished, he sighed heavily. "The blood is mostly old. The wound has scabbed over and will not require stitching. The swelling is mostly internal, I fear. Very little is present outside the skull and that is not a good sign. With head wounds, it is always better to bleed out than in. The brain cannot tolerate the increased pressure within the skull without being compromised in some way."

Viola's heart was heavy as she eyed the poor man's prone form. "Is he... will he recover at all?"

Nicholas did look up then, meeting her gaze directly and clearly, but his expression was impossible to read. "I do not know the answer to that. It is beyond my ability to predict. These types of injuries can resolve with no lasting effect or they may alter his functioning forever. At this point, I can only hope his skill isn't fractured. I've no notion how long Wells had been lying there but he doesn't show the telltale blackening of the eyes that I've seen in the past with more severe head injuries."

"So there's nothing you can do for him?"

"Try to keep him comfortable, make certain the wound doesn't begin bleeding again... monitor him for signs of delirium, but I'm afraid that's all. Medicine is not yet advanced enough to manage the inner workings of the brain or truly catastrophic injuries, I'm afraid. But for now, I'm going to leave him in the hands of the servants while you and I discuss why Timothy Cobb would have reason to attack one of the men involved in your rescue."

As they exited the small chamber, a maid rushed in. "The solicitor is here, my lady." The girl bobbed a hasty curtsy at a dark glower from the housekeeper.

"Our conversation will have to wait," she said. "But perhaps you'd join me for this one? I confess to needing all the support I can muster in hearing what I fear will be difficult news."

***

Frustrated by the interruption but well aware of the significance of what was to transpire, Nicholas nodded his agreement. Walking behind her, he noted that her posture had grown rigid, her shoulders back and her head held up as if she were about to face an executioner. As they neared the main hall, he placed a gentle hand on her elbow and stopped her. "This man is on your side."

"That may well be, but it could still be the losing side. And maybe I should lose. Maybe the best thing for Tristan would be to have nothing whatsoever to do with the Grantham or the Ramsleigh title... and that house of horrors I was forced to endure," she hissed. "I was so certain of my path when I left Aberdeen to return here and every day that certainty fades more and more. What if I'm wrong to pursue this course?"

Nicholas looked at her. He saw the confusion and uncertainty in her eyes. Her son was her entire world, as well he should be. "You are intelligent, wise and unaccountably brave... whatever you decide, will be for the right reasons and will be dealt with in a manner befitting your character and the kind of man you will raise your son to be. Wherever you are planted, my dear Viola, you will bloom, because that is simply your way." It wasn't precisely an admission of his feelings, but there could be no clearer expression of his admiration for her.

Looking down into her upturned face, Nicholas called on every bit of strength he possessed not to give in to temptation. Never in his life had he longed so desperately to kiss a woman. But it was not the time or the place. Those moments were for later, when they were locked in the safety of her chamber, far from prying eyes and the judgement of others.

"You should not say such things where they can be overheard," she admonished softly. "I am not the sort of woman most would see you with."

"Is it that, Viola? Or am I not the sort of man others would expect to see you with?"

She frowned. "I ran away from my husband… abandoned him and had a child while living in exile. You are well respected here, admired. The differences in our stations would be much less of a scandal than the differences in our levels of notoriety. I would not see your association with me do you harm."

"That is something else for us to discuss later… for now, the solicitor is waiting," he said gruffly. Whatever the man had to say, it could irrevocably alter the course of any future they had together. The least they could do was hear him out.

They said nothing further to one another, but made their way silently to Graham's study where the solicitor awaited them. Graham bade them enter at Nicholas' soft knock. Opening the door for her, he allowed her to enter first and followed close behind. If anyone thought their closeness odd or perhaps telling, no one would comment on it.

"Lady Viola Grantham, wife to the late Lord Ramsleigh, Dr. Warner, this is Mr. Pritchard, my solicitor. He's been well apprised of your situation, Lady Viola, and has made the necessary inquiries to advise you on your next course of action," Graham said. The introductions were as abrupt and to the point as most of his dealings.

Mr. Pritchard, in no way shocked or scandalized by the less than perfect manners of a lord of the realm, simply rose to his feet, sketched a bow to Viola and then offered his seat to her. When she'd settled herself in it, the tiny and bespectacled man began his long dissertation of what, precisely, he'd been looking in to.

"The law states quite implicitly that any child born to a wife during her marriage to her husband legitimizes the child, so long as the husband does not disavow the child as a bastard. In order to do so, he would have to show evidence that he was unable to complete his marital duties, as it were. So, regardless of any questions that might be raised about the boy's parentage, as long as he was born during your husband's life or he was born no more than nine months after you'd left your husband or nine months after your husband passed," the man paused, coughed uncomfortably, and stared resolutely at the floor. Then he blushed profusely as he asked, "How many months did pass between your departure and the child's birth?"

"Seven months, Mr. Pritchard. My son was conceived prior to me leaving my husband. It was because I carried a child and feared for his life and mine given the violent tendencies of the Grantham men that I fled," she answered softly.

It took great skill to tell the truth while still hiding it, Nicholas thought, and yet she did just that. She didn't tell an outright lie by saying that Tristan was her husband's child, nor did she state that her husband was the man who posed a danger to her. Both were carefully implied and the listener could draw their own conclusions.

"I see. And is there evidence to bear out the fact that you were reasonably frightened?"

"A woman fled that house with me, helped me to make my escape. She'd served as my maid and can attest to the fact that I was pushed down a flight of stairs resulting in the premature birth of the first child I'd conceived during my marriage. Is all this really necessary?" Viola demanded clearly distressed at having to bare such intimate details in front of all of them.

"It could be," the solicitor replied placatingly. "I cannot say whether the man who currently calls himself Lord Ramsleigh will challenge you in the courts. But if he does, it is precisely these sorts of questions that will be asked, much to my chagrin and embarrassment. At this point, he will be challenging you for the title alone, as the estate is all but bankrupt."

Nicholas watched her chin come up, her jaw clench and he saw the bitter flash of anger and disappointment in her eyes.

"Bankrupt?" she demanded. "How can he be bankrupt? I was to inherit a sum of thirty thousand pounds! Surely even he could not run through so much in only a matter of months!"

"Your hus—forgive me, your late husband, received your inheritance in its entirety. He then gifted your father a sum of fifteen thousand pounds. There is no recourse to recover that sum."

"Except that her father was the person who initiated the plot to have her declared dead and claim the inheritance when he knew precisely where she was," Nicholas protested. "It's blatant fraud!"

Mr. Pritchard nodded enthusiastically. "It is! It most assuredly is, and perhaps a refund of this settlement can be arranged privately with Mr. Daventry. I can only imagine that he would very much wish to avoid the scandal associated with such deplorable acts. I strongly urge Dr. Warner and you, as well, Lady Ramsleigh, to pursue these matters outside of the courts if possible... not because they cannot be won, but because the potential cost of them to your reputation and your standing in society would be irreparable."

"And if I elect not to challenge Randall, at all? If I decide to raise my son in peace and avoid the taint of all things related to the Grantham men?" she asked.

Mr. Pritchard's lips firmed. "I'm afraid that isn't really possible. There was a gentleman involved in your rescue, a Mr. Wells I believe, who has been entertaining travelers at the local inn with stories of the good doctor's heroic rescue and your resurrection, as it were. On my way here, I happened upon two elderly ladies traveling to a local spa, and they recounted the tale to me at great length and likely no small amount of embellishment. You are notorious now, Lady Ramsleigh, and as such, the subject of great scrutiny. Unless you plan to shuffle your child off to be raised by others and to change his name entirely, the truth will come out."

It was the missing piece, Nicholas realized. William Wells had been attacked and left for dead because he was spreading the truth of Viola's return. If Randall was attempting to keep it a secret, it meant he likely intended to do away with her, as well.

"I think Randall is plotting to kill you," he said softly. "If he knows about Tristan, at least he doesn't know that he's here. Not yet, anyway. We need to be certain it stays that way."

"What?" Mr. Pritchard gasped.

Nicholas didn't even look at the man. His gaze was locked on Viola who had grown pale. But she didn't appear shocked or in any way in disbelief. There was, in her face, complete acceptance of the notion that her late husband's nephew, the man who had fathered her child by force, meant to see both her and her son dead.

"William Wells is here in this house right now... I found him on the road this morning. He'd been attacked and left for dead. Currently, he's suffering from a head injury but I cannot say whether or not he will recover from it. He did confide in me in his last moment of consciousness that his attacker was a man by the name of Timothy Cobb," Nicholas said, addressing the small and now very nervous solicitor.

"And Timothy Cobb was frequently employed by my late husband to complete more—unsavory, as it were—tasks," Viola finished. "I imagine he is continuing in the same capacity for Randall."

Mr. Pritchard cleared his throat uncomfortable. "Yes, I quite imagine he is. Under the circumstances, Lady Ramsleigh, I will return to London and submit a letter to your father requesting the return of the funds settled on him by your late husband, as they were, in fact, not his to settle. I will offer to him to forgo the pursuit of legal recourse in exchange for his agreement, if that is acceptable to you?"

"It is," she said. "And submit a letter to Randall's solicitor, as well, while you are at it. Inform him that I have returned with my son and the rightful heir to the Ramsleigh title and fortune. It was what Percival wanted, after all."

Pritchard nodded. "As you wish, my lady. I do hope you are prepared for the ugliness that could ensue from this."

Viola stood, shoulders back and her head held high as a queen, "My dear, Mr. Pritchard, there has been naught but ugliness from the moment that my father bartered me to the late Lord Ramsleigh. I assure you, I am fully aware of what I am undertaking. If you will excuse me, I am going to check on my son... and Mr. Pritchard, I would not ask you to lie but, under the circumstances, it might be best not to be forthcoming with the fact that Tristan has now joined me at Castle Black."

"It will be handled with the utmost discretion, Lady Ramsleigh," the little man assured her. "Copies of all correspondence will be sent to you here in care of Lord Blakemore."

"Thank you, Mr. Pritchard."

Viola turned to leave the room. As she did, she locked gazes with Nicholas. He could see the fear in her eyes. It was one thing to know that Randall was capable of murder. It was quite another to be confronted with the very real evidence that he was, in fact, plotting it at that very moment.

"I'll check on Mr. Wells," he offered. "And join you and young Tristan later, if you are amenable."

She nodded her acquiescence and sailed gracefully from the room.

As the door closed behind her, Graham uttered the very sentiment that was stirring in Nicholas' mind. "Can't we just kill the bounder? I can challenge him to a duel. As a lord myself, there might be some scandal about it, but the law has no teeth where I'm concerned."

"I would not advise it, my lord," Pritchard protested. "There are still those not entirely convinced of your identity. To engage in such scandalous behavior would be to invite those naysayers and doubters to take action. It is best I think to continue as we are and focus our energies on providing protection for Lady Ramsleigh and her child."

"Fine," Graham relented. "But if he steps foot on my lands or makes any sort of threat against anyone in this house, I'll shoot him where he stands."

Clearly uncomfortable with such violent proclivities and strong emotions, the solicitor gathered up his papers, sketched a hasty bow and retreated quickly. After Pritchard left, Nicholas and Graham were alone in the study, free to discuss the matter without worry of being overheard.

"Scandal be damned. If it means protecting a woman and an innocent child, it's worth the risk," Graham vowed.

"It is. But it isn't your fight this time. It's mine. And I know what I have to do. Where is Lord Ambrose?" Nicholas asked.

"He's upstairs preparing for his departure in the morning, I think. You've decided to accept the bequest, then?"

Nicholas nodded. "I have. As a lowly country doctor, I can't challenge Ramsleigh. As a landed and wealthy bastard son of the late Lord Ambrose, I might fare better."

Graham arched one black brow. "You cannot challenge him over a woman who is simply your acquaintance. Not without ruining her."

"She is far more than an acquaintance, as you well know," Nicholas admitted. While they were making every attempt to be discreet, Graham was a man of the world and had eyes with which to see.

"And is this simply an affair, or is it something more?"

Nicholas laughed at that. "Are you trying to ask me what my intentions are?"

Graham shrugged. "Perhaps. You mean to marry her, then? Or will I be forced to issue a challenge to you down the road, as she is currently under my roof and, therefore, under my protection."

"I mean to offer," Nicholas said. "But the decision is hers. Too many men have made decisions for her already. I would not try to defy her will in this or anything else."

"You think she'll reject your offer, don't you? Nicholas, I think you sell yourself and Lady Ramsleigh short with that kind of doubt. It is obvious that the both of you have developed rather deep feelings for one another." Graham paused, cleared his throat, and then continued, "I know that you have become lovers. There is little in this house that I am not aware of. And I do not think she would undertake such a thing lightly."

"I don't think I'm selling either one of us short," Nicholas said, shaking his head. "And I won't lie to you and deny that our relationship has become more intimate than propriety would allow. But that doesn't mean she wishes to marry me. Women are just as given to fits of passion and to the longings of the flesh as are men—regardless of what society would have us believe!"

"But surely if you offer—"

"Given what they've put her through," Nicholas began, interrupting his friend, "and the lengths she went to in order to escape that hell and have her son safe, could you really blame her for never again wishing to place her life solely in the hands of another? I wouldn't if our situations were reversed."

Graham had no response to that. Instead, he simply reached into the drawer of the desk, retrieved two glasses and a bottle of brandy and placed them on the leather blotter. After filling both, and drinking liberally from one, he finally spoke, "Then do not ask her yet. Wait, until you can be certain of her response… women are unpredictable creatures. The moment you are certain you know what they will do or say, they change course like the wind. Eventually, a time will come when she will not be so set against such an entanglement."

Nicholas reached for his own glass and took a long sip, letting the amber liquid burn its way to his gut. "To be completely fair, I saw just how badly you mucked up your own affairs in trying to convince Beatrice to marry you. If you hadn't been shot and nearly died from it, you'd still be trying to maneuver her to the altar!"

Graham shrugged. "Then you have your answer. Do something dashing and heroic… and try not to die in the process."

Nicholas considered how much to share, and ultimately decided the answer was very little. It was not his story to tell, it was Viola's and he would not betray her trust by breaking a confidence even if there was an excellent reason to do so. Instead, he said, "I wish I could tell you the lengths of depravity and wickedness to which the elder Lord Ramsleigh and the current Lord Ramsleigh have actually sunk. But I cannot. I can only tell you that if an opportunity arises to rid this world of him, it should be taken and rejoiced at."

Graham took another sip and met his gaze levelly. "You do not have to sway me, my friend. I trust your judgement. If you say the man is a bounder, then a bounder he is, and whatever steps must be taken will be taken. I owe you my life, after all."

Nicholas placed his glass on the desk. "Then for the love of God, get some decent brandy and stop trying to murder me with that swill we used to drink aboard ship!"

Graham laughed then. "You've grown soft."

"I've grown unconscious! Blacked out cold from that rot gut that could turn a man blind drink with nothing more than a sip! You're a lord, now. A gentleman. Stop drinking like a bloody pirate!"

A shrug was Graham's only response. "Once a pirate, always a pirate... and to that end, if Ramsleigh needs killing, it doesn't have to be a duel. People have accidents all the time. I'm certain one could be arranged."

Nicholas had already considered it, and if it came to it, he wasn't above murder. Not if it meant keeping Viola safe. "I will certainly keep that in mind. Now, I suppose I should go and let my newly-discovered half-brother in on the fact that I've decided to accept my place as the resident by-blow in the Garrett clan."

Chapter Sixteen

VIOLA LOOKED IN on Tristan. He was napping and she didn't wish to disturb him. But she did stand there for a moment and stare down at him, sleeping peacefully in his ignorance of the plots and schemes that threatened them both. With a small, wooden horse clutched in his hands and his dark brown hair curling against his forehead, he had an angelic appearance that belied his willfulness and temper.

When she'd fled Ramsgate Hall, her only thought had been keeping her unborn child safe and protected. She hadn't expected that she could love anything or anyone as completely as she loved her son. Even while still in the womb, he'd become the entire focus of her being. But she hadn't been prepared for the wave of love and happiness that had suffused her when she'd first held him and stared down into the wrinkled, red and angry face of her newly-born son. Now, all she wanted was for him to be healthy, to be happy and to be a better man than the one who'd sired him—the very same man who now wanted him dead.

Coming back had stirred up a hornet's nest of trouble and it no longer mattered what she wanted to do as far as reclaiming what was left of her inheritance and seeking the title for him. Randall would come for them regardless of her actions. In her attempts to secure his future, she'd underestimated Randall and put them both in unbearable danger. And what if that danger extended to those who had offered her solace and sanctuary?

Easing from the nursery, she left him to sleep and retreated to her chambers, her heart and mind heavy. Nicholas would seek her out, but what they had left to discuss she couldn't be sure. Knowing what he did now, about her past, about Randall's insanity and dogged determination to see her ended once for all, surely the man would be sensible enough to flee and never look back. If he wasn't, did she have the strength of character to push him away for his own good? Or was she too selfish for that?

Settling herself at the dressing table, she plucked the pins from her hair and placed them in a small vessel. Brushing her hair was a mindless task that also soothed her frayed nerves. The silver-backed brush was yet something else gifted to her by Lady Agatha or Lady Beatrice, she'd long since given up determining whose largesse she was enjoying. Dragging the stiff bristles through her hair, she brushed the mass of it until she felt some semblance of calm begin to overtake her.

That was how Nicholas found her only moments later when he entered her chamber. She felt his gaze upon her without actually hearing him enter the room. Looking up, she noted how intently he watched her and the concern that etched his too-handsome face.

"I'm not about to fall into a fit of the vapors just because Randall wants me dead. It isn't the first time he's tried to kill me, after all," she stated, her mild tone easing the sting of the words.

"He'll not get close enough to you for it to matter. You can't imagine that either I, or Lord Blakemore for that matter, would ever allow harm to come to you?" His tone revealed not only his incredulity but also his anger. Whether it was directed at her or at Randall, she couldn't say.

"I don't know that. I trust that you will both do whatever you can to prevent it, but you cannot make promises, Nicholas. You've no notion what you're dealing with! The level of depravity, the sheer inhumanity of him! My God, he murdered his own unborn child to cling to his hopes of inheritance! Tristan and I are nothing to him but a threat... I was foolish to ever think I could come back here and simply take up residence. But then, I was unaware that my father had helped

Percival render me a legally dead woman! This entire situation has been complicated unnecessarily by their greed and collusion!"

He stepped deeper into the room until he was standing behind her. She couldn't see his face, but she could feel the tension emanating from him as he took the brush from her hand and placed it on the dressing table. His hands then delved into the thick, dark strands, mussing them terribly. She knew that he had an affinity for her hair, that he enjoyed the look and feel of it on his skin. It was one of the many things she'd discovered the previous night.

"I've accepted Ambrose's offer," he said softly. "I'm taking the bequest from my father. The world will know me for a bastard, but I'll be a noble bastard at least. Given that, my friendship with Lord Blakemore, my service in the Royal Navy and now Ambrose's public acknowledgement of me as his half-brother, I will be recognized as a gentleman."

"To what end?" She knew what he was about to say and she also knew that she would not be able to permit it. The risk was too great.

"If I challenge him to a duel, it can all end... immediately," he said. "His plots and schemes die with him and there is no one to challenge your assertions that Tristan is the rightful heir."

"And if he kills you? You assume he will fight fair, you assume that your time spent as a soldier—as a *physician* in the navy—offers some certainty that you can best him... but he's been dueling since he was practically in short pants. He's seduced his way through the ton, he's deflowered innocent and protesting young maidens, and he's affronted and cuckolded some of the most powerful men in society! Most of the society matrons of any importance at all refuse him entrance. He lives in disgrace because he is incapable of even feigning honor." Her protest was heated, her voice rising with it until she was all but shouting at him. Taking a calming breath, she forced herself to speak in a gentler tone, though the words were no less forceful and uncompromising. "He'll see you dead, Nicholas, and I won't have that on my conscience. I'd rather take Tristan and flee to the ends of the earth and certain poverty than to see you die at his hands!"

"Have you so little faith in my ability to protect you? Or is it that you're so used to him having complete power in his own little domain that you can't conceive of his defeat?" Nicholas challenged.

"You are a good man, Nicholas Warner. Perhaps, the very best of men… and my life hasn't allowed me to retain faith in the ability of goodness to survive the influence and the cruelty of the Granthams. They've turned me into an adulteress, a runaway wife, a liar, a defrauder, and a woman whose own family has turned its backs on her. How could I believe anything other than that they, in all their power, will prevail?"

"What would you have me do then? Simply walk away?" he snapped.

She faltered then. Was that what she wanted? A part of her screamed yes. He terrified her because he gave her the one thing she'd sworn never to have again—hope. He made her believe in and yearn for things she'd thought impossibly lost. The power he had to hurt her was far greater than Randall's because Nicholas possessed the ability, knowingly or not, to break her heart.

When she opened her mouth to speak, one single word escaped her. "No." Drawing a breath to steady herself she uttered again, "No. I don't think I could bear that."

"Trust me to help you, Viola. I can and I will. You had no one to stand for you in the past, no one to question their treatment of you. That is no longer true… you may be surprised at how little power Randall actually wields when the odds have been evened a bit."

"Why are you doing this, Nicholas?" She hated herself for asking the question, for needing the answers from him. "Is this all simply some overburdened sense of gallantry on your part?"

"I am not a gallant man. And I'm not the naive innocent you believe me to be, Viola. Just because I don't take joy in the suffering of others doesn't mean I'm unaware of how cruel the world can be or how evil men can be."

"I have never said you were naive… and I know you aren't innocent. But I fear that you have never encountered men like my late husband and his nephew! I fear for your safety, Nicholas. If something were to happen to you because you were trying to help me—"

"Being a physician in the navy did not spare me from the duties of a soldier. I fought and I killed. And then I took up with pirates while I lived in the Islands. That is where Lord Blakemore and I became acquainted, you see? He was a pirate, as well. I've done things that I'm not proud of, but if those past misdeeds put me in a better position to defend you now, then the path I have laid to hell has been well worth it," he asserted. "Because whether you are ready to hear it or not, I am ready to say it, and I have said it no other woman in my life. I love you."

Viola's heart stuttered in her chest, skipping erratically as the magnitude of what he'd said enveloped her. "What?" The question came out in an undignified squeak.

"I love you," he repeated, slowly and with far more patience than he ought to have had in such a circumstance. "From the very moment I met you, I was drawn to you. Before, even. There is no reason, Viola, that I should have seen you clinging to life in that dark water, much less been able to reach you and bring you back to the beach. I think I felt you before I even knew you were there. Fate brought us together. I've never been a believer in such things, but there is no other cause that I can think of. Fate brought Graham to me in the Indies, and then brought me here to you. I love you, and whether you return that feeling or not is of no matter at this time."

"Of course, it matters!" Viola interrupted. "Do you honestly think I would have taken you to my bed if I wasn't in love with you? After all that I have endured, do you truly believe anything less than love could prompt me to take such risks?"

NICHOLAS FELT AS if all the breath simply rushed from his body in one sharp exhale. For a moment, longer than was comfortable with, he was so stunned he was unable to replace that breath. He simply stood there, the enormity of their admissions weighting the very air around them.

Finally, managing to draw breath once more, he said, "Well, I'd rather hoped."

The sardonic answer drew a sharp burst of surprised laughter from her. "You are incorrigible."

"So, I've been told. Would you have an incorrigible husband, Viola?"

He saw her face shutter, saw the panic in her eyes. It wounded his pride, her lack of faith in his ability to protect her and the hesitation that he saw so clearly in that moment. But he wasn't so insensitive that he couldn't understand her reasoning. In her life, the Grantham men had been all powerful. The fear and terror they'd forced her to endure would loom large in her mind for many years, possibly forever. Why would she wish to marry again, to give another man that kind of control? So as much as it stung, he knew that lashing out at her for it was not the way.

"Are you asking me to marry you?" Her voice was tremulous, perhaps wary, but he thought, possibly, there was also hope buried within it.

"Not yet. I'm informing you that I would like to marry you. If and when you are ready to be asked, you may let me know. It seems to be the standard protocol for how our relationship progresses, don't you think?" he teased.

"It isn't that I don't want to. It's rather that I hadn't anticipated it would ever come up. There is Tristan to think of," she said hesitantly. "I could not leave him. I would not."

"There is Tristan," he agreed amiably. "And I would never ask you to leave him. I promise you that, little experience as I have with fathers, I will be the best one that I possibly can be to him... I will never treat him poorly. I will love him and care for him as if he were my own son. But now I must ask you another question, Viola."

"What is that?"

"I am a bastard, and soon there will be no denying it. Once Ambrose acknowledges me openly as his illegitimate half-brother and I accept my late father's bequest, the world will know. We will not be welcomed in society and both you and your son will be tainted by the circumstances of my rather ignoble birth. Can you live with that?"

"Do you honestly think it would matter to me?"

"I think," he said, "that it will matter for Tristan and for any children we might have. They will not have an easy time in society. You must know that. You must weigh that with your decision."

She walked toward the window and looked out to the sea. "My betrothal was easy. Not a hitch from our first introduction to the moment he entered my bedchamber on our wedding night. I even thought that I might come to love him. He was charming enough, handsome if somewhat older, and his manners were impeccable... though given the little of society I had seen, I had no real basis for comparison. Ease is not a guarantee of quality or happiness."

Never had he longed for anything more than to wipe away the sadness he saw in her lovely face. Viola deserved happiness. And whether he deserved her or not, he was selfish enough to take her and keep her for himself. But in doing so, he would devote himself to making her happy every day of their lives together.

Closing the distance between them, Nicholas placed one hand beneath her chin and tilted her face up to his. It was meant to be a sweet kiss, an expression of love and affection. But like so many things between them, it took on a life of its own. The very moment their lips met, desire flared hot and insistent. Pressing his lips more firmly to hers, he threaded his fingers once more through the mass of dark waves that cascaded past her shoulders. Her lips parted beneath his. It was all the invitation he needed to deepen the kiss, to explore the softness of her mouth and feel the gentle caress of her tongue against his own.

Without any thought of where they were, or that it was broad daylight and the servants were roaming freely through the house, Nicholas brought one hand up to cup the soft mound of her breast. She arched into his touch, kissing him back fervently as he teased that soft flesh until her nipple hardened to a taut point against his palm.

Kissing her until they were both breathless, it still wasn't enough. Reaching for her skirt, he tugged the fabric up until he could touch the satiny skin of her thigh. Her response, as she gripped his hand and guided it to the juncture of her thighs and the desire slicked flesh that was so eager for his touch, was more than any man could resist.

Breathless, so hard he ached with it, he eased his lips from hers. "This was not my intention in coming here."

"So long as your intention isn't to leave, I don't care," she said. "Make love to me, Nicholas."

He wanted that more than he wanted his next breath. "If only I could. But now is not the time. Tonight... I will come to you here after dinner."

She sighed and leaned back against the window casing. "I don't know how I'll wait so long."

He grinned. "That's part of my diabolical plan. You'll be thinking of it all day, as will I. Anticipation, my love, can be its own reward. And I do have a patient to see to."

"Is he going to recover?" Viola asked worriedly. "I hate to think he might suffer permanent damage simply for recounting the tale of your heroics."

"I have hopes that he will. Of course, if he does, I fully expect him to milk it for all the sympathy and brandy he can get out of it... Wells is quite good at that, no doubt. I believe he was telling the tale and exaggerating it to great and romantic detail in order to con passing travelers into paying for his ale and whiskey."

Viola shook her head. "Still, he doesn't deserve what has happened to him."

"No, he does not. I'll see you in a few hours... and I have a request."

"What?"

He grinned again, knowing that he was about to shock her. "When I arrive, I want you completely naked... not a stitch covering you but the fall of that glorious hair. My very own Lady Godiva."

She blushed furiously. "That would be scandalous."

"You've come back from the dead, Viola. Everything you do is scandalous," he reminded her.

Her lips tightened as she attempted to hold back her laughter. "So it is."

Nicholas left her chamber and made his way back to the small room off the kitchen. Wells was more alert than before, responding to requests to squeeze his hand and move his limbs, but he had yet to open his eyes. Still, it was a good sign.

"You may go," Nicholas said to the maid. "I'll sit with him a while, I think."

"I don't mind, Dr. Warner, sir," the maid said.

Nicholas realized that watching over the patient was likely keeping her from other chores that were even more unpleasant. "What's your name, girl?"

"Dora, sir," she said, bobbing a little curtsy that was totally unwarranted for someone of his standing. As if she recognized her mistake, she blushed furiously.

"Take a walk in the garden, Dora. Or sneak up to your rooms and have a nap. I won't tell," he promised.

The girl's eyes widened. "Oh, no, that isn't—I wouldn't… oh, cook would skin me alive!"

"Only if she finds out," he said. "I can distract her if you'd like, while you slip out the back?"

"No, sir. I'll just go back to the kitchen and see what needs doing," she said meekly. "But I do thank you for the offer."

Nicholas leaned back in the chair and propped his feet on the edge of Wells' bed. "I hope you wake up. And I hope to hell you remember Cobb's attack well enough to convince the magistrate of it."

Chapter Seventeen

TIMOTHY COBB HAD spent the day earning every shilling that Ramsleigh had given him. He'd gone far and wide in the small village, carrying the same tales from one farm to another as he preyed on the superstitions of the poorest amongst them and fueled their already intense anger and bitterness toward anyone of the upper class. If the truth were told, he despised Ramsleigh as much as anyone else did. But Ramsleigh was a steady stream of income, and he'd not bite the hand that fed him.

"I've amassed a group of about ten men, give or take. That ought to be enough to take her without raising too much of a fuss... especially after I set the mill on fire and lure his lordship and the good doctor away," Cobb said.

Ramsleigh smiled. "That should do quite well I think. Make certain she tells you where the boy is hidden away before they hang her. Are you squeamish about killing a child, Cobb?"

"Not squeamish about nothing, m'lord," he answered readily enough. It didn't much matter to him who he killed—man, woman or child—so long as he got paid. He'd have shoved a knife between Ramsleigh's ribs right there on the spot for the right price. "I'll make her talk and when it's done, I'll be making a little trip to snuff out the rightful heir."

Ramsleigh laughed. "Rightful heir, indeed! I wish I'd managed to kill the bitch the first time she bred!"

"She's a right looker, ain't she?" Cobb asked. "Too bad about all them witnesses or maybe I'd sample her refined charms myself."

"They're not so refined. She fights like a wildcat, though," Ramsleigh admitted, his lips twisting into a chilling smile.

That was something he hadn't considered. "You tupping your old auntie?" Cobb asked.

"It's mine, you know? The whelp she delivered while in hiding. My dear old uncle could have plowed her ten times a day and not put a babe in her belly... so he asked me to do it. Her bastard—my bastard," he said with a laugh, "isn't the rightful heir to anything. Just another by-blow. I'd leave him to the workhouse like I did the others, but I fear it might be a mistake given her powerful allies. No doubt, they'd search high and low for the brat. You'll kill him and be certain the body is found. I won't have an imposter showing up in twenty years claiming to be the long lost anything."

"I'll make sure the boy is dead, and that there's no doubt about it. I'll kill him and whoever's caring for him in their own home, so there can be no question of who he is," Cobb said. "And I'll be paid extra for my trouble."

Ramsleigh opened the desk drawer and withdrew another pouch of coins. He tossed it to him. "Not a tuppence more."

Cobb opened the pouch, examined his loot. "Seems a fair price. I've got to go and make sure everything is ready. She'll be dead by the morning, and then I'll go for the boy."

"You're not a good man, Cobb, but you're a good man to know," Ramsleigh said by way of parting.

Cobb nodded again and left, richer for his trouble.

IT WAS A wonder Viola had survived dinner. Every time she looked across the table, she'd seen Nicholas and recalled their earlier conversation and the more intimate aspects of their abbreviated encounter. He'd said anticipation was its own reward. The truth was that it was more akin to torture. She felt fevered, her body burning for things she barely understood but craved nonetheless. When the meal was done, she excused herself hastily enough that Lady Agatha became concerned for her.

"My dear, are you quite well?" Lady Agatha asked.

"I'm quite well, Lady Agatha. I simply wanted to get Tristan settled and into bed myself. It's a task I've missed since leaving him behind in Aberdeen," she said. It wasn't a lie. She was actually going to tuck her sweet boy in, but that wasn't the ultimate reason for her hurry. It was the man who sat across the hall, drinking brandy with his newly-found half-brother and his friend.

Lady Agatha nodded. "It is the best time, isn't it? When they're tired and let you cuddle them as you would when they were babies? It's terrible when they start being independent and demanding to do things for themselves. I believe we would, all of us, keep them small forever if we could."

"Yes, I most certainly would," Viola agreed.

"Go see to your son, my dear, and I shall see you in the morning. I think I will retire early myself. I've a new novel waiting for me," the older woman said. It was obvious that her concern was for Lady Beatrice who had been somewhat wan throughout dinner.

Viola turned to the younger woman, "Let me help you upstairs, Lady Beatrice. I vow when I was as far along as you, there was not a part of my body that did not ache... and steps were impossible to navigate because I simply couldn't see them anymore!"

Beatrice smiled. "Nonsense. You go on ahead. I'll wait here for Graham. I'd make him carry me, but I fear his poor back would not survive the task."

Lady Agatha made a tsking sound at her. "Now who is speaking nonsense? You are the picture of grace and beauty, my dear. But I shall leave you to my son's tender care."

Walking up the stairs with Lady Agatha, they parted ways at the top and Viola made her way to the nursery where Tristan was safely ensconced. Stepping inside, she found him sitting up in his small bed, chattering to Belinda as he excitedly showed her the small, wooden toys in each hand.

"He will not wish to leave here," Viola mused. "This room is a veritable treasure trove for a small boy."

Belinda grinned at that. "Those are new and just for him. Lord Blakemore brought them to him today. I believe he carved them himself. Apparently, he spent a great deal of time working on such things while aboard ship in his previous endeavors."

A pirate lord who carved toys for children, Viola mused. The man was full of surprises. But she believed him to be cut from the same sort of cloth as Nicholas. They were not gentleman by society's definition of the word, and yet their behavior and treatment of others far surpassed those who were supposed to represent the best society had to offer.

As Belinda moved away, Viola took her spot on the edge of Tristan's bed and listened to his chatter until it finally began to slow. She hugged him close then, snuggling him as she would have when he was so very small. Singing softly, the familiar lullaby did its work. She held him until he drifted to sleep and then tucked him back beneath the covers and made her way back to her own room.

Nicholas' request from earlier was still ringing in her mind. In truth, it had never been far from it. But she couldn't refuse him. Embarrassed as she was by it, it excited her as well. Loosening the simple tapes of her gown, she removed it and then her petticoats and stays. Removing the pins from her hair once more, she loosened the braids that had been the base for her chignon and allowed the waves of her hair to fall over her shoulders. Only then did she free the ties of her shift and let it fall to her waist. When she pushed it past her hips and the garment puddled on the floor, she spared a glance at her reflection.

It was more than a cursory glance. She took stock of every flaw. From the marks on her stomach and breasts that had bloomed there during and after her pregnancy, to the slight protrusion of her stomach that would never go away, or so she'd been told—there was much changed about her appearance. Yet, he insisted that he found her not just beautiful but desirable. Given how devilishly handsome he was and that he was, as far as she could see, a perfect specimen of masculinity, it caused her no small amount of insecurity.

She didn't hear the door open. Viola was unaware that anyone observed her as she stood before the mirror frowning disapprovingly at her reflection.

"I CANNOT IMAGINE what you would see there to prompt such an unhappy expression," Nicholas said by way of announcing his presence. He made no move to cross the room and close the distance between him. If he was near enough to touch her, things would progress too quickly and rob him of the alluring vision of her naked before him.

She blushed furiously and he knew that it was pride more than anything else that kept her from shielding herself from his view. Instead, her hands dropped to her sides, though they were still clenched nervously. "I was simply cataloguing all the ways in which I have changed."

It didn't surprise him that she saw flaws where he saw perfection. In his experience, even the most beautiful of women were often never satisfied with their appearances. Of course, in a society that valued them predominantly for that, he could easily see why.

"That you are free now and happy, I hope, that you now know your body is capable of indescribable pleasure?" he asked.

She shook her head, the dark cascade of her hair swaying seductively over her bare skin. "I was thinking in more visual terms. I had a very enviable figure once upon a time."

"You had the figure of a girl, once upon a time. Now you have the body of a woman, and there is nothing inherently better or worse in either of those... but I can tell you that you are beautiful, I can tell you that you are desirable, and you will still doubt. Leaving me to wonder if words are simply not the appropriate course of action here."

"And what is, then?" she demanded.

Nicholas moved forward then, easing away from the door and

stalking toward her with purpose. "This," he said simply, before capturing her hair in his hand and tugging her close enough to claim her mouth in a searing kiss. He could feel the softness of her body against him, the silk of her hair tangling about them both, as he parted her lips and swept inside the soft recesses of her mouth.

To that point, he'd been careful with her. He'd held his own desires in check for fear of frightening her. In that moment, he was no longer capable of such altruism. His own baser urges had overwhelmed, driving him to take, to claim, to conquer. Maneuvering her backwards toward the dressing table, until the backs of her thighs bumped against it, he lifted her onto it. Nudging her thighs apart with his knees, he stepped between them, pressing against her in a blatantly carnal manner. There was no mistaking his intent and he waited with bated breath for her to protest. But she didn't. Instead, she tugged his shirt from his breeches and slid her hands beneath it, sliding them tentatively over his fevered skin.

"I don't want to do anything to frighten you," he whispered against her skin. "But my will is gone, Viola. I need you too badly."

"I'm not some broken thing that you have to tend, Nicholas. I know what you want... and for the first time in my life, I want it, too," she replied.

That whispered admission was his undoing. Nicholas stripped off his shirt and tossed it aside, eager for the crush of her breasts against his chest. Sliding his hand along her inner thigh, he moved upward until he could touch her intimately, stroking the soft folds of her sex. Her flesh was slick with desire, her body as burning and eager as his own.

Her hands roamed his back, his chest, and then he felt one soft hand cupping him through the fabric of his breeches. It was the sweetest of torment, but not nearly enough. Then she freed each button, one by one, and he thought he might die from it. Forcing himself to back away from her, he uttered, "Bed... we should be in bed for this."

"Does it matter?" she asked as she stroked him gently.

"Christ, yes. If we have a hope in hell of lasting more than a minute, yes," he said, gripping her wrist and pulling her hand from him as he stepped back, "Get on the bed, Viola."

Thankfully, she did as he asked. Lowering herself from the dressing table, she crossed the chamber and paused at the side of the bed. She looked back at him over her shoulder. Her dark hair brushed the small of her back, highlighting the flare of her hips and her perfect, heart-shaped bottom. Whether she intended to torture him with such an erotic and sensual image of her was irrelevant to the impact it had. Like a punch in the gut, the need was so sharp and so irresistible that he had no choice but to follow her.

Shucking his breeches he climbed onto the bed and pulled her down with him until she sprawled atop his body. Whether it was instinct or simply that she was attuned to his desire, she immediately parted her thighs and sat back so that she was astride him. Nicholas reached between them, guiding his aching member to her entrance. He watched with bated breath as she lowered herself, taking him inside her.

It was glorious and agonizing at once. Resting his hands on her hips, he guided her gently, urging her to move, to set a rhythm. And she did—slow, maddening and so sweet it robbed him of breath. Every subtle movement, every undulation of her hips against him and the soft, wet heat of her surrounding him pushed him closer and closer to that edge.

IT WAS NOT lost on her that even in this he'd managed to give her the illusion of control. But that was not what she wanted from him. Slowing her movements, she stopped entirely and waited. He looked up at her, eyes dark and blazing with desire.

"What would you do right now," she asked, "If you didn't know about my past?"

"Everything," he said.

"Then do it... because when I'm with you, I'm not that girl anymore. I'm not broken or shattered by them."

It was all the urging he needed. Somehow, he flipped them so that she was beneath him and he was still inside her. One of his hands hooked behind her knee, hitching it higher on his hips. She raised her other, the slight shift opening her fully to him. To say that it was a wonder was the biggest of understatements. He filled her completely, consumed her. And when he moved within her, she closed her eyes and gave herself up to the beauty of it. Her thighs trembled as the familiar tension stole through her. When her stomach began to quiver with it, his own movements became sharper, his control breaking as his own need for release drove him.

It was that which pushed her over that precipice. As she looked up at him, his face etched with desire, she shattered completely. Waves of pleasure rocked her, ebbing and flowing within her as her body shuddered beneath his and a sob escaped her. He stiffened, his body drawing taut and a harsh groan erupting from him as he jerked within her.

When he collapsed atop her, sweat slicking his skin and his breath a harsh rasp, Viola clung to him. She wrapped herself around him and savored the moment. It was the first time since the night of her wedding that she felt whole, as if the broken pieces of her had finally fused together once more.

"I love you," he whispered.

"And I you," she replied, stroking his back. "Let's hope it will be enough for all that we must face."

Chapter Eighteen

It was the wee hours of the morning when a commotion woke the entire household. Viola sat up in bed, Nicholas was still beside her. He'd stayed because she'd asked him to.

"What is it? What's happening?" she asked as she listened to servants shouting. One word penetrated the sleep-induced fog. *Fire.*

"Tristan!" she shouted and jumped from the bed.

Nicholas grabbed her and pulled her back. He shoved her nightrail at her with a terse order to put it on. "The fire isn't here, Viola... it's at the mill, and Graham can't afford to lose it. Not now when the estate is on the verge of being profitable again!"

Viola turned back to see that Nicholas was already more than halfway dressed. He'd donned his breeches and was struggling into his shirt.

"Are you certain? There's no danger here?"

He paused and looked at her sharply. "I can't say that. I have no reason to believe otherwise except for the same instincts that have kept me alive for all these years. Stay here. No matter what happens, no matter what you might hear, do not leave this house. I'll have one of the maids fetch your nurse and Tristan and bring them here. You should go below stairs when you've dressed and join Lady Agatha and Lady Beatrice. I can't help but feel there will be safety in numbers for you all."

Viola watched him leave, a sinking feeling settling into her gut. Was it Randall? Had he done something horrible to avenge what he perceived as Lord Blakemore wronging him by sheltering her? She wouldn't put it past him. The man had always been petty and vindictive. It pained her to think that people who had shown her such kindness and hospitality would suffer for it. Or was it something even more sinister, she wondered. Was this all part of some devious plan to gain access to her and Tristan?

The one saving grace was that he didn't know about Tristan yet, she reminded herself. No one could have told him yet that her son had joined her. She couldn't imagine that if he did know, he wouldn't have been shouting from the rooftops that she'd not pawn off her bastard as the heir. If she was wrong, the danger to both of them would be too high. They'd have no choice but to flee. And she didn't want to run.

She didn't want to leave what she'd found with Nicholas Warner. It wasn't just passion, or the indescribable pleasure that he'd shown her. It was the love they'd confessed to one another. It was the teasing moments, the fact that he could see straight through into the very heart of her it seemed. No one had ever known her as he did. The sad truth of her life to that point was that no one else had ever cared to. She'd been a commodity to her father, something even less than human to her husband, and her own mother hadn't been able to pull herself out of her laudanum-induced haze to care enough. It wasn't self-pity, but honest reflection that had led her to those conclusions. She didn't bemoan her fate either. Whatever she might have suffered, those steps had led her to her current place, with her child who was her entire world and a man that she prayed with her whole heart would be part of that world, as well.

After a moment, the door opened and Belinda came in carrying a sleepy-eyed and fussy Tristan. The moment he entered the room, he reached for her and Viola took him into her arms. As always, it soothed her soul to hold him close. Whatever else she might have done wrong in her life, he would always be the most perfect thing she'd ever do.

"What's all the commotion about?" Belinda asked worriedly.

"There's a fire at the mill on the estate. It could be an accident," Viola offered.

"But you don't think it is," the nurse surmised.

Their relationship was quite off for mistress and servant, but Viola wouldn't have altered it for the world. Belinda had been her trusted confidante and had nursed her back to health every time Percival's drunken rages or temper had gotten the better of him. Those days, trapped inside her own bedchamber by the ugly and vicious bruises that she'd been too embarrassed to allow others to see, had decimated any social barriers between them.

"No. I think it was Randall. I think he resents Lord Blakemore's assistance and interference on my behalf. It would be just like him to do something so reckless and destructive in order to exact his own petty revenge for any perceived wrong," she admitted, though it pained her to do so.

Belinda shook her head. "Whatever you're thinking of doing, don't. He's not a reasonable man. That vile temper of his and his own inflated sense of worth and entitlement will not allow him to be reasonable. You cannot deal with him."

"I should at least try," Viola stated firmly. "He doesn't know about Tristan. And I won't let him. I won't take that risk... but if I offer to go away again, to simply vanish, in exchange for a small portion of my inheritance, then perhaps no one else will be harmed." *And Nicholas would go with them.* Was it too much to hope for a happy ending for herself?

"No. Because he'd never consent to it... and I don't need to remind you that he's as capable, if not more so, of violence as his uncle was. And even worse, I think he enjoys it. Lord Ramsleigh had a temper and acted out of anger, but that boy, he's cruel for the sake of it. He takes pleasure in inflicting pain on others, and you perhaps more than anyone."

Viola turned away. The reminder of the humiliation she'd suffered at Randall's hands, of all the different ways he'd terrorized and bullied her while they resided under the same roof brought too many fresh and painful memories to the surface. She didn't want to think of those times, not while standing next to the very bed she'd occupied with

Nicholas only a short time earlier. It felt as if Randall's contagion was spreading, seeping out into areas of her life that she longed to protect from the stench and filth of him. Those moments of joy, of completion with Nicholas, seemed further and further away.

"I know you're right... but I can't just let him destroy these people when they've done so much to help us!" Viola protested.

"I'm begging you," Belinda urged, "for Tristan's sake, don't fall into his trap. If he were to get his hands on you, what would become of the boy? Think of him, my lady!"

That argument swayed her, brought her crashing to her senses. It was too much to risk.

"Let us go below stairs, at least," Viola said. "No doubt, Lady Agatha and Lady Beatrice are beside themselves with worry."

TIMOTHY COBB WATCHED from the shadows of the trees that lined the long drive to Castle Black. The group with him was not large, only about twelve men in all, but as he watched Lord Blakemore and Dr. Warner flee the house with a bevy of footmen in their wake, he had little doubt that it would be enough.

"How many bloody servants do they have?" one of the men asked.

Cobb shushed him. "Keep quiet or we may find out. When the call goes out that there's a cottage burning on the other side of the estate, then the rest of the servants will go to put it out. That'll leave the women alone and unprotected. If we don't get that devil-witch out of that house while they're away, we'll not succeed at all."

"Never known you to be so devoted to the good Lord before," someone else groused.

"Aye. Right enough. Maybe I don't go to the church and play nice before the vicar as some do," Cobb replied in a heated whisper. "But that's a far cry from suffering the presence of a witch... a woman clearly in league with devil hisself and responsible for bringing bad luck and misfortune to all of Blackfield!"

As if on cue, a young boy came running from the other side of the forest, onto the drive, shouting fire at the top of his lungs. He'd neared the top of the hill when the butler stepped out. The wind carried his words easily enough through the darkness.

"We know about the fire, boy. His lordship is already on his way to the mill as we speak," the man offered.

"No," the boy said, gasping as his sides heaved from the exertion. "Not the mill, sir. Old Nan's cottage has gone up... they've got her out, but the other cottages are too near it and the wind is picking up!"

The butler was off then, shouting orders. Within minutes, the remaining servants from the castle were gone, buckets in hand. They followed the boy through the woods toward the burning cottage of the old midwife.

"Now's our chance," Cobb said.

They didn't go directly up the drive. Instead, they cut back through the trees and came up along the cliff's edge to the single room on the lower level where light blazed from the windows. No doubt, in the wake of such turmoil, they would have gathered to drink their expensive sherry and pity the poor folk displaced by the tragedy, he thought bitterly.

Stepping onto the terrace, he peered through the window. He could see two women, the old lady and the wife of Lord Blakemore. Lady Ramsleigh had not yet bothered to come and commiserate with them, it seemed. It was no matter, he decided. With little fanfare, he used the butt of his pistol to break the glass pane nearest the lock on the terrace door. Both women screamed as he let himself inside, the small but effective mob following behind him. All of them had done as instructed and tied a cloth over their faces.

"Where's the witch?" Cobb demanded.

"What is the meaning of this?" the old woman shouted. "You will be hanged for this! Leave now while you still may!"

"We'll leave when the dead woman goes with us!" another man shouted from the back of the group. "And if you don't hand her over, you jus' might burn with her!"

"You set the fires to draw the men away."

The statement was made, more calmly than it should have been, from the doorway.

Cobb glanced over and grinned behind his mask. She was a right looker, he thought. Hair black as night, tousled from bed and wearing naught but her nightrail and a wrapper, she was a sight to behold.

"Maybe we did and maybe we didn't," he said. "The Lord do work in mysterious ways, after all. You're comin' with us, Lady Ramsleigh... taken into our custody for the crime of witchcraft."

"Witchcraft is no longer recognized by the crown as a crime," she replied. "If you do this, it isn't justice of any sort. It will be nothing short of kidnapping and murder. No doubt committed at the behest of my late husband's nephew, Randall Grantham."

"Seeing as how you've been dead for nigh on two years, I doubt we'll be swinging for sending a corpse back to her grave. Come with us now and we won't have to hurt the others," Cobb warned as he raised his pistol and pointed it directly at Beatrice, who'd half-risen from her chair. "Put up a fight, and there'll be no heir to inherit this den of iniquity."

VIOLA WATCHED IN horror as the masked man pointed his gun directly at Lady Blakemore. "Do not risk it, Beatrice!" Lady Ramsleigh hissed. "I'll go with them."

Lady Agatha sobbed loudly. Beatrice lowered herself back down, but glared daggers at the intruders. "Where are you taking her?" she demanded.

"To the square in the village," one of them answered. "She'll be tried. If she's found guilty, she will hang for her crimes! Too wet out to burn her as she likely deserves."

Viola's one consolation was that Tristan was safe. Belinda had made away with him and they didn't know he was in the house. "It will be all right. I'm certain that Lord Blakemore and Dr. Warner will get things sorted out in a timely fashion."

"You'll be dead before the dawn," the leader swore. "The sun won't rise on you again, Witch!"

The words were uttered with conviction, but the gleam in his eyes was something else entirely. Not even triumph, Viola thought. It was greed and nothing more. Whoever he was, he'd been well paid to see her life end in such an ignoble way. *Randall.* No one better than he understood the power of gossip. He'd used her so-called resurrection to bring about what would likely be her actual death.

"Then take me on and let's be done with it," she insisted. She couldn't afford for them to linger in case Tristan should cry out. If they heard him, all would be lost.

Two of the men stepped forward. They grabbed her arms roughly, binding her hands behind her back and marching her through the same terrace doors they'd entered through. No sooner had they stepped outside than the heavens opened and rain began to pour in thick sheets. It was fitting and would at least hide her tears.

As they pushed her forward, Viola didn't look back. If she did, they might wonder what she was looking back for. Her own safety was of little import. She would not bring death and ruin to those who had helped her so selflessly and she would not risk her child's life by rousing their suspicions. With her head held high, she allowed them to march her through the rain and into the darkness.

WILLIAM WELLS HAD stirred earlier. He'd managed to get himself out of bed and was standing in the hall staring at a terrified maid and a small boy with brown curls and terrified, blue eyes. Beyond the door, he could hear angry voices and one of them belonged to Cobb. There were too many of them to fight, even if he'd been at full strength. So he waited in silence. When at last it seemed they'd gone, he asked the maid, "Where's his lordship and the doctor?"

"They've gone to the mill... you take the boy, and I'll go get them," she said.

"And you know how to get there?" he asked.

She faltered then. "No. I don't."

"I've ridden a horse drunk as a stoat for nigh on two decades. I reckon I can do the same with my head busted up a little," he said. Turning on his heel, still dressed in his bloodied shirt and breeches, he returned to his room long enough to tug on his boots and made for the stable. He faltered a few times, nearly cast up his accounts twice but, finally, he reached the stables. He saddled the first horse that looked like it wouldn't murder him and still seemed to have a bit of spirit. Rather than try to hoist himself up, he used the mounting block and managed to get himself on the horse's back without doing too much damage. Leaning low over the saddle, he urged the horse forward and once clear of the stable, into a gallop. He had one thought and one thought only, to reach the good doctor.

Chapter Nineteen

THE FIRE HAD not been as much of a travesty as it might have been. The heavy downpour had done most of the work in taming the blaze before they even arrived. Comprised almost entirely of stone, the mill had sustained damage to a few interior walls made of wood and its thatched roof. Otherwise the structure as a whole remained sound. He should have felt relief but, in spite of their relative good fortune, Nicholas could not shake the strange sense of foreboding that swept through him. There was a strange prickling sensation along his skin, a disturbance of his senses. Something was terribly wrong but he couldn't fathom what it might be.

"It's well under control," Nicholas said, shouting to be heard over the downpour. There was a sense of urgency riding him, a need to get back and assure himself of everyone's safety. "We should return to the house. I dislike leaving the ladies there alone. I cannot help but feel either Randall Grantham or Daventry had a hand in this."

Graham nodded. "I do not believe the fire was an accident either. One of the tenants reported that they saw a man slipping about earlier, his face covered with a cloth. It's hardly the sort of thing one does when not engaging in criminal activity."

Ambrose was shaking his head. "I agree that this was far too convenient. I can't help but feel it was nothing more than a distraction to lure us away. If it's all the same to you, Blakemore, I'll head back to the house and keep an eye on things there while the two of you finish sorting all of this out."

"I think that's a fine idea," Graham agreed. "Warner?"

"Agreed. I think Randall is making a play… whether it's petty vengeance or something worse, I cannot yet say," Nicholas replied, taking in the damage with a sweeping glance. "I have a very bad feeling about all of this and I wonder if we are not already too late."

No sooner had the conversation concluded than a horse emerged from the trees at a speed that was beyond foolish. Bent low over its neck was William Wells, looking as pale as death and streaked with mud and dirt.

"They took her, m'lord!" he shouted as he brought the horse up so suddenly it reared.

"Beatrice?" Graham demanded.

"No, m'lord! Lady Ramsleigh… men from the village came and took her!" He was gasping, clearly in pain and half-dead from his exertions. "Said she was a witch raised from the dead and bringing misfortune to the town. They've taken her to the village for a trial."

Nicholas didn't hesitate, but immediately mounted the nearest horse. "Where did they take her?"

"To the square, sir! They mean to try her tonight!" Wells shouted, but his voice was growing weak with exhaustion and he swayed atop his mount before managing to right himself.

To Graham, Nicholas said, "Come with me… Lord Ambrose, get him back to Castle Black and tie him to the bloody bed if need be before the fool kills himself. Then see to it that Lady Beatrice and Lady Agatha are safe!"

Graham replied, "I'll be along as soon as I rally some men here. I doubt the mob is overly large, but it'll take more than the two of us to stop them. Delay. Stall. Distract. Keep them occupied until I arrive with reinforcements!"

"I'll see that the ladies are safe," Ambrose vowed, as he mounted his own horse and brought it round near the sweating mount that William Wells had ridden hell bent for leather.

Nicholas didn't acknowledge the responses. He whirled on his mount, nudged it into a gallop and sped off into the night. He could hear Graham shouting orders behind him and saw Lord Ambrose from his peripheral vision making for the castle with his charge in tow.

Nicholas' first thought was to get to her before the unthinkable happened. His second thought was that he needed weapons. He wouldn't be able to fend off the entire mob, but he might be able to make them hesitate if he was heavily armed. There was only one place he could think of to get them and that would be the inn. He knew the innkeeper kept a stash of weapons there that had been "confiscated" over the years. In truth, that was only euphemism for being a storage facility for the local smugglers. Since it worked to his advantage at the moment, he couldn't really have cared less about the origin.

The horse's hooves thundered over the damp earth, splattering mud onto his boots and clothes as he rode toward the inn. As he was already soaked to the skin and covered in soot and dirt, it mattered little. It wasn't a great distance to cover. But given his urgency, he'd done it in record time. Nearing the village, he'd reach the inn long before he'd reach the square. He was immediately unnerved by how still the night was. No one stirred and all the nearby houses were dark. Whether all the local folk were truly abed, or simply hiding out in fear of whatever wickedness the night had brought into their midst, he could not say.

Tethering his mount, he dismounted in the inn yard and stepped inside. It was deserted. That alone would have been cause for concern as there had always been one or two souls tucked in by the fire and nursing a pint, no matter how foul the weather. But the overturned tables and broken crockery told the truth of it. There had been a struggle and he couldn't imagine that Tarleton would have gone quietly along with whatever scheme had been hatched within the walls of his establishment. Concerned but no less determined, Nicholas made for the cellar and what he hoped would be a decent stash of weaponry.

Unlocking the door to the cellar, he grabbed the candle and flint from the shelf by the door. Striking the tinder quickly, he let the flame settle before easing down into the darkness. What he saw there confirmed his suspicions. Tarleton, or Tarley as the innkeeper had asked to be called, had been bound to a chair. Cloth had been shoved in his mouth and bound there with the man's own neckcloth. Crossing the distance, Nicholas untied him quickly.

"They were setting off to take Lady Ramsleigh, sir!" Tarley gasped.

"And they have her already," Nicholas replied, his tone tight and his words clipped. "I need weapons, Tarleton. Any that can be spared."

"They're in that chest on the far wall. A couple of muskets, a few pistols and swords... do you know how to handle them, Doctor?" the innkeeper asked worriedly.

"I wasn't always a physician, Tarley. I started out in the navy, if you must know," Nicholas answered, already lifting the heavy lid of the chest in question. He began arming himself heavily, pistols, extra shot, a musket and a sword. "How many of them are there?"

"He had six with him when he left here, though I suspect there were more waiting to join up. I'd say maybe twelve in all. Lots of folks round here are superstitious like, but most are not foolish enough to rise up against a lady. It was that Timothy Cobb what did it! And I think the bounder has done something with William Wells. Haven't seen hide nor hair of him in three days now and that man, mark me on this, has not gone more than the span of a single day without darkening my door in all the years I've known him!"

Thinking of the good-natured drunkard, Nicholas fumed. He didn't question that Cobb, and ultimately Ramsleigh, were involved. He simply wondered how it would benefit the other. "I know about Wells. I found him on the road just this morning, knocked senseless by Cobb days ago and left for dead. He's back at Castle Black now after riding out to tell us that Cobb had come for Viola—for Lady Ramsleigh."

Tarleton didn't miss the slip, but he was wise enough not to comment on it. He merely raised one eyebrow as he replied, "I reckon Cobb is working for Lord Ramsleigh... seems to be the only thing what makes any sense. Like as not, Ramsleigh don't want others knowing that her ladyship ain't really dead. And Wells was telling the tale for any that would buy him a pint," Tarleton explained.

If Ramsleigh's plan was to play off Viola and her disappearance as that of an imposter, it would be easy enough to do so if no one outside of their area knew of it. But if gossip reached outlying areas, or worse—all the way to London—he'd have to provide some sort of evidence to that or be ruined. He was simply trying to contain the information to avoid questions. It was the very same conclusion he'd reached earlier.

"Not to be intrusive, Dr. Warner, but I reckon it'll take more than one man to stop a mob."

Nicholas glanced back at Tarleton. He was bruised, a little worse for wear, but appeared sound enough. "Can you fight?"

"I reckon I was fighting them bloody Yanks before you'd even donned your first pair of short pants, now wasn't I? I'd not have been tied up in this cellar if there hadn't been half a dozen of 'em that took me off guard!"

"Fair enough," Nicholas said as he passed the man a musket and a brace of pistols, primed and ready. The sword came next and he was relieved to see that Tarleton handled all with no small amount of reverence and skill. "Infantry?"

"Cavalry," Tarley corrected. "I earned enough money to buy my own commission and availed myself quite well. There's a handful of dusty metals upstairs to prove it. I won't let you down, Doctor. I know you what you do for the people of this village and I know we're a damn sight better off with you here than that old sawbones, Dr. Shepherd."

"It's not me that'll be let down, Tarley. It's Lady Ramsleigh," Nicholas corrected.

The older man continued checking his weapons as he said, "Seen her once... in the old lord's carriage. Pretty as a picture, but I reckon the saddest woman I'd ever seen. Seems like maybe she won't be so sad anymore, once we clear up this mess."

Nicholas said nothing. He simply took his cache of weapons and climbed the steps out of the cellar and into the tap room. As he entered, the door swept open and Randall Grantham, the not quite

Lord Ramsleigh entered. "I saw that poor lathered beast out front and thought perhaps it might be you," he said. "Rescuing my dear aunt once more, it seems?"

"You'll get out of my way, Grantham," Nicholas warned, "Or I will shoot you where you stand."

"And hang for it. I'm a nobleman!" Grantham laughed, though his eyes were completely cold and devoid of anything remotely human.

Nicholas had seen a shark attack once. A sailor had fallen overboard and before they could haul him back in, the massive beast had taken the poor bastard's leg. The shark had been coming back for the rest of him when they finally managed to haul the poor man up. Those cold, flat eyes reminded him of the man before him.

"No," Nicholas replied. "You aren't a nobleman. You're the heir apparent to a small boy who will be safe from all of your plots and schemes even if it means I swing from a noose to ensure it!" It was uttered as a vow, and accompanied by the raising of one of his pistols.

"Heir apparent?" Randall asked with a wicked grin. "I think not. Not when her beloved son is naught but my bastard offspring. Or did she not tell you that before she invited you to warm her bed, as well?"

It wasn't a surprise to hear the admission. It was uttered for no other reason than to goad him into being brash and stupid. But it still fueled his rage to greater heights. Knowing that Randall had forced himself on her with full permission from her own husband, it was all Nicholas could do not to put a pistol ball in him where he stood.

"A convenient rumor to help you hold on a bit longer to all the things that do not actually belong to you... a title, an estate, the inheritance from her grandfather that your uncle and Daventry schemed to take from her by fabricating her death. Tell me, Randall, is that an empty box in the churchyard? Or did some poor, unsuspecting girl meet an untimely end at your hands?"

"Dig it up and find out, then. In the meantime, I'm heading for the square. It's not every day that one sees a witch burned for her crimes against both man and church." Ramsleigh turned on his heel as if to leave.

"And William Wells? Did you know that he lived? Cobb failed in his efforts to end the poor sot's life. He's recovering at Castle Black as we speak and can identify Cobb as his attacker."

Randall paused. "What if he can? He and Cobb are both of a similar ilk. What care I for the conflict of two illiterate drunkards?"

"You'll care a great deal, I think," Nicholas added. "Because when Wells names Cobb to the magistrate, I've no doubt that Cobb would be only too willing to sell your worthless hide down the river if it means being transported rather than being executed. There is no honor among thieves, Grantham, and that's what you are."

Randall Grantham looked back over his shoulder, glaring with his strange, pale eyes and glacial manner. "Your low opinion of me will not save the bitch you've been rutting with. It really is a pity she has to die. As much as I despise her, there is no denying her beauty or the sweetness of all her feminine charms. If I had the time, I'd take her once more, just to spite a base-born bastard like you!"

"You'll never touch her again," Nicholas warned and stepped forward, ready to end Grantham's reign of misery and terror once and for all.

At the door, Grantham whirled, pistol drawn. "Perhaps you are more of a gentleman than I will ever be, Warner. It appears you made the mistake of assuming this would be a fair fight. I'm smart enough to know that I can't possibly overpower you. So I'll simply shoot you instead."

Grantham raised his weapon, but Nicholas was quicker. Nicholas dove to the right, the shot going wide, as he fired his own weapon. He prayed the shot would only wound and not kill. He needed Grantham alive, at least for the time being.

Randall dropped his gun and clutched his bleeding arm with an anguished cry. "You bastard!"

"That I am," Nicholas agreed. "But a bastard with a noble half-brother who is more than eager to acknowledge my existence. The circumstances of my birth are such that I can never claim a title, but I can claim a connection to one. We are on equal footing there."

Grantham glared at him, "We will never be equals."

"Perhaps you are right. But at this moment, you have more to fear from me than I from you." The truth was, Nicholas didn't care if he hanged for it. So long as he managed to save Viola, nothing else mattered. "You're a worthless coward and all those small-minded, sheep-like bastards who are doing your bidding will see you for the wretch you really are. Your power here is done, your sway on the people of this community is done... and any chance you had to ever hurt Viola again has ended on this day!"

The last statement was accompanied by him gripping the back of Randall's coat as he made for the door and dragging the other man behind him. He didn't bother mounting his horse again, but cut through the garden and stable area behind the inn, through a small copse of trees, and emerged near the churchyard. It was the same churchyard where Viola was supposedly buried. The fear that he might have to actually bury her incited a panic in him like nothing else.

Dragging the bleeding and protesting *nearly-a-lord* Grantham behind him, Nicholas accepted the inevitable truth of his situation. He loved her—had probably loved her from the moment he looked into her pale face on that beach—and there was nothing he would not do to protect her. It seemed as if fate had thrust them into one another's paths regardless of the strangeness of both their stations, and he didn't mean to let that stroke of good fortune be stolen from him now.

RAIN PELTED HER, soaking through the wool wrapper she'd donned and the linen nightrail beneath. Her hair, plastered to her face and neck, obscured her vision, but then Viola wasn't entirely certain she wished to see what lay ahead of her. It might be more of a blessing not to know. A shiver wracked her but it was not necessarily caused by the cold. She'd long since stopped feeling it. It was fear that prompted that visceral response. Thus far, no one had been especially cruel, but she knew better than anyone that cruelty was something men excelled at.

The haphazard and motley mob had marched her from the grounds of Castle Black, hauling her up roughly when she stumbled, but she hadn't been struck or abused in any other way. It seemed they were intent on only one purpose—to see her hang. It was an ignoble death but, given the kinds of torment those accused of witchcraft had suffered in the past, it seemed the least objectionable. Viola thought of Tristan, of the weight of his small body pressed to hers, the way he'd snuggle against her when he became fatigued. She didn't want to leave her son. She didn't want to see him raised by someone else who would never love him as she did. The very thought of him alone in the world created more terror in her than any mob could.

Still, despite their disheveled appearances and their backward thinking, they'd shown themselves remarkably capable. One amongst them, likely Cobb, was a master strategist if the fires set on the Blakemore estate were any indication. If their single-mindedness resulted in equal efficiency, her fate would be inevitably tragic. But, she reminded herself, Tristan was safe for the moment, at least, and Nicholas was far away, battling the blaze that had likely been no more than a distraction perpetrated on Randall's orders. She offered up a silent prayer of thanks for those two small blessings.

Abruptly, the rather small mob stopped moving. She stumbled again, her slippered feet sliding in the mud that had once been a road. The man she fell against pushed her roughly away, so much so that she fell onto her side, sinking into the muck and mire. Despite the soft consistency of the soil beneath her, the impact made her gasp as pain exploded in her hip and thigh. She lay there for a moment, struggling to regain her breath and wondering if she would even be able to support her weight after such a fall.

It was their leader who came for her, hauling her up roughly, his grip bruising. "Quit your messing about! We'll not be delayed in seeing justice served, Witch! If you've anything to say in your defense, say it now!"

"I am no witch. A fact you well know, Timothy Cobb. Don't think

"I don't remember you," she said. "I know what you did. I know that you were the perpetrator of all my late husband's dirty deeds and are likely serving in the same capacity as henchman for Randall! How many of these poor people that are doing your bidding tonight have felt your wrath and viciousness in the past? How many of them have been threatened and bullied by you before when they could not pay their rents? They're following you now because they fear you and I know that he sent you for me because he's terrified my return will impact his fortunes!" Viola accused. To the rest of the amassed crowd, she demanded, "He set fire to a mill that tenant farmers, your peers, are dependent upon for their livelihoods! He set fire to an old woman's cottage! And all of this to attack me when I've done nothing but rest and recover in a private home after nearly dying in a shipwreck! How many of you were there, combing those same beaches yourself looking for survivors or any goods to be scavenged?"

There was some shuffling of feet. Some of the accusing stares leveled at her skittered away. Others remained locked on her, unflinching, ungiving, and completely without mercy. It wasn't her that they hated, but her station. Resentment and years of poverty had sown the seeds of hate in them.

"You'd say anything to see your life spared!" Cobb spat.

"As would you in my circumstances," she fired back. "I've done nothing wrong. I did not come back from the dead as some have accused. I left my husband. If you wish to accuse me of crimes, at least let them be those I committed. Yes, I left him! I'd already lost one child due to his cruelty and to Randall's, to the beatings I endured while in residence at Ramsgate Hall. When I was blessed to conceive again, I knew the only way my child and I would survive was to flee... and so I did. The tales of my untimely death were put about by my late husband and my father to spare them the embarrassment of my absence and to allow them to procure an inheritance left to me by my grandfather. It was naught but greed and pride that prompted their actions. I'm innocent of what you accuse me of!" Her voice had risen to a shout by the end of it. She didn't expect them to be swayed, but the righteous indignation that she felt would not be stifled.

"And do you deny putting the evil eye on several of our local farmers, resulting in loss of livestock and sickness?" one of the men shouted from the back of the group.

"How could I have done such a thing when I have not left Castle Black? I was injured in the wreck, half-frozen from the cold sea water. I've only just become well enough to even traverse the house itself without assistance much less leave the grounds and do such wicked and impossible things!" Viola snapped back. She turned back to the small gathering of men, "Can you not see that you're being manipulated? That all of this is an elaborate ruse to get rid of me permanently so that Randall, whom you all know to be a cruel and wicked man, may continue his reign over this village just as his uncle did? He has already run through his portion of my inheritance! How long will it be before he raises your rents again? Before he charges you more and more until even the most meager of existences becomes impossible?"

There was more grumbling amongst the small mob gathered, several looking back and forth to one another as if questioning their actions. Seeing an opportunity, Viola continued. "If this was truly the Lord's work you are doing, what need would you have of lies and subterfuge? Why would you need to destroy the property of an innocent man and increase the difficulty of the lives of your friends and neighbors? Surely God would not require such actions in His name! You're doing the work of Randall Grantham and he might as well be the devil himself!"

More grumbling and, from the back, two or three of the dozen men drifted away. They slipped off into the shadows, not willing to participate further in a debacle that would surely see them hanged, but not willing to stand up to the angrier men who appeared to be in charge. Perhaps, it was the misery of the rain which cooled their fiery tempers and also tempered some of the drunkenness that appeared to be impacting the judgement of others still. It seemed they were less inclined to follow through on their bloodlust than at the outset of their journey.

"You'll not talk your way out of this," Cobb said, reaching for her.

Viola tried to back away, but her slippered feet were mired in mud and he grasped her bound wrists easily. Tugging her forward, he half-dragged her to a large oak tree. "I thought I was to be tried!" Viola protested.

"I'm done talking with witches," Cobb said, persisting in his subterfuge. "I'll not listen to any more lies from the likes of you. Get a rope, lads."

"You're making a mistake," Viola whispered. "Whatever Randall promised you, he will not deliver. It is not in his nature to keep his word!"

"Ain't in mine either... but here's one promise I mean to keep. You'll swing before the first light of dawn!" Cobb said and there was a sadistic gleam in his eye.

Viola knew that look. She'd seen it on Percival's face, on Randall's. It wasn't simply the money that motivated him. He took gratification in hurting others, in holding power over them to the point of life and death. "You are well suited to your work, it would seem," she said flatly.

Cobb smiled then and whispered close to her ear, just loudly enough to be heard over the driving rain, "If it weren't for this damned rain, I'd burn you instead. I always wondered what it would sound like to hear a woman screaming from within the flames."

Viola shuddered once more as the farce of her trial began.

Chapter Twenty

NICHOLAS APPROACHED THE square dragging the bleeding and protesting Randall Grantham with him. Tarleton was behind him, keeping from view of the others and he was well armed. Having surprise reinforcements was never a bad plan.

"Halt your screeching, Grantham, or so help me, I'll halt it for you," Nicholas hissed.

Up ahead, he could see the crowd of men, some with torches. The flickering light caught a flash of white in their midst. *Viola's nightdress.* They'd pulled her from the safety of the castle, half-dressed, and dragged her through heaven knew what to take her there at the behest of the worthless coward now wailing at his side. The fury he felt was overwhelming, but it was second to the fear that consumed him—the fear that he was too late, the fear that he would fail her.

As he neared the men, one turned back to look at him. A flash of panic crossed the man's face but before he could shout a warning, a shot rang out from the trees. Tarleton hadn't overestimated his deadly aim, it would seem. The man dropped to the ground, a bright red stain spreading across his shoulder.

"Let her go," Nicholas said, his voice ringing out through the darkness. "If you harm her any further, so help me, not a one of you will walk away from this. By pistol ball or noose, each one of you will pay the price!"

"If it isn't the good doctor himself... come to the rescue," Cobb said, turning to face them. He caught sight of Randall, bleeding and sniveling at Nicholas' feet. The man's bravado faltered, but he quickly regained his composure. "Beat a confession out of him, did you? Dragged him out here to tell everyone that he paid us to see the witch hanged? Hard to believe a man when he's held hostage at the feet of one what's about to do him in!"

Nicholas dragged Randall up to his feet and hurled him forward with enough force that he careened directly into Cobb. "I shot him when he tried to kill me at the inn. Thankfully, I'd already raided Tarley's stash of weapons and was armed for just such an event... that's right. Tarley. The very same man whose tavern you've frequented for decades. The same man you beat, bound and left for dead in the cellar of that same establishment. You're as lacking in honor as the man you serve."

"Can't afford honor, now can I?" Cobb challenged, twisting Viola's wrist in attempt to show his power.

The man hadn't counted on Viola's history, on just how much she'd already suffered at the hands of ruthless and dishonorable men. She neither cried out nor sank to her knees to beg for mercy. When Cobb turned back to her in shock, Nicholas sprang forward, tackling the larger, beefier man and taking him to the ground. The other men converged as if to stop any escape attempt from Viola, but the sound of hooves, a great number of them, slapping against the wet, muddy earth halted them in their tracks.

As Nicholas struggled to subdue Cobb, locking his arms about the man's head in an effort to render him unconscious, Graham and a host of his servants—from footmen to stable lads—descended on the square. Mounted, armed with pistols, swords and even a pitchfork, they far outnumbered the pitiful mob Cobb had gathered. Bringing up the rear of the Blakemore cavalry was the local magistrate. Still wearing his dressing gown and a hastily-donned wig that hadn't been fashionable in half a century, the man was clearly unhappy at having his slumber disturbed.

"What is the meaning of this?" the magistrate thundered. "Who in the village of Blackfield would dare to usurp my authority?"

"It were Timothy Cobb, sir." The admission came from one, if not remorseful then at least opportunistic, member of the small mob. "He said that Lady Ramsleigh was a witch in league with the devil and that we should see her punished for her crimes. Said she put the evil eye on local farmers to strike their livestock down!"

The magistrate raised one eyebrow high enough that it disappeared into his skewed wig. "Did he now? And were you foolish enough to believe such drivel? Perhaps a jail is too good for you then... surely only Bedlam would suffice for such an imbecile!"

The man blanched and quickly backed away, saying nothing else that might further raise the ire of the magistrate who continued his tirade. "And who is this Timothy Cobb to decide the fate of someone in my domain? And who are the lot of you miscreants to assume to do his bidding? Not only that, to think that you might lay hands upon the person of an aristocrat and mete out justice as if you had the right! I will see you all in the gaol!"

"She did come back from the dead!" The protest came from the back of the small group.

"She most assuredly did not!" the magistrate bellowed. "People do not simply resurrect themselves! Like as not, her death had been feigned by her scoundrel of a late husband! Had the bunch of you a single brain betwixt you, you'd have reached the same conclusion!"

Cobb finally succumbed. The man had a neck like an oak tree and it had taken Nicholas far longer than he liked to admit to subdue him completely. Shoving the man's prone form aside, he rose to his feet. He was panting from exertion and, perhaps, from the same sort of rush he'd always experienced in battles. It left his pulse racing, blood rushing in his veins.

"We are putting a stop to this nonsense once and for all. There will be no more guesses, no more rumors and no more conjecture! We are going to that blasted churchyard and opening that grave! I'll not have Lady Ramsleigh looking over her shoulder or being stared at askance by every person she passes. And no one will ever again accuse her of being a resurrected witch!"

There were gasps all around. Even the magistrate appeared to be flummoxed at the suggestion. To exhume a body was no simple thing. Only grave robbers and resurrection men did such things. Even then, to do such a thing in the full darkness of night, when superstition would have everyone believe that evil was most rampant and good at its weakest—well, that bordered on madness. But Nicholas was beyond caring.

"Now, Doctor, we've no need to be desecrating graves—"

"It's not a grave, as you just said," Nicholas insisted. "Or if it is, the late Lord Ramsleigh was guilty of far more than simply being a terrible husband! One way or another, by dawn we will know who or what is buried there."

Nicholas turned to Viola. Drenched through, mud splattering her face and clothes, she looked slightly worse for wear, but still hearty enough. His heart was in his throat as he considered how very different the outcome could have been. Had he not arrived when he did, had the rain not doused the flames at the mill so others could ride to the rescue—there were a dozen ifs and all of them meant the very same thing. He'd come far too close to losing her to something more permanent and tragic than their own reservations about the future.

Taking her hands in his, feeling just how cold she was, his jaw clenched with renewed anger. "Graham will see you returned to Castle Black and it will be well guarded… you will be safe there. Nothing like this will ever happen again. We will not make the same mistakes again," he vowed.

She shook her head. "No one could have foreseen such a thing as this. There have been no witch trials in England for a half-century or more! They've been outlawed entirely, I think. It's simply unimaginable."

"And yet it happened. They would have killed you, murdered you as certainly as I stand here now," Nicholas said. He paused then, swallowing convulsively as the enormity of that statement sank in for both of them. "I would go with you, but this must be seen through to the end. There needs to be proof that you are not deceased as your late husband and now his presumptive and presumptuous heir would have others believe. It's the only way to ensure your safety going forward."

Viola shook her head in protest. "No. I want to stay. If it's all the same, I'd prefer to go to the churchyard with you. I have a rather vested interest in finding out precisely what was buried there."

"You've had a—"

"I've had nothing but shocks since returning to England," she interrupted. "I'm fine, Nicholas. Really. I can do this. I'm already soaked through! It's not as if my clothing will get any wetter!"

He didn't make the mistake of telling her she shouldn't, or heaven forbid, couldn't. Nicholas recognized that loving Viola, and he did desperately love her, would mean always allowing her to make her own decisions. She'd earned the right to do so, clearly. Men had been abhorrently disappointing in that regard in her life. He did, however, make a suggestion. "Your clothing was hardly appropriate for entertaining to start with. But you are in a nightrail that has been rendered all but transparent by the rain. And your wrapper only covers so much, my dear. I'm sure someone here would be willing to lend you a greatcoat or cape that would preserve your modesty and provide some warmth… and help to stave off any of my own jealous inclinations when I catch them looking at you."

Viola looked down then at the soaked, white linen that clung to her legs. "Perhaps a borrowed greatcoat would not be amiss," she agreed.

Graham stepped forward then, doffing his own coat and offering it to Viola. "This should do. Let us get this done, then. No better time to desecrate a possible grave than the dead of night!"

"Beggin' your pardon, m'lord," Tarley said. "If we could not be talking so much about the dead, I'd much appreciate it. I'm as happy to dig as anyone else since I don't believe we'll find anything but an empty box. Still, no point in stirring the ire of any ghosts that might be lingering on this side of the veil!"

As they made their way across the muddy lane that served as the village's main thoroughfare, Ramsleigh in tow and the magistrate accompanying them, it was Viola who provided much needed levity.

"I'm more concerned about the ire of the vicar than any that are buried yon."

"Well said and heartily agreed," Nicholas smirked. In a quieter tone, one meant for her ears only, he said, "You aren't hurt? You swear?"

"I'm unharmed," she offered with a slight turn of her lips. For just the briefest moment, she reached out and touched his arm, squeezing reassuringly. "Shaken, tired, cold, certainly! But I am also bitterly impatient with this entire debacle—I need it to be done, Nicholas. I need it to be finished so that my son and I can have a normal life."

A normal life. He could offer her love. He could offer her the protection of his name, as it was. But he couldn't give her normal, not when he was the bastard son of one of the most scandalous libertines the ton had known and when, as a physician, he was viewed as little better than a tradesman. If they married, she would be renowned as having married beneath her. He'd be labeled a fortune hunter if not worse. It was a risk he was willing to take, however.

As if sensing his thoughts, she added, "Or any life, so long as you are part of it."

Relieved beyond words, he took a torch from one of the remaining members of the small mob and made for the churchyard, the motley group following at his heels. It wasn't difficult to find the plot for the Grantham family. The headstone on Viola's grave was the newest. Plain, without any ornamentation, it matched those of Percival Grantham's first two wives. Even in death, real or feigned, he'd thought little of any of the women in his life. They'd been disposable to him—an expedient means of refilling the family coffers or slaking his lust. Discarded like the scraps of his dinner, he'd tossed them away without fanfare or ceremony in graves that looked as if they'd belonged to paupers.

Tarley appeared ahead of him, having raided the caretaker's shed. He carried two spades. Passing one to Nicholas, he said, "It's a tight space here. I figure we ought to take turns until we reach the box."

Nicholas gripped the spade and, after Viola had stepped back, stabbed it into the sopping wet earth. Several of Graham's servants had taken custody of Randall Grantham who was watching the scene with a look of fear and horror on his face. It was that more than anything that told Nicholas the grave was not empty at all. Whatever they would find there would see the man hanged or imprisoned. Without a title, he would not have the right to claim privilege of peerage.

Spurred on by the knowledge, Nicholas dug with a vicious energy, one shovelful of wet earth after another piling up behind him. When Nicholas had dug down until his shoulders were aching from the strain, he stepped back and Tarleton took over. At some point, Graham relieved him for the last bit of it. When the tip of the spade struck wood, everyone grew silent and all the chattering of the assembled crowd stopped. Light was just beginning to filter through the trees as the sun began its ascent.

Scraping the rest of the mud back from the heavy, oak coffin, ropes were wrestled beneath it until it could be hoisted up. The lid was pried open and the putrid smell of decay hit him squarely. There was, in fact, a body. Bracing himself for what they would find within, Nicholas gave a curt nod and the loosened lid to the simple coffin was pulled away.

The body was little more than a dried husk, unrecognizable by appearance save for a halo of blonde curls so pale they were almost white. The dress, or what he could see of it, was plain and free of any ornamentation. It was the dress of a maid or farmer's daughter, perhaps.

"That's Rose Wilkes," Tarley said and his voice held a note of such sadness. "She worked up at Ramsgate Hall. When her parents asked after her, they was told she'd run off to London with a soldier. It fair broke their hearts. I reckon this will do it for good. She was a sweet little thing, always with a smile and just as pretty as you please."

"What do you know about this?" the magistrate demanded of Randall.

"Not a thing. It was my uncle's secret and he took it to the grave with him, it seems. Unless you mean to dig him up as well," Randall replied snidely.

"I don't think so," the magistrate said. "I am placing you under arrest, Randall Grantham. I won't call you Lord Ramsleigh again as Blakemore has kindly informed me that Lady Ramsleigh has borne a son who is now the rightful heir to that title. I remember when the girl first went missing because her parents, bless them, didn't give me a moment's peace. Your uncle was in London, likely cooking up this scheme with Daventry. He might have helped you cover up the crime, but I'd lay my money on you being responsible for that poor girl's death. And I will not rest until you hang for it."

"We'll bury her here. It don't seem right to move her," Tarley said. "But we'll get a different marker put up and let the vicar know so the records can be stricken."

Graham nodded. "I'll see to that, Tarleton." Turning to the gathered men who'd been part of the mob, Graham shouted, "That'll be a task for the lot of you! Clearly you haven't enough to keep you occupied."

Nicholas was helping to lower the body, to return it to its final resting place, when a prickling feeling of unease overtook him. He glanced up to see that the men who'd been guarding Randall had turned their backs on him long enough for him to draw his remaining pistol. "No!" His shout rang out, but it was too late.

The pistol went off, the blast echoing like thunder. Before him, Viola slowly sank to her knees. Graham's greatcoat parted to reveal a growing red stain spreading over the white of her nightrail. Another shot rang out and Randall sank to the ground, as well. Whoever had fired the shot, it had been true. His eyes were fixed and sightless as he came to rest in the mud.

The men rushed him, tackling him to the ground but the damage was done. Men stepped forward, took the rope from him and Nicholas moved toward Viola. In truth, he was running, but it felt as if he were mired in the mud that surrounded them, as if time itself had slowed to nothing. When at last he reached her, he sank to his knees beside her, heedless of the mud. Pulling her to him, he cradled her close. In that moment, he did not, indeed could not, think as a physician. He was simply a man overwhelmed with fear and grief as he contemplated losing the woman he loved.

"We'll take her to the inn. It's closer... I'll send someone to fetch your bag," Graham said as Nicholas reached her fallen form.

Nicholas didn't respond. He was incapable. He simply held on to her. But Graham knelt before him, forcing the man to meet his gaze. "Nicholas, she needs you now. You must put aside what you feel, what you fear, and do what must be done. Or the outcome you are most afraid of will certainly come to pass."

Those harsh words, the brutal honesty of them, pulled him back to himself. With more fear than he'd known in his entire life, Nicholas pressed his fingers to her throat. When he felt the steady beat of her pulse beneath his fingers, he could have wept with it. But he knew there was no time to waste. She was bleeding profusely and if he meant to keep her alive, he needed to focus only on the task at hand. Lifting her in his arms, he made for the inn as fast as he could. Tarley was running ahead of him, throwing open the doors, shouting orders at the serving girl who'd come in and was weeping in the corner.

"There's no time for that, girl! Get water and bandages," he shouted.

"Mr. Tarley, sir, you're alive!" she wailed.

"I am, but if you don't move your arse, Lady Ramsleigh might not be! Go!"

Nicholas placed her in the first chamber he reached. Peeling away the coat, he tossed it aside and then ripped her borrowed nightdress at the neck to reveal the ugly wound in her shoulder. It had entered the fleshy part of her shoulder but there was no exit wound. The ball was still in there. Palpating the wound as gently as possible, he stopped when she cried out. Her eyes opened but they were glazed, filled with pain and fear.

"Am I dying?" she whispered.

"Not this day" he vowed. "The pistol ball is lodged at your ribs. It didn't pierce them so your lungs are intact. But I have to remove it and clean the wound."

"This is too much for you," she said. "I can see it in your eyes, Nicholas. And your hands are shaking. Surely a task such as this can be entrusted to Dr. Shepherd."

"First you try to terrify me half to death and now you insult me," he teased. "A bit of brandy to steady my nerves and yours will work wonders. I would never let Dr. Shepherd near you, not after—not after everything I've learned of him. I will take care of you, Viola. Trust me."

"I do. More than you know… but… just do it then. Let us get the thing over with."

"We'll wait until they fetch my bag," he insisted. He took one of the bandages that had just been deposited by the serving girl. He pressed it over the wound to slow the bleeding. The blood was flowing far more freely from the wound than he liked. Given all of her recent traumas and injuries, that was even more concerning. "I have laudanum which will keep you from feeling the worst of it."

"I don't want it. I hate laudanum," she protested.

"You are not your mother," Nicholas insisted. He understood that fear only too well. "This will be painful. If you do not have it, the shock of the pain could kill you."

"Then I will likely lose consciousness from the pain before that happens. The bandage is already soaked through. I know I'm losing too much blood. The longer the ball is in there, the more blood I will lose. Just do it, Nicholas," she urged.

Tarley entered the room carrying a piece of rolled leather. "These were my mother's. She was the midwife here before she passed."

Nicholas nodded for him to open it. There were some tools he recognized, others which simply terrified him, but they would do the job. "Pour whiskey over them and hold them in the fire until they glow."

Tarley frowned. "What on earth for?"

"It was a trick I learned while in the navy… and it worked most times. I lost far fewer men to infection than most doctors," he answered. "And when you're done with the whiskey, bring it here."

Placing his arm beneath Viola's shoulders, he lifted her from the bed and held the bottle to her lips. "Drink as much of it as you can."

Viola coughed and sputtered as the fiery liquid burned its way through her. "Good heavens! Why would anyone willingly subject themselves to that?"

"In about five minutes, when it hits you, you'll understand," he said. "Now, drink a bit more."

She did, grimacing in distaste. When she'd had enough that he knew it would leave her languid and incapacitated, he laid her back on the bed and took the tools from Tarley. He doused his own hands with the whiskey and then poured a liberal amount onto the wound. She didn't scream, but a soft whimper escaped her and she bit her lip hard enough to draw blood.

"We can wait, if I get the bleeding slowed—"

"Nicholas, I can feel it. I know what has to be done," she said.

So did he. The blood had already soaked through the second bandage. If the wound wasn't closed soon, then all would be for naught. To Tarleton, he said, "Hold her down. Don't let her thrash about. Get someone else in here to help."

Tarley shouted for the serving girl who was lurking in the hall. She held Viola's legs as he pressed her shoulders back against the mattress. Nicholas used the smallest of the forceps to penetrate the wound. Viola did scream then. The cords of her neck stood out in stark relief as she struggled against the pain. The sounds that escaped her were like that of an animal, no longer even human. It made the hair on his body stand up and transported him back to those few occasions on board ship when the battles had raged. Severed limbs, burns, pistol balls buried in guts. He'd seen it all, treated it all. But nothing in his experience had weighed as heavily on him as the pain he inflicted on her in those few seconds. It seemed to go on forever.

Despite his distorted perception of time, it was not a difficult extraction, in truth. He located the ball easily enough and he removed it. And he began stitching the wound with the supplies the serving girl had brought in. But by the time it was done, Viola was unconscious and he felt near it himself. He was sweating profusely and it was all he could do not to cast up his accounts. Every part of him was shaking. Like a leaf buffeted by strong winds, he was without any sort of control.

"You've got nerves of steel, Dr. Warner," Tarley said in admiration. "Though I'd say hers might even be a might stronger. I've seen grown men not withstand the digging out of a pistol ball without laudanum. Wailed like babies they did."

"Now that the bleeding has stopped, and assuming the wound doesn't fester, she should recover," Nicholas said. It was automatic, that assessment of her condition following the surgery. Yet he knew that the words were uttered more as a means of soothing his own battered soul than anything else.

The room fell silent. He remained by her bedside and Tarleton stood sentry at the door, staring out into the corridor. It was only after hours of that routine that Nicholas realized the man was still armed. Tarley had set himself up as their guard.

"Thank you," Nicholas said softly. "For everything you have done overnight. If she lives, it will be largely because of you."

The innkeeper glanced back at him. His old and grizzled face, covered with bruises and dried blood caked into his beard, cracked with a grin. "I reckon William Wells had the right of it. He told the tale of her rescue like it was a love story for the ages. And from the looks of it, seems he knew something before the rest of us did," Tarleton observed.

"Is it so laughable then that a man of my lowly station could be in love with a lady such as Viola?" Nicholas asked. The conversation was settling his nerves more than the whiskey he'd just drained from the bottle.

Tarleton's grin faded. "I don't find it laughable, not at all. I reckon she deserves some happiness after what she's been through. Married the way her family demanded the first time around and look what that got her!"

Nicholas didn't laugh, but a small smile did tug at the corners of his lips. "I suppose that, my station aside, there really is no place to go but up from there."

Tarleton let out a cackle. "Right enough that. Never liked old Ramsleigh. Never much cared for the younger one, either." The man paused then, his expression growing thoughtful. "I fear what'll become of the female population of Blackfield, now. Given how most of the women in this town take on after you, there'll be a whole bushel of broken hearts from it."

At that, Nicholas did laugh. "You are a salve to my battered pride, Tarleton."

"I try, Doctor. I do try," the man said. For the first time since they'd returned from the cemetery and the wretched events that had taken place there, Tarleton left his post. He opened the door wide and, just before stepping out into the hall, said, "We'll be below if you need us. Come on, girl!"

Nicholas remained there, sitting on the edge of her blood-soaked bed and watching her sleep. The room was silent save for her breathing and it was the sweetest sound he'd ever heard. Content to listen to it and yet vigilant for even the slightest change, Nicholas was prepared to sit there as long as necessary.

VIOLA AWOKE TO a dull ache in her shoulder that was easily surmounted by the pounding of her head. Her mouth tasted foul and she wondered what on earth could have happened. Bleary eyed, she peered around the unfamiliar room. Memories, disjointed and foggy began to creep in. She'd been watching Lord Ambrose ride up when pain had exploded in her shoulder. Randall had shot her.

Turning her head slightly, she peered out the window. The sun was setting, silhouetting the spires of the church. She was at the inn, she realized.

A serving girl bustled in. "Oh, you're awake! The doctor will be ever so relieved."

"Where is he?"

The girl smiled. "Tarley made him go next door and take a bath. He's sat by your bedside for two full days. Tarley said if the doctor didn't have a bath and a shave, you'd not recognize him when you did awaken!"

Viola attempted to lever herself into a sitting position but failed horribly. Embarrassed, she asked, "Will you help to me sit up?"

The girl nodded and fetched extra pillows from the trunk at the foot of the bed. Wrapping her arms around Viola's shoulders, she helped her to sit up and then shoved the other pillows behind her, allowing her to recline against them.

"It's been two days since Randall shot me?" Viola asked. The time was simply gone. There was not even the faintest stirring of memory.

"Yes, my lady. You burned a fever something fierce. It's only in the last few hours that it broke. Poor Dr. Warner hasn't left your side since!" The maid appeared to be on the verge of swooning as she relayed the tales of Nicholas' devotion.

Before Viola could respond, the door opened and Nicholas entered. Freshly bathed, with his face clean shaven, he still did not look well. It was clear from the gaunt appearance of his face and the shadows beneath his eyes that he hadn't slept. "Dear heavens! You look horrible," she blurted out.

His answering grin alleviated some of the hollowed appearance of his face, but did nothing for the dark bags that had formed beneath his eyes. "Is your love so fickle that it will fade in the face of my newly-developed hideousness, Viola?"

Her lips firmed in disapproval. "You've made yourself ill taking care of me! You look as if you're about to fall over yourself at any moment!"

"I assure you, I'm made of sterner stuff than that," he replied. He gestured for the maid to go.

The girl did so with a blush and a giggle. At the door, she glanced back once more, her expression so blatantly adoring that Viola could practically see the stars and hearts dancing in her eyes. Her own eyes rolled in response. "Well, clearly you've made a conquest. I should not be difficult to replace if you feel so inclined."

His brows arched upward and his gaze settled on her. It felt as if they were the only people on earth in that moment. "On that point, I must beg to differ. It would be impossible to replace you. Ever."

Her breath caught. She couldn't think much less speak when he looked at her in that way.

"Are you in pain?" Nicholas asked, his expression shifting to one of concern.

She shook her head slightly. "My head hurts and my shoulder aches a bit but, otherwise, I am quite well. What of you? I can tell that you are exhausted, but you were not injured?"

He shrugged as he moved nearer to the bed and settled himself on the edge of it. "I was not injured, other than having my heart nearly ripped from chest. I'm better now. Yesterday, when your fever was at its worst, I was rather like a madman."

"I'm sorry to have worried you."

"I'm sorry to have allowed you to be shot... I did promise to protect you, after all. I failed at it rather miserably," he replied.

Viola could not believe how obstinate he was being in not seeing just how heroic his actions had been. The man had risked everything and very nearly sacrificed everything to save her. "And yet here I am, recovering quite well thanks to your skill. No one could ever fully anticipate the evil that is Randall Grantham unless they've experienced it firsthand. I failed myself in not anticipating that he would do something so underhanded. That poor maid! Has her family been notified?"

"They have," he said. "And they held a service for her yesterday with a vicar who seemed entirely uncertain how to conduct such an affair."

Viola reached for his hand, needing to touch him, to feel the comfort of his skin against hers. "What happened to Randall?"

"Ambrose shot him," he said simply. "He'd arrived from the castle after having settled Wells once more into bed. Lady Agatha and Lady Beatrice would not have it but that he should come into town and help."

"Is he—" She stopped abruptly. She hoped he was dead. If he were dead, so many of her problems would simply die with him. They'd be able to live in peace.

"Quite dead. Ambrose has left for Bath. The magistrate says there will be no issue for him legally, but the scandal will be quite ugly. So Bath will be far better for him than London at the moment," Nicholas offered. "I was very unfair to him, I think. I made assumptions about him and what sort of relationship we could develop as two grown men suddenly discovering they are half-brothers. Yet he has been loyal and staunchly supportive when I have been reluctant, ill-tempered and, at times, quite rude."

Viola smiled at that. "And yet he persevered. Because he understands the importance of family... and because he sees you for what you are. Kind. Just. Honorable."

Nicholas leveled her with a sidewise glance. "You will turn my head, Lady Ramsleigh."

"Then allow me to turn it more, Dr. Warner. I love you," she said. "I know I told you before, but I just really needed to say it again. I love you more than I ever dreamed was possible."

"And I love you. I knew I loved you from the first, I think, even when I wasn't quite willing to admit it," he said.

"You told me that I should let you know when I was amenable to answering your question. I find that I'm quite ready to do so," she said.

Tired, haggard, worn out from days of grief and anxiety, he was still the most handsome man she had ever seen. And as his gaze settled upon her, and his lips turned upward in that half-smile, her heart stuttered just a bit. But then he uttered a single phrase that made it skip altogether.

"Viola Daventry Grantham, will you marry me?"

Viola couldn't hide her smile, nor did she wish to. For the first time in her entire life, she was free to feel what she wished to, to express those feelings as she desired. Without fear, without hesitation, without concerns of reprisal—and he had given her that. "Do you think the vicar has ever performed a marriage ceremony for a resurrected woman recovering from a pistol wound?"

"Possibly, though I doubt the groom in question would have been the illegitimate offspring of a notorious libertine," he said. "Between the two of us, we should be able to scandalize him thoroughly."

"Then get us a license and we'll be married tomorrow morning," she said.

He raised one eyebrow at that. "I think we could give it a few days, at the very least. You did almost die, after all."

"And that's all the more reason not to waste another day," she said. "I've been so unhappy for so long… and I don't want another day of it. I mean to live my life to the fullest—free of fear and full of love—with you at my side."

In the end, he relented. He was unable to refuse her anything.

Epilogue

NICHOLAS AND VIOLA had elected not to live at Ramsgate Hall. It was a place of darkness, after all, and neither wanted that in their life. Ambrose, as a wedding gift, had granted them a small estate not far from Blackfield. He was still in hiding in Bath as the scandal raged through London. Nicholas' half-brother, the once upright and staid son of a notorious libertine, had been painted by that same tarnished brush in the eyes of society.

Branded a murderer, cut by some of the more respected members of the ton, Ambrose insisted that he minded not at all in the letters he'd sent to Nicholas, letters that her husband had shared with her. But Viola had read between the lines and shared her concerns with him. It was clear to her that Ambrose minded very much. She'd urged Nicholas to speak to him about it more honestly, but he refused, saying he did not wish to press. Of course, Viola understood. They were half-brothers, but they did not have the lifelong bond that would have come from being raised together. In many ways they were still strangers who happened to share the same blood. Their relationship was not such yet that Nicholas could feel comfortable prying into Ambrose's affairs.

Thinking of the small estate they had been granted, Viola smiled as she envisioned what it would be for them. It was a place where they could make a life together. They had traveled to it to inspect the property only the day before and make the necessary arrangements to take up residence there, but were postponing any move until the Blakemore heir made an appearance. As Beatrice had taken to her bed with pains in her back that morning, it was unlikely to be much longer. Thinking of what it felt like to hold her son in her arms, after the pain of childbirth, Viola felt a pang of longing.

A childish giggle pulled her attention and Viola turned to see Tristan playing with a small, wooden horse. It was his favorite toy. Beyond the open door of the nursery, Viola could see Lord Blakemore pacing the length of the hall. Lady Agatha was with Beatrice and Nicholas was attending the birth. It was an uncommon thing for a birth to be overseen by a physician rather than a midwife, but then the Blakemore family was nothing if not unorthodox.

"He'll wear a hole in that carpet before the day is done," Belinda said smartly.

"It is his carpet, after all," Viola replied. "And I think it's rather sweet. He's so clearly smitten with her and so very worried for her and the babe. I didn't think that sort of love existed. I certainly never believed that kind of man existed!"

Belinda looked at her. "Far cry from the way you gave birth to this one," she said, pointing to Tristan. "Not a doctor or midwife in sight, and only your old aunt and uncle to care what happened. But I reckon that's all changed now. Hasn't it, Mrs. Warner? You've found the best of everything now that you've come back here."

Viola smiled. She was quite happy to never be called Lady Ramsleigh again. "I suppose we shall see when I am blessed enough to present Tristan with a brother or sister... and yes, it feels almost sinful to be this happy."

Belinda smiled at that. "Nothing wrong with being happy. It's how the good Lord intended for us to be. It's the devil what gets in the way of it. But about this brother or sister for that wee demon... I don't suppose that's coming anytime soon, is it?"

Viola laughed. "We've only been married for a week, Belinda!"

The other woman cackled at that. "You don't get the babe from standing in front of the vicar. And I don't think I need to be telling you that!"

Viola blushed to the roots of her hair, unable to deny it. "I don't know is the only acceptable answer I can offer."

"Is it wrong to say that I hope it's a sister? I know every man wants a son, but I'd quite like to see Dr. Warner bowing and scraping to a little scrap of a girl who looks like you," Belinda mused.

As Viola had often thought the same thing, she said nothing.

Just then, a sharp cry pierced the air. It was the indignant wail of the newly born and a sweeter sound she had never heard. A relieved smile tugged at her lips and she uttered a small prayer of thanks. That smile spread to a grin at the thundering of Lord Blakemore's steps as he ran down the hall.

Moments later, Nicholas entered. Having discarded his coat and cravat, his shirtsleeves were pushed back and waistcoat undone. He was so handsome he took her breath away.

"Mother and babies are both doing quite well," he offered with a grin.

"Babies?" Belinda asked, her shock sharpening her tone.

Nicholas grinned. "Yes. It appears Lady Beatrice is something of an overachiever and felt the need to present her husband with twins… a boy and a girl. Both quite perfect, though the boy does seem to have his father's more stoic nature. The girl is quite the hellion already, I fear. That was her caterwauling you heard."

Viola laughed, "Lady Agatha must be simply beside herself with joy… Lord Blakemore is probably in a dead faint."

"If ever anything could prompt him to swoon," Nicholas agreed with a laugh of his own, "this would likely be it."

Belinda rose and picked up Tristan. "I'm going to take him down to the kitchens for a sweet, I think. He has been awfully good today."

Alone with her husband after the maid left, Viola shook her head. "She's not going to the kitchens for Tristan's sake!" It was, in all likelihood, to pay a visit to William Wells who'd stayed on at Castle Black to recuperate and then to work for Lord Blakemore. In the last weeks, they'd become quite taken with one another.

"We need servants for Ashton Hall… Belinda will accompany us, of course. What do you think of Wells as a butler?"

She blinked at that for several seconds. Her reply was cautious at best, "He'd be quite unorthodox. In that regard, I suppose it makes him perfect. But I suppose it might depend on whether or not Belinda can entice him more than a cask of brandy."

Nicholas chuckled at that. "And that, my dear, is one of the many reasons I love you."

What a miraculous thing it was, she thought, to be loved so completely and to love him so completely in return. "I feel very sorry for people who aren't us," she said. "Everyone should know this kind of happiness in their lives."

Nicholas stepped forward, tugged her up from the floor where she'd settled to play with Tristan and kissed her soundly. "While Belinda is making cow's eyes at Wells and Tristan is chaperoning them, we could take advantage of the situation."

"What do you have in mind?"

"I think you could likely outdo Lady Beatrice. Triplets at the very least, no?"

Viola laughed at that. "Absolutely not. Twins perhaps, but I draw the line at three. It would be bad form to show off so terribly!"

"Then by all means, Mrs. Warner, let us retire to our room and get to work," he urged, his voice low and roughened with desire.

Looking up into his eyes, dark with desire, Viola felt an answering surge of longing within her. He could seduce her with little more than a glance. "Lead on, Doctor. But hurry… one of those babes will hiccup and Lord Blakemore will hunt you to the ends of the earth to ascertain their state of health."

She didn't need to ask again. As they hurried down the hall and into their chamber, it was all urgency and need. The door closed, locking out the world, as they succumbed to passion.

The world faded to nothing around them and the only sounds in that chamber were soft cries and earthy moans as the desire that had brought them together only strengthened the bond between them.

In the aftermath, Viola lay in the circle of his arms and marveled at the good fortune that had washed her ashore only a short distance away. "I thought God had forsaken me. Years ago, when I suffered the pain and humiliation at the hands of Percival, and even worse, at the hands of Randall... but now, as horrible as it is to say, I wouldn't change a thing. Because all that I suffered allows me to see just how rare and precious this is between us."

Nicholas kissed her then, his lips moving over hers with such tenderness that it brought tears to her eyes. When he drew back, his own eyes were curiously damp. "I never thought much about fate, destiny, or even God. Because surely nothing less than divine intervention could have brought us together... I love you. More than my own life."

"Just so long as you plan to live for a good long time. I'm not very good at being a widow," she teased, an attempt at levity. "The last time I tried it, I embarked upon a scandalous affair with a handsome, young doctor."

Nicholas moved over her once more, pressing intimately against her. "Tell me again just how handsome this doctor was."

Viola couldn't stop her laughter as her husband fished for compliments. But the laughter faded as passion flared again. It was not a bad way to live, she thought, lost between moments of humor and the pleasure they could bring to one another.

The End

About the Author

Chasity Bowlin lives in central Kentucky with her husband and their menagerie of animals. She loves writing, loves traveling and enjoys incorporating tidbits of her actual vacations into her books. She is an avid Anglophile, loving all things British, but specifically all things Regency.

Growing up in Tennessee, spending as much time as possible with her doting grandparents, soap operas were a part of her daily existence, followed by back to back episodes of Scooby Doo. Her path to becoming a romance novelist was set when, rather than simply have her Barbie dolls cruise around in a pink convertible, they time traveled, hosted lavish dinner parties and one even had an evil twin locked in the attic.

If you'd like to get in touch with Chasity or learn more about her current and upcoming projects, you can follow her on social media or contact her via the links included here:

Facebook Profile:
facebook.com/ChasityBowlinRegencyRomance

Facebook Author Page:
facebook.com/ChasityBowlinAuthor

Reader Group:
facebook.com/groups/chasitysbooknook/

Instagram:
instagram.com/chasitybowlin/

Pinterest:
pinterest.com/chasitybowlin/pins/

Bookbub:
bookbub.com/authors/chasity-bowlin

Website:
www.chasitybowlin.com

Amazon:
https://amzn.to/2GGB2mH

Made in the USA
Las Vegas, NV
09 February 2021